ALSO BY SHELLY CAMPBELL

Under the Lesser Moon 2020
Voice of the Banished 2022

Making Myths and Magic: A Field Guide to Writing Sci-Fi and Fantasy (co-writer Allison Alexander) 2022

Knowledge Itself (co-writer Megan King) 2022
Madness of People (co-writer Megan King) 2024

Breach: Book Two of The Dark Walker Series (2024)

Feed Your Imagination!

GULF

BOOK ONE OF THE DARK WALKER SERIES
BY SHELLY CAMPBELL

Campbell

INCLUDES THE NOVELETTE
THE DARKNESS

EERIE RIVER PUBLISHING

GULF

Cover art by Shelly Campbell
Artwork by Shelly Campbell
https://www.shellycampbellauthorandart.com/

Edited by David-Jack Fletcher - Chainsaw Editing

Book Formatting by Michelle River

978-1-998112-34-0   Gulf   Electronic book
978-1-998112-33-3   Gulf   Paperback Book

To my parents who endured many uncomfortable meetings with elementary school English teachers to discuss why Shelly had written another disturbing story. Apologies. I never did stop writing them. Thank you for all the wonderful, happy childhood memories (including that old Gulf station of our own) and for always making me feel important, cherished, and loved. All the things my main character is desperately searching for... I had in spades growing up! Thank you.

CHAPTER ONE

The first time my parents forgot me, I was six years old—the first time that I know of. God knows how many times it happened unnoticed before that, me in my car seat left in the back of the van, or napping in my stroller at the park as a baby. Six was the big one though, the first one I remembered, crammed in the rear of our brown 1974 Ford Econoline, with only the tinted portal window offering us fishbowl glimpses of outside. My family headed to the summer cottage.

I had to pee, bad. My knees pressed together as I asked, "Can we stop at the gas station?"

Dad slouched in his captain's chair way up front, piloting our hulking craft. Across from him, Mom fingered through a glossy magazine with Princess Diana on the cover. I squirmed, wedged between the twins, Jord and Jess, in the far back seat. Rows of chattering heads with matching severe bowl cuts filled the space between. Seven kids altogether, and not a chance anybody up front heard my tentative plea.

I recalled a recent conversation with Dad. I'd been sitting on his lap in our living room with tears drying and itchy on my cheeks, still whimpering over some injustice—there were countless ones in a family our size. Dad pointed out our bay window at the robin's nest under the eaves of the garden shed. "You see that, David?"

Even before the mother bird arced into the nest, I counted four wobbling heads with twiggy necks and yawning mouths stretching toward her. "Where's the fifth one?" There'd been five baby birds the day before. We'd snuck out to peek at them, Dad and I. At first, they were just a messy tangle of pink, bristling feathers, knobby wings and dandelion yellow beaks. But we'd counted five.

"Oh, he's in there. But look at who's getting fed," Dad whispered. His name was David too. I was David Junior, probably because my parents ran out of ideas for new names by the time they got to me. He was tall and thin, and he cleared his throat more often than anyone else I knew.

"All the other ones are eating," I said as the mother robin stuffed segments of dirt-battered worm into four eager mouths. "The loud ones."

"Exactly, David. The loud ones. You want to eat? You want to be heard in this family? You've got to be loud, Pipsqueak." He poked my ribs until I giggled and then kissed the top of my head. His chest deflated as he sighed, and I thought, *You too, Dad. Be loud.*

I thought about that as my bladder swelled and the noise of my family piled up like a mudslide in the confines of our van, clogging my ears and squeezing my chest. I blinked at Dad hunched over the steering wheel, inhaled a sour breath of B.O. and socks and announced, "I have to pee!"

Nothing. No-one turned. Julie laughed like a horse from the middle seat, her head pressed close to Justine's.

Wriggling straighter, I shouted, "I said I have to pee!"

"Great." Jord spat and shook his head.

"What?" James swiveled back to face us. Mom said I shouldn't have favorites, but the twins had each other, plus they were jerks, and Jeremiah was just way too old. James listened.

"Snotface has to piss." Jord sneered.

"Stop it." I scowled.

"Dad," James relayed to the front. "David has to pee."

Mom's magazine flopped onto her lap. She didn't wait for Dad to answer. "Can he hold it? We're almost there."

"No. I need to—"

Jess shoved my head into Jord's armpit, bellowing, "Yeah, he can. All good."

Choking on sudden tears and mortified that the twins might see them, I ducked out from under Jess's hand, tucked my chin to my chest and went rigid between them. *You've got to be loud, David.*

"Aw, widdle baby." Jord reached to flick my bottom lip.

I bit his finger as hard as I could. He screamed, yanked his hand back and cuffed the back of my head.

"I have to *pee*!" I screeched at the top of my lungs.

We stopped. Being loud worked.

Dad pulled into the Gulf gas station about five miles away from the cottage, the one where we never stopped for milk because it was too expensive. Dad insisted on packing two jugs from home, sandwiched in blocks of ice. Us kids took turns balancing the Styrofoam cooler on our laps, howling that our legs were falling off and later, at the cottage, whenever Mom plucked the milk out of the Philco fridge, she'd wrinkle her nose over the open container and demand, "Smell this." Every. Single. Time.

We poured out of the van onto the oiled parking lot as the slowly spinning, battered orange-and-blue sign beckoned us inside. I shadowed James as he sauntered toward a cracked glass door with sleigh bells hanging from the handle. Mom inspected Jord's extended hand before pursing her lips. "*You* take him to the bathroom and wash that wound off while you're there, lots of soap. Bites infect easily."

Crap. I ducked my head as Mom's shrill order, "Stay together!",

cut through the baked air like a crow's call. By the time Jord collect-
ed the men's room key— they chained it to the handle of a toilet
plunger—Jess had already stuffed his cheeks with pilfered Hubba
Bubba, and I was jangling those bells so loudly that the owner, Mr.
Morrison, hoisted his huge belly over the register counter to bellow
at me like a walrus.

"What's your damage, dickwad?" Jord flicked my ear and
prodded me with the plunger. "Come on."

In the john, cherry air fresheners and urinal pucks did a terrible
job of masking the smell of stale piss. A guy the size of a refrigerator
stood in a wide stance at the urinals, so I bee-lined for the single,
lonely stall. Jord snorted, dived past me, and slammed the stall door
behind him.

"Jord!" I squealed, one hand clamped over my crotch, and the
other smacking the blue dented door. "Jord, come on!"

"Can't hear you," he drawled.

I blinked back fresh tears, poked at the wadded up wrapper
stuffed in the hole where the door latch once lived, and sounded out
the only legible word on it. "Tro-jan."

Jord giggled, so I poked past the wrapper and yanked on the
door. He smacked my finger so hard that it went numb.

Stumbling back, I clamped a hand over my tingling finger and
wailed as the pain came pouring in. "Asshole!" I howled, face hot,
eyes swimming with tears.

Boots scuffed from the direction of the urinal, hinting that the
man there was turning toward us, but I didn't care. Screams spooled
out of me in hiccupping waves.

"Shut up," Jord barked, opening the door, but I couldn't.

I started crying, and it pulled me along like a wave I couldn't
stop. My only hope was to gulp for air and ride it out until it lost
momentum. Warmth bloomed at my crotch, and I looked down
and wailed louder.

Jord snatched my shirt collar, yanked me into the stall and shoved me against the door to hold it closed. "Shut up, David," he hissed into my ear. "If you know what's good for you, shut the hell up!"

I hate you. I wanted to say it, but the crying wouldn't let me. My finger throbbed and piss ran down my leg and into my sock no matter how hard I tried to stop it.

"Jesus."

Through the tears, I saw Jord's nose wrinkle as he looked down at the puddle between us. He steered me toward the toilet and ducked out the door. The guy at the urinal left. Jord headed to the sink shaking his injured hand and muttering something about rabies.

At the sound of running water, I gulped, "Wait for me?" As soon as the words left my lips, I hated them, and I hated Jord. *Wussy. Don't be a wussy, David.* I yanked my fly down, but it stuck, wadded up in soggy fabric. *Goddamned hand-me-down pants.* Forcing the zipper halfway down, I wriggled out of the pants like a snake shedding corduroy skin. Next I peeled off my underwear, then my wet sock.

The main door to the bathroom whuffed open and closed, and I cringed, backed my bare bum against the stall door and balanced on one foot. Tossing my undies and balled-up sock onto the floor, I twisted my bare foot back into my shoe, yanked a generous swath of toilet paper from the roll, and balled it up against the crotch of my pants. I left the bathroom with a ruined zipper, untucked shirt, and still-damp corduroys stinking of piss.

Squinting into the afternoon sun, I trotted around the front of the station and, halfway across the gravel lot, realized the van wasn't there. My stomach felt like the Styrofoam cooler, food sloshing around in there with a big block of ice. Wandering a half circle, I scanned the lot, but there was nothing that could hide an entire

Econoline. It was gone. They'd left. Without me.

The realization froze me. My eyes ached from staring down the gravel road that ambled toward the cottage. Surely any second the roof racks on that God-awful van would pop back over the hill and everyone would laugh as I climbed in.

Big joke.

The orange-and-blue sign rotated overhead. I stared down the road and counted the revolutions in my head, but lost track somewhere past one hundred and forty. Pretty soon everything got fuzzy. Wiping my nose, I glanced back at the gas station. Nobody back there but Morrison-the-Walrus, and he probably ate crybabies.

I shuffled closer to the waxing and waning shadow of the spinning sign and stood cocooned in it for awhile before I heard the chirping. Squinting up, I spotted a bird hovering at the uncapped end of a cross-pipe clamped below the main sign. A faded piece of tin with the words *Oil and Lube* stamped on it swung from the horizontal support. As I watched, the bird neatly tucked its wings and disappeared into the end of the pipe.

A nest. Just like the one at home. Tipping onto the balls of my feet, I cocked my head. Sure enough, the chirping stopped, and shortly after, the bird popped out of the pipe and zipped away. When she returned, the peeping crescendoed, just like the baby birds in the nest at home. *How do they know it's her?*

They didn't, as it turned out. The fourth time the mother bird flitted away from the nest, a larger shadow swooped in, and I caught a blur of white and iridescent black.

Magpie, my mind registered.

Pale lids flicked over the bird's black eyes as the chicks squeaked louder.

"Shhh." I fanned my hands, but the sly birds hover only wobbled for a second before it poked its head into the end of the pipe. The chirping cut off. "No," I yelped.

Back-winging, the magpie emerged with a wriggling nestling clamped in its thick beak. It landed on the oiled gravel pad not ten feet away from me, with its tail cocked, and started pecking. The baby bird was still alive and flopping as its assailant gouged its belly and teased out its innards.

Can they see it from up there, the other baby birds? Do they know what's happened to their brother? My throat ached. They must have known, because not a single chirp sounded from the nest the entire time the magpie gorged, and when it flew up for seconds, it couldn't reach the rest of the chicks. They stayed quiet until the mother bird returned.

Shut up, David. If you know what's good for you, shut the hell up.

CHAPTER TWO

I'm seventeen now, but I still flinch when we drive past that old Gulf station on the way to the cottage. We've summered here since before I was born. That's how Mom says it: "Oh, and if you need to reach us in July, we'll be *summering* at the cottage." Turning that noun into a verb somehow makes up for the fact that we've never had the cash to fly somewhere warm.

We still drive the same damned old van. My throat closes as the Econoline coasts under the burled log arch with *Honey Bear Hollow* branded across its face. Most other years, driving under that cheesy sign marked the euphoric start to a summer filled with the smell of coconut sunscreen and beach barbecues. But this year, I know it for what it is.

A dead end.

It was supposed to be your last summer here. One last hurrah before you turned eighteen and enlisted against your parent's wishes. Good thing you found out how gutless you were before then. I ball the thought up and press it to the back of my mind, forcing a smile as Jord and Jess poke their bleach blond heads out the open window.

They're looking for Evie Tyler and her sister Veronica, future inheritors of Honey Bear Hollow Resort. They chop firewood. In short-shorts. And midriff baring v-neck tees. Can I get a Hallelujah?

My twin brothers graduated two years ago, but still live at home. They are proof positive that my parents will tolerate free-loading, useless adults in their home, and they only tag along to the cottage for the Tyler sisters. Hell, James is a year and a half older still, and he came home from trade school for the same reason. All three of them gaze toward the woodpile as we pass, but alas, no-one's there. Dad nudges the faded Ford Econoline toward a metal Quonset with a clapboard lean-to clinging to its side.

A giant of a man, poured into Carhart coveralls, spritzes Windex onto the plexiglass square in the door, just under the branded wood 'Office' sign. I know for a fact that the red hankie he scrubs the window with is the same one he uses to blow his nose.

Angus Tyler, proud proprietor of Honey Bear Hollow Resort, and father of the lovely, leggy Tyler sisters, is easily the largest human I've ever met. Not fat like Morrison-the-Walrus, just big, you know? Stubble peppers his chin like a neglected lawn. He has an angular, rat-like face, like God just lost Angus's original noggin and threw on a spare. His hair reminds me of a doll my sister Julie had as a kid, her favorite, and therefore on the receiving end of obsessive bouts of hair-brushing. It got to where Jules would ram that flowery Barbie hair comb into a mangled mess of abused clumps and just scream because she couldn't get it to comb through.

Has anyone ever tackled Angus's hair like that?

He turns, holding the Windex like someone just ordered him to *Draw, Pardner*.

"Afternoon, Sir Rawlingson." Angus bobs his head at Dad. He calls everyone Sir, and not as in: Yes-sir, No-sir. Sir, as in *Sir* Elton John. Yeah, and the wives get a 'M'lady.' Oh, the perks of staying at Honey Bear Hollow—five cent pepperoni sticks, and complimentary knighthood. "Been, 'spectin you."

"Long drive." Dad says it like he says everything. Like he's apologizing.

Angus nods. His chin wrinkles as he pokes his face through the open window like a cop surveying our vehicle.

I raise a half-swigged can in greeting, and he frowns like he's just seen Hitler.

"It's root beer," Mom chirps. Officially, Honey Bear Hollow doesn't allow alcohol, but that isn't what drew Angus's quizzical look. I can tell when people register my presence by that odd stare, like I just interrupted an important conversation with an asinine comment.

"S'pose your regular cottage will do for this year?" He continues, gaze sliding off me to refocus on Dad.

"Sure, that'd be fine, Angus." Dad smiles. We've stayed in the same cottage since God made Adam.

"Owner renovated this year."

"Oh." That one throws Dad. Throws all of us. "Oh, I thought—I mean—we thought you were..."

'Oh, I own 'em, but they're all on ninety-nine-year leases to other folks." Angus winks as if he's just offered up the savviest business secret ever hatched. "They come an' stay in the off season. Everett's been fixin' up yours for twenty-sem years, Sir Rawlingson."

I shift in my seat, scanning my brother's faces to determine if I'm the only one uncomfortable with the idea of someone else staying in our cottage. I mean, I know we aren't the only ones who've ever set foot in the place, but it seems intrusive, this permanent resident with enough pull to scab an addition onto the building that held all our summer memories.

Who the hell is Everett and why did he change our cottage?

"He added a room on this year, back on the east side, before his missus died."

Simultaneous exclamations spill out of the van.

"Frigginserious?" yelps Jess.

"What?" Mom chokes.

"In-in the cottage?" stutters Dad.

"Naw, naw." Angus guffaws, glances at Mom and peals into laughter so hard, he has to wipe tears from his eyes with the Windex rag. "Naw, don't you worry, M'lady. Annie *was* feeling sickly when she was here this spring so Everett ended up takin' her home early. She had a heart attack in their house in Sudbury. Died in her bed, Everett said when I called. Real shame. Funny thing is though, the door to that bran' new room is locked tight. That's why I phoned up Everett in the first place, but he cain't find the key nowhere, and I cain't neither, so a lot of good it'll do ya. Renovated cottage. Same size." He spreads his meaty hands in appeasement. I think he expects us to laugh, but we're all still digesting the existence of Everett and the death of his wife.

Angus sobers and scrubs the back of his neck. "Didn't sound like he was keen on coming back this winter. Figured this fall, once y'all are cleared out, I'll just knock the wall right down to the new room, open the place up, but I gotta warn ya, rate'll go up after that. Place'll be twice as big, an' you can bring the whole family without knockin' elbows. How's that sound?"

"G-good." Dad grips the steering wheel and nods like a bobble-head.

"Well," Angus whistles through his teeth, grips the windowsill, and pushes away from the van. "You go on up. Vee and Evie'll be there in a bit with some firewood."

"Got a fire burning right now," Jord whispers, lolls his tongue out and pretends to jerk off.

Nice. I wrinkle my nose and turn away to peer out the window. *This is what I have to look forward to now. A life with my perverted brothers in my parents' basement.*

Gravel crunches under our tires as we roll up the familiar fork in the road, bearing left at Sweet Bee Circle—I shit you not, that's the name of the road. At the end stands the cottage, clapboard coated in butter-yellow paint, lace curtains hanging behind rattling six pane windows.

I brighten. *Even if my life is a dead end, this still feels like coming home.*

We can't see any addition from the road, but of course we all pile out and circle around the house to take in the new awkward growth on the east side.

"No windows," James reports, scratching the stubble on his chin. "Jesus, it doubles the size of the place. What was he gonna to do with it? Can't be a bedroom with no windows."

"Maybe his wife died before he got to put them in," I offer.

"David, shhh!" hisses Mom. Like I just spit on the old lady's grave.

We file back to the front of the house in weighted silence, like a funeral procession. The front door, armored with dozens of coats of chipping ivory paint, swings open on well-oiled hinges, and I smell it. Best smell in the whole world, and I don't even know what it is. Some combination of mothballs and freshly cut wood, peeling wallpaper and Orange-Glo polish, sun-baked rooms and hot cast iron. That mixing of old and new, citronella summer nights and front porch iced tea wraps my mind and relaxes me in a way nothing else can.

They should just bottle this smell, give it to that damned psychiatrist the school counselor referred my parents to.

Jord and Jess barrel past me to what used to be a closet door on the addition-side of the living room, just left of the Home Comfort woodstove. It's a five-panel with a crystal knob. Jess cranks on it, and then the pair of them elbow each other, alternately squinting through the keyhole.

"Yeah, it's locked alright," Jord grumbles.

"Goddamned Hardy Boys." James smirks.

Jord crams his eye closer to the keyhole. "Used to be the towel closet, didn't it?"

"It's called a linen closet, genius," I contribute.

"James, get me a flashlight," Jord presses, and Jess drops to all fours and pokes his nose under the crack in the door.

"Jesus." I shake my head. It's hard to believe the twins are semi-functioning adults sometimes.

James strides to the kitchen and starts rattling through drawers. "How 'bout a candle?"

"How are you gonna shine a candle under the crack in the door, Einstein?" I snort, but James ignores me, and so do the twins. "Just look for the key, James." I press.

Mom pokes her head over two bulging, brown paper bags and rasps, "If any of you want supper, get the groceries in here *now*."

After supper, we slouch at the Formica table, sucking half-melted mango sorbet off our spoons and staring down the former closet door.

"Let's just bust it down." Jord slams his palm down and spoons rattle. He gets through life busting everything he sees. Bull in a china shop sort of thing. Only there are two in our house. No wonder Mom never had any Royal Doulton.

"No!" Mom preens her cloud of hair back from her face.

"We'd lose our deposit," Dad echoes faintly.

"And Angus'd sit on you for sure." James winks at me.

"Well, we're getting in there. Old man's probably got a huge pot stash in there. Be a great summer." Jord flashes Mom that apologetic gee-I-can't-help-myself grin, and she goes for it.

She always goes for it. How many children has she been through now? This woman who's policed every toy-snatching incident, candy shoplifting heist and counterfeit ID operation, yet inexplicably lets the twins get away with proverbial murder.

As excited as they are about the door, none of my brothers volunteer to sleep on the green foldout couch in front of the stove. House rules are whoever sleeps closest to the stove keeps it fired up—or risks an early morning lake-dunking. My brothers happily jam through the door to bring in armfuls of firewood delivered by the dreamy duo of Evie and Veronica. But I take the post of furnace boy.

Dead end summer, dead end job to go with it.

I wriggle into the sweet spot between the mattress's prodding springs and squint up at the kaleidoscope pattern of open log rafters overhead. One beam close to the loft has a series of knots and curved patterns that look just like a horse's head. How often have I stared up at that knot-eyed, solemn lipped face and categorized my day, decompressing from the relentless, clamoring noise of my cramped family? The horse's head and I, we have an understanding. The way his wood grain ears press back, I can tell he longs for quiet moments too, and I imagine how quiet the cottage is when we're gone and do not fill its nights with snoring and unapologetic farts.

Past midnight, with the old cast-iron stove crackling merrily, I wake up with frozen feet. Groaning, I flip out of the clutches of the sagging hide-a-bed and stub my toe hard.

Air hisses out of me as I fold in half, clutching my foot. That's when I realize the stove is still hotter than hell. Cold air sluices over my ankles. My hands slip from my throbbing toe, and I straighten.

Where the hell is that coming from?

Grinding the heels of my hands against my eye sockets, I yawn and shuffle toward the draft. My gaze slides down the closet door to the generous crack beneath. It's so bloody cold that mist slithers over the hardwood, and I take a step back.

He must not have insulated the addition.

Since I'm already standing, I hook the handle into the stove's burner cover plate, lever it aside and feed some fresh wood to the glowing ember bed within. Then, I worm back into the hide-a-bed, tuck the blanket under my feet, and fall asleep.

CHAPTER THREE

The next day, James, Jess, Jord and I blow up these cheesy inflatable float toys we bought from the dollar store back home. We spend the day at the lake, puffing our chests out, and grinning as we drift past the firewood pile on pink flamingos and rainbow-maned unicorns, while the Tyler sisters shake their heads and laugh behind their hands. It doesn't last long, and when the girls leave, we sag into our squeaking crafts, breathe in the smell of cheap vinyl, and trail our fingers in the water.

I wake up alone several hours later, beached on the far west shore, my skin sunburned a shade of pink that rivals that of my sadly deflated flamingo. When I limp barefoot back to the cottage, my brothers roar at the sight of me.

Assholes.

At bedtime, I slather on layers of aloe gel and ease onto the couch under a single sheet. At first, when I wake up shivering, I figure it's just the sunburn, but then the draft curls over me, cold and painful as one of Jess's freezer aisle tittie twisters.

"What the hell?" I wince as I peel the sheet back and my chest stings, tight and itchy. Kneeling down, I press my cheek against warped floorboards, and am rewarded by another icy blast.

Christ, it's nearly July. Where is the wind coming from in a room with no windows?

"Everett, you suck." I zombie-walk to the kitchen, whip the dishtowel off the oven handle, and cram it under the door crack with my toes. I forget about the whole thing until the next day when Mom asks for the towel, her hands dripping dishwater.

Leaning back from the kitchen table, I peer over the couch to where the towel lies wadded under the locked door. "I'll get it," I mumble.

Jord crams a spoonful of Cheerios into his mouth and crunches loudly, his forehead wrinkling as he watches me bend to fish the towel out from under the crack. He swallows and points his spoon at the door. "What the hell's it doing down there?"

"Nothing." I shake my head. *Aw, come on Jord. Just leave it.* "Just a cold draft."

"Oooh." Jess snorts and wriggles his fingers around his face. "Bogeyman." But Jord stands so fast, his chair squeals as it scrapes back.

"Where?" He crosses the living room, drops to all fours, and squints under the door. "Where's it coming from? I don't feel anything."

"Under the door. It only comes out at night." I wince as the words fall past my lips, handing the dishtowel to my mother. *It only comes out at night. You sound like a six-year-old who's pissed his pants.*

James grins at me from across the kitchen table, holds his cereal spoon up to his mouth like a microphone, and breaks into song. Hall and Oates. 'Maneater'.

Great. Just friggin' great.

Jess slaps his hands on the table, picking up the drumbeat and joining in.

"Shut up, you dicks." I blush.

Jord belts out the chorus. The three of them actually harmonize.

I grin as they crumble into laughter, but my cheeks feel stiff, like setting concrete, and my chest stings. It isn't just the sunburn. James started the ribbing. He's usually in my corner.

Not you, James. I can't handle an entire summer of all three of you picking at me like crows. You'll break me this time.

"You about done, assholes?" I ask, hiding my true thoughts.

That night, same damn thing happens. Same draft from hell frozen over, sliding under the door. This time I grab the flashlight from the top kitchen drawer and flick it on. With my ass in the air, I peek under the crack. Nothing but more crooked pine floorboards, but damn it's cold. Wrapping my blanket over my shoulders, I creep out the front door, struck by the humid warmth of the summer night. It's a hell of a lot warmer than that draft. I circle outside the recent addition, aiming the pale beam of light under the raised foundation. Not any holes I can see.

After the five-hundredth mosquito bites my ankles, I retreat inside. I approach the door and shiver. I'm not imagining it. The door is shuddering, just enough to rattle gently in its frame. Tentatively, I rest a palm against the cold wood and it stops, but starts again as soon as I pull my hand away. "Jesus, he build a freezer in there?" *It doesn't sound like that. It sounds like...*I cock my head. *Like knocking or scratching.* Shaking my head, I jam the dishtowel back under the door until the rattling stops, and dream about sides of frozen beef slung on meat hooks, swinging slowly in the linen closet.

In the morning, I hang the dishtowel back over the oven handle before anyone else wakes up. Good thing, because Jord and Jess, after three days of unrequited flirting with Evie and Veronica, have renewed their focus on the door. They spend most of the morning easing credit cards and butter knifes along the doorframe, and manipulating wire clothes hangers into the keyhole beneath the crystal knob, to no avail.

"Is that *my* credit card?" Dad glances up from his crossword puzzle, centers his coffee cup on a coaster, and purses his lips at the twins.

They straighten and nod in sync, like cartoon characters.

Dad turns to Mom. "This is what I mean about consequences, Madeline."

"Fifty-eight down," she jabs at the newspaper, "is Engulf. E-N-G-U-L-F."

I grin, watching them from the couch. Dad hates it when Mom ignores him, hates it even more when she spells out her crossword contributions, and she knows it.

"No, I'm serious." Instead of filling in fifty-eight down, Dad just flicks his pen. "I read this article that says the rational part of the male teenage brain doesn't develop fully until they're twenty-five. They've got no concept of consequences, absolutely none." He straightens and refocuses on the twins. "That's why you haven't given any thought at all to what would happen to the pair of you if you snapped my credit card in half in that door, have you? Are you like this at work? Is this why you can't hold a job?"

"Enough." Mom presses a hand against Dad's forearm and gives him a long look.

Jord and Jess can do no wrong, remember Dad?

James saunters into the awkward silence with a toothbrush dangling from his mouth. "What?" he slurs, scanning faces.

"Fine." Dad leans back, scoops up his cup and takes a large swig of coffee. "James, why don't you do something useful with that credit card. Go to the Gulf station and buy some fireworks before they sell out, would you?"

The Gulf station up the road from Honey Bear Hollow hasn't actually pumped gas since the mid-eighties, but Morrison, the station's ancient proprietor somehow keeps afloat stocking nothing but cigarettes, gum, and an impressive inventory of pyrotechnics: sparklers and snakes, roman candles and screamers. The works.

"Wanna come?" James nods toward me, his words slurred around the toothbrush still dangling between his lips.

"Nah, I'm good." As much as I'd love some one-on-one time with James, I just can't. Ever since that summer, back when I was six, the mere sight of a Gulf sign makes the hair on the back of my neck prickle. They are rarer, those signs, since Gulf sold out to PetroCan, but Morrison has never taken his down. Even now, the place still gives me the creeps.

"OK, buzzkill, suit yourself." My older brother shrugs and crosses the room to pluck Dad's credit card from a sulking Jess's hand, before returning to the kitchen to spit toothpaste into the sink.

It pours in the afternoon. I curl into the beanbag chair in the tiny loft above the kitchen to read while Mom heads to the flea market in town. The pie lady there makes these deadly chocolate cream pies, so Mom never has a hard time convincing Dad, Jess and Jord to go with her. James isn't much of a pie man, though. He stays behind and makes us both toasted BLT's before falling asleep on the couch.

Steven King's *The Long Walk* rests in my lap until the words blur. I tip my head back and luxuriate in the rare silence. It almost never happens in our family—silence—especially when I was younger and couldn't escape to be on my own. Christ, when all seven of us kids were still at home, it had been downright excruciating. Dad, when he noticed how much noise bothered me, had walked me to the garage, opened a small, square drawer in his tool chest, and revealed his secret stash of earplugs like he was showing me a pile of gold. I think that's how I survived. Dad, too. We'd stuff those bright foam plugs in so far, Mom couldn't even see them. It wasn't silence, but it muffled the chaos of my family just enough to make it bearable.

"You awake up there, Einstein?" James's voice makes me jump.

I let the book flop to my chest and press my head back into the beanbag. "Yep."

James says nothing else for so long that I turn to peer down at him on the couch. His gaze focuses on the five-panel door. Without turning, he asks, "Mom and Dad ever come round to the idea of you in the military?"

Aw, shit, James. Not this. Anything but this. My throat closes and I swallow against the tightness. "Nope."

"You gonna do it? Enlist this year? You turn eighteen, right? Screw Mom and Dad, that's still the plan?"

"Screw Mom and Dad is *not* the plan," I sigh, picking at dog-eared pages.

"You know what I mean."

I stare up at the ceiling, my throat aching. *Say it, you wuss. Say the words out loud.* "Changed my mind. Not going."

"No? Why not?"

"Dunno." I shrug, but tension ratchets tighter between my shoulders.

James rolls toward me and levers up on one elbow. "Bullshit, David. What changed?"

What changed? Someone shoved a gun in my face last month, and I pissed my pants, James. That's what changed. Not really cut out for the military, am I? I swallow the heat in my throat, feel my nostrils flare, and turn my face so my brother can't see the flush in my cheeks, then I answer quietly, "None of your damned business."

James backs down. "OK. OK. Don't get your panties in a twist." He pounds the couch cushion, flops onto his side and re-focuses on the door. After a long yawn, he asks, "Wanna find out where that draft is coming from tonight? I'll stay up with you."

Thank you, James. He never pushes too far. He always seems to sense when I'm ready to collapse inward like a hermit crab. "Yeah, sure." I smile.

As night closes, every cottage on the lake blazes, bedecked with patio lanterns and red-and-white flags. People sing 'Oh Canada' from their balconies and salute the night with roman candles, comets, and pop-rockets. Reflections ripple like submerged fireflies in the lake, and, since it's Canada Day, Dad lets each of us crack a contraband beer, despite the rules and Mom's half-hearted admonishment.

Our cottage doesn't succumb to sleep until three-thirty a.m. James and I sit on the couch until we hear snoring from both bedrooms off the kitchen. Jord and Jess still sleep in the bunkroom across from Mom and Dad's room. Two unused bunks line the walls where James and Jeremiah used to sleep when they were younger. I don't remember Jeremiah ever being a kid. That's the thing about big families. There're different generations of kids. My oldest brother had already moved out by the time I was born, and for a short time, I bunked with the other boys in Jeremiah's old bed, while Justine and Julie shared the hide-a-bed couch in the living room. Now, James prefers the cot in the loft when he comes—he says the twin's farts are enough to kill him—but I know it's because of the sleepwalking. James has always wandered at night, and the twins love to scare him awake when they catch him.

Assholes.

I guess James feels more corralled in up in the loft, safer. Sometimes, late at night, I hear him shuffling around up there, aimlessly, and I hold my breath, terrified of him crashing down the ladder. It hasn't happened yet.

"OK, they're out cold, I think." James slaps his thighs, pushes off the couch and pads to the kitchen, breaking me from my thoughts. He pulls two of Dad's beers out of the fridge, and eases the caps off, before offering me a bottle.

I stare down at the mist curling off the bottle and inhale the crisp barley smell. "You know Dad counts them."

James's grin flashes in the dark. "Still?" He shrugs. "He'll think it was the twins. Does he know you smoke?"

I shake my head and crack a smile. "He thinks it's the twins."

James clinks his bottle against mine and we both take big swigs, smiles still bunching our cheeks. There are distinct advantages to having idiot brothers.

We sit in the dark. The stove soaks us with warmth as we sip our cold beers. Wordlessly we peel the labels off in long strips, wad them up, and take turns tossing them into the ash bin. Am I stupid to love moments like this so much that my heart hurts?

"So what are you going to do after school then?" James finally ventures. The question's not mired in autocratic expectation, like when Dad asks it. My brother just sounds genuinely curious.

"Don't know." I answer truthfully, mellowed by the beer.

"Just don't become a dickwad, jobless loser like Dumb and Dumber over there." James nods toward the bunkroom.

"No guarantees." My smile sags on my face and we settle into silence, staring at the crack under the door. *That's exactly what's going to happen. A dickwad, jobless loser, that's what you have to look forward to, David. That's what you've built for yourself now.*

The draft never comes. James and I have time to clean up all evidence of our pilfered drinks, and even sleep for a couple of hours sitting up, bare feet stretched in front of us like early warning devices against the cold, but nothing happens.

"I'm sorry, man." I mumble in the morning.

"No worries." James stretches and yawns. "Maybe tonight?"

I nod, knowing James will forget. James is special, like Dad. But I know full well I can only pull on any family member's attention for so long before it unravels like a loose thread and gets tangled up in some other sphere of our family circle. I can't hold on to attention in my family. It slips through my fingers every time, and I do nothing to stop it.

James does forget about staying up with me the next night, but it doesn't matter. The draft doesn't materialize anyways, not all night or the night after when the outside temperature drops the coldest it's been since we arrived last week.

Maybe you dreamt it, or the sunburn just made the air feel cold against your skin.

But the excusing thought is bullshit, and I know it. I had felt it, hadn't I? And I'd felt the door rattle, like the clacking of a distant train.

A few more draftless nights would have been all it took for me to forget about the strange door, and drift aimlessly into summer, I'm sure of it. But this morning, it happens. The discovery that changes everything.

When I'm cleaning the ash pan, something heavy clunks against my shovel. I fish through the ashes and my fingers close on something cylindrical, so I pull it up. A skeleton key with a scalloped cloverleaf handle. Swallowing excitement, I blow soot off, revealing a solid shank and a single rectangular tooth.

The key.

It rests, still warm, and oddly heavy in my hand.

Might not be such a dead-end summer after all, David. I grin like an imbecile as I heft the key in my palm before pocketing it. "Who's the Hardy Brother now, boys?" I whisper.

CHAPTER FOUR

After my family forgot me at the Gulf station, and the magpie came, I couldn't stay in the parking lot, not with the spiny wing feathers of the picked-clean baby bird waving at me in the wind. So I walked down the gravel road toward Honey Bear Hollow. It seemed welcoming, lined with tall, jack pines and dappled sunlight. I figured I'd head toward the cottage and, when my parents came back for me, I'd meet them halfway.

But they didn't meet me halfway. It was dark, and I was still miles away from the cottage, mosquito-bitten, with snot and tears running down my face, by the time I saw headlights bouncing down the road. Scared by how fast they were coming, I shuffled into the ditch as the van came barreling past. The brake lights flashed, the wheels locked up, and the behemoth skidded to a stop.

Mom's frizzy hair looked like steel wool against the red lights. She sprinted toward me, calling my name, and I don't know why, but I just stood there. I didn't even go to her.

Dad backed up the van, and Mom crumbled to her knees, clawed at my back, and squeezed me so hard I coughed. Grasping both my arms, she examined me. She looked funny. Her face was puffy. I guess I expected her to look happy, or relieved, but it was something else. My six-year-old mind couldn't quite grasp it. She kept asking if I was OK, but no matter how many times I mumbled an answer, she asked again. When she herded me into the van, Dad's face was tight and he didn't say anything for a long time.

"Don't put this all on me." Mom's voice was cold as we bounced down the gravel road.

"I was sleeping, Madeline," Dad snapped back. "I drove all the way here, and I was taking a Goddamned nap. You were the only other adult in the house, and you didn't even realize he was gone for three hours. Who exactly would you like me to blame?"

My parents didn't speak for the rest of the van ride.

We pulled into the cottage, and James gripped me in a headlock and messed my hair. "Hey Skippy! Where'd you go, dig a hole to China?"

He kept winking at me and making funny faces as we folded out my sleeping bag, ignoring Mom and Dad's harsh whispers in the kitchen.

That night I laid awake amidst the noise of eight other people sleeping, swallowing against the fiery ache growing in my chest. *They didn't even come back for me until after supper. They didn't even think to fold out my sleeping bag or bring a jacket.* My stomach growled as I lay there blinking at the ceiling, but then I remembered the magpie, and I wasn't hungry anymore. *If I hadn't screamed in the bathroom, if I hadn't pissed myself, Jord would have waited for me. They left because you're a big, loud cry baby.*

It rained the next day. I holed up in the tiny loft beside Justine, who sat folded in the beanbag chair, thumbing through a paperback with no cover. I didn't even think of her as a sister. She was *ancient*, even older than Jeremiah. But she was nice enough.

She smiled as I hauled a massive dictionary off the bookshelf, the kind with thumb tabs pocked into the pages in a diagonal pattern. It thunked onto the floor and flopped open to 'G'.

Proudly, I sounded out bold-lettered words to myself. I was a pretty good reader.

"What are you researching, lil' man?" Justine drawled.

"Look." I stabbed halfway down the page. "I found Gulf."

"So I see." Her long hair tickled my neck as she read over my shoulder. "Gulf: A portion of an ocean or sea partly enclosed by land. A deep hollow; chasm or abyss. Any wide separation, as in position, status, or education. Something that engulfs or swallows up." She raised her eyebrows, green eyes twinkling. "That's some pretty deep stuff."

I flipped a page back, circled my finger and stabbed at another one. "What about this one?"

"Sound it out, buddy."

Hunched over the dictionary, I rolled the word around in my mouth. "Goo-ii-llt. Gewilt."

"You got 'er. Guilt: The state of one who has committed an offense, especially consciously. Feelings of culpability, especially for imagined offenses or from a sense of inadequacy."

"What's culpability?"

"Um, it means you feel responsible. Like it's your fault something happened the way it did."

"And inad....Inady?"

"Inadequacy? Jeez, David." Justine grinned. "I think I'm inadequate to answer that one."

"What?"

"It's how you feel when you don't think you can do something. When you think you're the wrong person for the job."

"Read the guilt again. The second one."

"What, feelings of culpability?"

"Yeah."

My sister straightened, shook out her shoulders and recited in a booming voice, "Guilt: Feelings of culpability, especially for imagined offenses, or from a sense of inadequacy."

That was it. My stomach dropped, and I fidgeted to make sure Justine didn't notice my lip trembling. *That* was the look in Mom's eyes as she'd knelt in the ditch. Guilt. Like she thought she was the wrong person for me, or maybe I was the wrong person for her. Later I circled the word with red crayon so I'd never forget it again. I circled Gulf too.

The key digs into my hip, heavy and awkward in my pocket, radiating heat, warmer than it was when I first pulled it from the ash pan.

Is it actually getting hotter?

I shift uncomfortably on the foldout couch as my family whirs around me in a flurry of clattering dishes, frying bacon, dripping coffee and slouching pajamas. I want to stand and pace, am overwhelmed by the urge to clasp the key in my pocket, like it might worm out of some unseen hole and disappear if I don't hold it secure. But I clamp my teeth, slouch further into the couch, and stare at the keyhole in the five-panel door. I want the house to myself when I open it. It's *my* discovery.

Jord and Jess will bulldoze me if I let them in on the secret. They shanghai any adventure they're a part of, and James is too laid back to reclaim the wheel once the twins have it. I scratch my chest and dry skin flakes off beneath my fingers.

Your last outing with them ended with you marooned on a beach and sunburned to a crisp. Not this time.

After a lifetime of hand-me-down clothes, inherited mattresses, and feeding-frenzy meals, Goddamnit, I deserve *something* that is just mine.

Being forgettable isn't all disadvantages. I've had years of practice to perfect it, and I can use it when I need to, like now. If I sit still enough, and say nothing, I'm as good as invisible to my bleary-eyed family milling around the kitchen. Their loudness covers me like a blanket, and I sink between the cracks of these cushions and watch them like a hunter from a blind. I'm here. If they look really close they'll see me, but I'm confident my camouflage will hold. It always has. Only a sudden, stupid move, or thoughtless spoken word will betray me now, and I've paid for enough lapses in judgment this past month to keep me good and quiet now.

James rounds the sofa, scoops the blue enamel percolator off the cook stove burner, and pours the last of the coffee into a chipped mug with lily pads on it. He likes his coffee black, and hot enough that he winces every time he slurps it. A smile pulls at my lips as he stands before me, scratching his balls and looking over the back of the couch, blue eyes squinting in distaste. By the sounds of it, Jord and Jess are deep into their fried egg eating contest.

"Foul!" Jess's cry is muffled, his mouth full. A glass clicks against his teeth and I hear a large swallow. "Asshole put hot sauce all over mine. How the hell am I supposed to keep pace, cheating prick?"

"Language," Mom sighs hopelessly from the sink, scraping a frying pan.

Someone gags. James laughs and Dad mutters, "For the love of Pete," before his chair clatters back and the sound of paper rustling signals him retreating to the front porch with the Sunday news. As soon as the door slams, Jord slurs past a mouth crammed with half-chewed egg, "I win. Ha! Twelve." He slams the table. "Twelve eggs in under ten minutes. Beat that, jackass."

"You gonna put that on your resume?" James grins.

"Shit, yeah. Destroyer of a dozen eggs."

"You're buying the next three cartons, Destroyer." Mom quips. "Farmer's market starts in twenty minutes, and if we're late, Georgia will be all sold out. Get dressed."

Jord groans like a fat cow pressing to its feet. "No fair. Dick-weed over here ate a bunch too. How come I'm the only one paying?"

Don't fold, Mom. Come on.

"Swear jar." Mom chirps and Jess snorts. "Get going, both of you. James, you coming?"

Come on, James. I stare at his shoes, willing him to go, or at least move away from the couch. If he gets much closer, he's bound to notice me. James and Dad can see me flying under the radar sometimes. It's harder to dupe them. I ignore the jab of the key in my pocket and press my tongue to the top of my mouth. *James. Just bloody go.*

Mom unknowingly saves me. "There's this new local coffee roaster set up by the ginger jam stand. Smelled just divine last time I walked by."

"I'm in." James nods and walks past without seeing me.

A long exhale threads out of me, and my hand slips into my pocket, thumb stroking the cloverleaf handle. Something embossed on the end, like Braille or lettering, is catching under my thumbnail, and I'm dying to pull out the key and investigate this detail that I missed before.

Dishes rattle in the kitchen sink for an abysmally long time. Eventually, Mom sighs and drains the water, despite the still-towering stack of dirty dishes to her left. She can only tackle so much at once. I brighten when the front door opens and the jingle of van keys sounds, but I deflate, just like Dad does, at the sound of the hissing shower sputtering to life in the bathroom.

"Who on earth is showering now?" Dad hollers. "I thought we were going."

"Mom is." Jess reports.

"Hurry up, Madeline. There's hardly any hot water."

"Mmm hmm." Mom's voice echoes faintly. "I'll only be a minute."

Liar. I bite the inside of my cheek and fight to keep my restless leg from jiggling. Mom has never taken 'just a minute' her entire life. She operates in a different dimension, flustered, but agonizingly slow. When she parks a bloody car, she takes five minutes just to gather her wits and the contents of her purse before she's ready to exit.

"I'll be outside." Dad's sentence trails off like a balloon deflating. The door closes behind him.

Jord and Jess thud around the bunk room for a few more minutes before sauntering out, pulling shirts over their heads. James shaves at the kitchen sink, mouth gaping at his reflection in the window. The shower shuts off with a snick and the whir of a hair dryer takes its place.

Holy shit, are they ever going to leave? God, I need a smoke. I want to run my hands through my hair, but hold my breath instead, as James towels off his face and scans the room, frowning.

"What?" Jord asks.

"Nothing." James hangs the towel on the oven handle and checks his jean pocket for the bulge of his wallet. "Feel like I'm forgetting something, that's all."

Shit. I freeze on the couch.

"Prolly that twenty bucks you owe me," Jord quips.

"Asswipe." James snorts. "I don't owe you twenty bucks."

"Swear jar!" Jess sings in a falsetto voice, and all three of my brothers jostle each other out the door. It slams behind them hard enough to rattle the windows.

I exhale through my teeth and crack my neck. *Four down, one to go.*

Mom, as always, is last. I roll my eyes and stroke the key until its handle burnishes and the bumpy raised lettering digs into my thumb pad. *What the hell does she do in there?*

Drawers fly open and contents clatter around as she paws through them, mumbling to herself. Mom always sounds so damned disappointed. Finally, she pads into the kitchen in a green summer dress and bulky crocheted shoulder bag. Her hair is frizzy as always, despite her herculean efforts to tame it. She smells like citrus.

I don't have to hold my breath when she crosses behind the couch, still speaking under her breath. I'm not careful with Mom like I am with James and Dad. Busy in her own frenetic head, Madeline overlooks me easiest of all, always has. I'd like to say it doesn't hurt anymore, and that I'm used to it, her ignoring me, but damn it, it pulls at me like an embedded fish hook every time. I'm no Momma's Boy, furthest thing from it. So why does it hurt then? How can you miss someone you were never ever close to?

The front door clicks shut and my knee bounces as I stare at the gap under the five-panel door. When the van growls to reluctant life outside and recedes down the driveway, I pull out the key and squint down at the handle. Stamped in small plain print on the end of the cloverleaf handle is the word 'Pithos'.

Who the hell is he, one of the three musketeers? I trace the small letters under my finger and count to sixty. Certain my family is gone, I cross to the five-panel in two strides, twist the key into the lock, and push the door.

It doesn't open.

Of course it doesn't, idiot. It's still hung like a closet door. It opens out, not in.

I pull.

Mirror.

That's the first thought that strikes me as I take in the exact duplicate of the living room I'm standing in. Same green, crushed velvet sofa bed sagging behind me. Identical chipped melamine cabinets. Same painted windmills on the porcelain tile backsplash—wait.

No me.

No reflection of me. Tentative as Alice in bloody Wonder-land, I pull the black skeleton key from its hole and crane my head through the doorway. No dirty breakfast dishes, but when I look over my shoulder, there's still stacks of egg-yolk spackled tin plates beside our sink. Crumpled under one arm of the hide-a-bed is my plaid blanket, but the one in front of me is empty. Looks dusty.

"What the hell, Everett?" *This is creepy.*

The ole bugger's built an exact mirror image of the room next door. Where on earth did he find the twin to that green monster of a couch? There's even a spring beckoning through the same spot in the back cushion.

Got an eye for detail, hasn't he?

Same woodstove too, only this one has a cold, crusty frying pan on it. I can still feel the heat on my back from ours across the wall.

The pine planking creaks under my next step, and I jump and then smile, but I'm pretty sure it ends up as a snarl. An odd feeling consumes me whole, the one I had just before Sam Ren and his go-rilla wingmen beat the piss out of me behind the Dairy Queen. A curdled sense of approaching doom slithers through my lungs.

Get out.

Primal instinct presses me back a step toward the door, but I hold fast there, like a dumbass, like I waited while Sam Ren eased toward me in the Dairy Queen parking lot.

Shaking out my hands and hissing through my teeth, I scan the room trying to identify what's wrong, because *something* is. Something is very wrong, and it's not just the duplicate room, or the draft emanating from here at night. It takes a few seconds to pin it down. The out-of-place thing. My throat spasms when I see it. I swallow and shift to the balls of my feet.

"Window," I whisper.

There's a window above the sink, just like the kitchen behind me. A *window*, in a room with no windows. Cold curiosity needles me. It has gotta be a mirror, some sort of TV screen. I squint at it, crack my hip against the back of the couch as I stumble by, and effortlessly ignore the pain.

Jesus Christ, it looks real.

Trees, pinecones, boughs all waving in the wind. Sunshine winking off the lake. Leaning over the dishless sink, I pocket the skeleton key, thumb the sill lock over and grunt with the effort of jamming the pane up its hundred-year-old slides.

When it flies open, I fall into the sink, recover, and rub my elbow. A breeze puffs against my cheek. How did we all miss a window on our backyard tour of the addition? All of us. We'd actually noted the omission, hadn't we?

James said it couldn't be a bedroom with no windows, and Mom gave you shit for suggesting the old man didn't have time to put them in before his wife croaked.

I stare out at the lake and realize I'm panting. That harsh, hiccupping sound an animal makes when it's cornered, I'm doing that. Something squeaks from the tree outside and my gaze locks onto the tight round of a bird nest wedged in the branches. I gape in horror at the four nestlings inside, craning their scrawny necks, membrane mouths opened like tiny umbrellas. Visceral memories flood up my throat, tasting of bile. I can't move. Paralyzed, I stare at the peeping birds until a fat fly corkscrews through the open window. I blink and backpedal away like it's Satan. When my ass hits the back of the couch, I twist toward the door.

"Shit!" My voice cracks into choir boy octave.

It's shut. The closet door is shut, and I didn't shut it, and I didn't hear it close.

Plunging toward the door, it's all I can do not to claw at the paneling. I crank the knob, but the door doesn't give so I yank the key out of my pocket, stab at the keyhole, but miss. Stab again. Miss.

"Come on," I wail, and on the third try I get it. Twisting the key so hard my wrist twinges, I hear the bolt click, grab the cold crystal knob and shoulder the door hard.

Nothing.

"Shit," I squeak and try again. Halfway through the third body check, I fumble and turn the key the other way, twist the knob and the door swings open, *thank Christ,* it swings open. Biting my lip against a hysterical laugh, I pour into our warm living room.

When the door is safely closed and locked, I flop back onto the couch. Staring at the keyhole, I murmur, "David-Shit-Your-Pants-Hardy Boy." I laugh again and it echoes high and horse-like in the rafters, but it isn't funny. There's something wrong with this place. There's something wrong with me.

CHAPTER FIVE

I blink at the five-panel for a long time before my legs revert from mushy to al dente. The cottage creaks and clicks around me, stretching as the morning sun filters through the trees. I trot out the front door. Pine branches slap at my face as I round the east side of the cottage. A blank, fresh yellow clapboard wall stares back at me. No window. No windows on the other sides of the addition either.

"What the hell?" I mutter to myself, scuttling down onto my belly and peeling aside a piece of skirting so I can squint between the building's pilings. Pine needles press through my shirt as I scan between the floor trusses for wiring, vents, ducts...something. But the underside of the building looks stripped bare, all wooden ribs and cobwebs. A stack of extra siding rests tucked against the cottage foundation. Something else skitters across my brain, a spider of a thought.

The lake. I saw the lake out the window in the Bizarro closet. I saw the sun off the waves on the lake.

Out the *east* window. And the lake is most definitely on the *west* side of the cottage.

The back of my neck tingles as I stand. I resist the urge to rub it. Instead, I shake out my hands, crack my knuckles and turn to scan the widely spaced trees. Needled branches laced with dew wink tiny reflections of the sun back at me. A robin trills from the canopy top.

I imagined it then? A window? A bird's nest? It had to have been some sort of recessed TV screen. A hidden fan to simulate the breeze coming through, but there's no wiring. It feels wrong to turn my back on the blank east wall, so I crash back toward the front of the house.

Tucked under the front porch steps, out of sight, is a rusted coffee tin. I fish it out, peel off the brittle plastic lid, and peer inside. A faded pink lighter and a crumpled half-pack of cigarettes lie among the rust flakes. My secret stash. Sometimes James tops it off for me. The label on the package is not one I recognize.

"God bless you, James." I ease a cigarette out of the sleeve, pinch the filtered end between my lips, and cup my hand over the lighter, flicking three times before inhaling successfully.

Fly fishers tease their lures over the flat, dark surface of the lake, and chimney smoke rises in lazy spires over the sleepy cottages lining the banks. The comforting sound of someone—most likely the Tyler sisters—chopping firewood thuds like a steady heartbeat across the water. I breathe in the cold smell of the lake and the warm comfort of nicotine and try to settle my jack-rabbiting heart.

What's wrong with you? Go back in the house. But I nurse the cigarette for a long time before facing the front door.

The heavy, stale smell of fried eggs surrounds me as I ease the door shut behind me. I'm cold despite the crackling of the settled fire in the cookstove. The door to its left pulls at me with a strange gravity and as I round the green couch, my cold fingers find the warmth of the key in my pocket.

I perch on the lumpy armrest and pick at the threadbare crushed velvet, staring at the crystal door-knob without blinking. The floor seems to tilt, like the whole quiet cottage is leaning into me and pushing me toward the five-panel. I press my heels into the hardwood, brace my thighs and tuck my chin to my chest. When I pull the key out of my pocket, it smells like a hot iron poker.

"Right then, figure this out." I murmur and dive for the door.

The tumbler turns with a clack, and I hold my breath as I pull on the wobbly crystal knob, opening the door to reveal...

A normal guest room.

There's a bed, a thick mattress with a multi-colored crocheted blanket folded tightly over it, an ivory, metal bed frame, chipped, simple and clean. The room yawns around it, all warm hardwood floors, braided rag mats and chunky nightstands with matching hurricane lamps. Above the bed, on a thick curtain rod, hangs a tufted rug wall-hanging of a pair of black-and-yellow birds, their wings raised in stiff vertical flight.

Where's the window that was here before?

I swing the five-panel wide open, prop the fire shovel against it, and cross the bedroom. The rug is heavy as I lift its stiff corner to peer at the wall behind. There's nothing but vertical pine paneling behind it. I run my palm over it, searching for seams, but can't detect any. Wrinkling my nose at the smell of dust, I drop the edge of the rug and scan the rest of the walls.

No windows at all.

To my left, there's a crib, old, metal-framed like the bed. A round crocheted pillow and a floppy sock horse sit propped at one end. To my right, a plain, narrow door that looks like it leads to another closet. I shuffle to it, press a palm against the smooth wood and hold it there.

What the hell are you listening for, David? Bogeyman? Maneater? Snorting, I force a smirk onto my face, wipe my sweaty palm against my jeans, and grip the metal knob. I crank open the door, standing to one side.

It is a closet, a small one. A few ladies' wool winter coats slump on wire hangers and stuffed above the wooden shelf are extra pillows and quilts in zippered clear plastic bags. It smells like mothballs.

People still use mothballs?

I move the coats and poke around the empty closet, digging under the blankets on the shelf, but find nothing of interest. It's just a normal room. Nothing out of the ordinary here. Closing the door, I swing back toward the entry, ensuring it's still wide open.

Beyond the doorway, the foldout couch stretches before the woodstove like a green, sleeping dog.

Calm down, you freak. I breathe in through my nose and out through my mouth twice, hand still clamped over the key in my pocket. *What's wrong with you, David? It's a bedroom. Just a bedroom. That's exactly what's wrong. What the hell was it before? What did I see? The mirror room, the window, the bird nest. It felt real. Jesus, why the hell would I imagine all that?*

I scan the room, looking for some flaw or explanation, but find none. The crib across from me looks lonely, like a set piece in a movie where a couple lovingly sets up a nursery for the baby that never comes.

"Jesus," I shake my head at the random thought and refocus on the bed.

There's a book there I hadn't noticed before, at the foot of the bed, a hefty, thick monster of a thing with a brown cover, gold-leafed pages and half-moon thumb tabs carved diagonally into the side.

I know that book.

It's a dictionary. Pursing my lips, I edge toward it and hook a finger under the 'G' thumb tab. Someone highlighted it with scribbled red crayon. My neck tingles as I hoist the cover open and smooth out the tissue-paper thin pages stamped with tidy fine print. Two words stand out, circled in scrawling red wax.

Gulf. Guilt.

"Shit." I sag against the bed. *I circled those words that day with Justine in the loft. What the hell?*

I trace the red crayon swirl in the dictionary with my finger and skim the description, even though I know it all by heart.

Gulf: A deep hollow. A wide separation in status. Something
that swallows us up.

I've had enough years to pin it down, what it is about me that's
wrong. It's the gulf. It's the unexplainable distance between me and
the rest of the world, and no matter how many bridges I try to build,
they all burn. I'm forgettable. I've accepted that long ago. There's
something off about me. I know that.

*But is it too much to ask for some friggin' direction? A purpose?
One Goddamned thing that makes me feel like a part of something?*

Slamming the book shut, I scoop it off the creaking bed and
carry it out the door to the green couch. I close, lock, and double-check the five-panel's latch before sliding the key back into my
pocket and sitting beside the dictionary. Then, I place a palm on the
cover and stare the door down.

Be a part of something bigger. Wasn't that the whole allure of
the military? *You don't have the balls for it. First gun in your face,
you pissed your pants. That's what happens when you try to be part of
something bigger, David.*

The door feels like something bigger. Whatever I saw behind
it this morning, whatever that was the first time, it was big. *That's
why it scared the shit out of you.*

But what had I seen?

"Hallucination?" I whisper to myself.

Soldiers with PTSD sometimes hallucinated. Could you get
posttraumatic stress disorder from a gun pointed at your head? I
mean, students at school shootings got therapy for that kind of shit,
but I'd always figured it had only been the ones who saw their buddy's brains sprayed across a desk. Something like that. Besides, why
would I imagine a Bizarro world in the spare room? What the hell
was that supposed to signify?

"You're just psycho," I sigh, scrubbing my creased forehead.

Frowning down at the dictionary, I open it to the 'P' tab and trace my finger down the words. *Pipe, pitch, pitcher, pity.* There's no 'Pithos'. Whatever the word on the key is, it must not be English. I close the cover and heave the dictionary off the couch with a grunt. The ladder to the loft is difficult to climb one-handed with the massive tome tucked under one arm, but I need to put the book back on the shelf it came from. My brothers had broken out into a spontaneous teasing song over a dishtowel blocking a draft. God knows what torture they'd come up with if they think I'm moping around here reading a bloody dictionary.

I squeeze between James's unmade cot and the beanbag and slide the dictionary into the empty slot on a bookshelf full of ratty paperbacks and recipe books.

Who took it down and put it on the bed? Everett?

The way Angus had talked about him, I'd pictured a skinny old man, but I was out of breath after wrestling the dictionary up here. Why would an old man haul it all the way down the ladder to lock it in the guest room he'd just built? Why did it seem like someone had left it there just for me? Only Justine ever knew about the dictionary, no-one else.

The world isn't about you, dickwad. How many lessons you need before you learn that? I stare at the twisted sleeping bag in James's cot for a few more seconds before descending the ladder.

Dad's half-finished crossword sits on the kitchen table, and I pick out all the mistakes as I shovel down a bowl of Shreddies. The milk is so cold it hurts my teeth. The old Philco fridge, chugging away to my right, keeps everything colder than the fridge at home. I wash the rest of the dishes, dry everything and put them away, before the weight of the key in my pocket, slapping against the side of my thigh, gets too heavy to ignore.

Of course, I open the door again. I do it a few more times

before everyone gets back from the farmers market, but it's just the big bed and the lonely crib on the other side each time. I feel like more of a fool every time I check, so I pocket the key, head outside and walk toward Angus's office, hoping for the distraction of his daughters and maybe a five-cent pepperoni stick. There's a sign in the window with the cardboard hands of a clock turned to 11:15, so I settle for a walk around the lake instead. Dogs bark from fenced yards as I pass, but none of the people raise their heads or wave back when I hold up my palm in greeting.

People like to keep to themselves here. That's what I used to think, but that's bullshit and I know it. It's the gulf.

That night, the draft under the door comes back. The hide-a-bed squeaks as I shift to face the cold, clammy air, holding my breath, like it's toxic or something. A soft creak and thud sounds from the loft. I roll over and squint at the dark triangle of space above the ladder.

"James?" I whisper, and his silhouette swims into milky focus. "You awake?"

He turns from me and shuffles toward the bookshelf, picking up a book and tucking it under his t-shirt. Then he tucks another into the waistband of his boxers. He does weird shit like that when he sleepwalks. Once he took a bag of frozen peas to bed with him. Another time he ate an entire T-bone steak from the refrigerator. It was raw and still in its cellophane package.

"James?" I try again. "Wake up, James. It's back."

I need someone else to feel it, to experience the icy breath of air from under the door and see if it's as foreboding to them as it is to me, or if they can sense it at all.

Maybe it's just messed up circuitry in my mind.

James doesn't wake up, just shuffles around in the loft like a slow-motion pinball. Eventually, I climb the ladder and pull the beanbag across the gap in the railing. He'll break his neck one of these nights. When my feet hit the main floor, the draft washes over them and makes me flinch. I lick my lips and ignore the soft rattle of the five-panel door in its frame.

It's James. He's walking around up there and the vibration's carrying through the beams, that's all.

Shuddering, I back into the kitchen to ease open the second-to-top drawer, grabbing a wooden spoon. I swipe a strawberry-print dishtowel off the oven door handle and use the spoon to wad it into the crack under the five-panel. I don't want my toes anywhere near there.

"I'm taking the boat out. You wanna come fishing?" James asks me through a mouth full of scrambled eggs and hot sauce. When I don't answer, he jabs me across the table with his fork. "Hey Skippy, you wanna come friggin' fishing or what?" I thought he was talking to someone else. People rarely start conversations with me unless I start first, so I guess I wasn't expecting the question.

"Ow. Screw you." I rub my chest. The key pokes me through my back pocket, and I shift in my seat.

Somewhere from one of the bedrooms, Mom shrills, "Watch your mouth!"

"You coming or what?"

"Nah." I fold two pieces of bacon into my mouth at once.

"Why not?"

"I can't bloody swim, James. I'm not coming on a boat with you."

"What?" James waves his hand at me dismissively. "You float-ed around on the flamingo just fine. You don't have to lie, dickhead. Just say you don't wanna come. Won't break my heart."

"I'm not lying. We stayed in shallow water with the flamingo. You *know* I can't swim." *And you pricks let me fall asleep and float away anyways.*

"Quit shitting me. We took swimming lessons together."

"Yeah, and I nearly drowned, remember?" Course he doesn't.

James leans his chair back on two legs and scratches his hair with his fork. "Fifteen summers at this lake, and you can't friggin' swim?"

"Seventeen. And you can't remember I never learned to swim." I punch him in the shoulder. "How brotherly of you. I'll pass."

I turn toward the oven door handle, intending to swipe a dish-towel off to flick it at James, and that's when I notice the towel is missing. I look at the five-panel door, and there's just an empty gap where it was. James follows my gaze but says nothing.

CHAPTER SIX

Ironically, other than being forgotten, there's not much else I remembered about that summer at the cottage when I was six. Everyone seemed to deflate on the van ride home. Mom bawled and squeezed Justine for too long when she loaded her tiny car to head back to university.

On my very first day of school, Mom slipped James's old backpack over my shoulders. I breathed in the smell of new pencils. A brand new set of twenty colored Crayolas nestled in their glossy sleeve next to my bagged lunch. They were *all* mine. I didn't have to share with anyone.

Mom herded all of us out the door. I turned back to wave, to see if she was crying like she'd done for Justine, but she just looked relieved. My siblings plodded down the sidewalk ahead of me in second-hand Keds and jelly shoes.

My teacher announced her name in a pert voice, Miss Martin. She wore a fitted blue dress and a tight smile, and she liked rules. When she raised her hand, if you didn't pipe down right away, you had to stand in the corner, underneath the flag, with your nose pressed against the wall. If you were quiet as a mouse, she'd pry open a round tin of hard candy she kept on her desk, and you could pick one: spearmint green or peppermint red pinstriped logs, raspberry-shaped drops, or these pillowy chalky squares. I'd earned one of each kind by the end of the week, and the inside of my mouth got all cut up from sucking on sharp shards all the way home.

One November night, my dad gathered us around the TV. The twins flopped onto the couch while Julie and I perched on the curved armrests and James leaned in from behind. The Channel 9 news intro flashed by with its neon cityscape and forcibly cheerful jingle. Peter Jennings was hosting a special called 'JFK' to commemorate the twentieth anniversary of the president's assassination.

"Miss Martin taught us about JFK. His name is John Fitzgerald Kennedy," I announced proudly. I only remembered because the name Fitzgerald sounded so smart, I'd moved it to the top of my list of dog names, if I ever got a dog.

"Was. His name *was*." Jess grinned and cocked a finger against the side of his head like a gun.

"Jessie Aaron Rawlingson!" Mom shouted loud enough to make us all jump and gape at her.

She stared back, rigid in her rocking chair, the tendons in her neck popping out, and her crocheting a frozen tangle in her hands.

"Show some respect, boy." Dad grumbled, and Jess's ears turned red. The smirk fell from his face as he slouched into the couch.

A collage of candlelight vigils, some from as far away as Berlin, flickered by on the screen. Then a soft, lilting voice spoke with quiet authority. Kennedy, in one of his speeches. I only caught one odd phrase: "I think it will be a very dangerous time for us all."

Mom snorted and blinked down at her crochet hook, fingers frantically busy. "Little did he know. He should never have gone down there, should never have taken Jackie. He knew how anti-Kennedy they all were down there."

"That's why he went," Dad sighed.

"What's that mean, anti-Kennedy?" I peered at the president's wife mincing down a set of aircraft stairs in a pink dress and fancy little hat. She reminded me of Miss Martin. No-one answered me, so I inhaled and tried again. "What does anti-Kennedy—"

"It means they didn't like him," James whispered from behind me.

But everyone in the video clips was cheering at his speeches. His polished car looked like liquid metal gliding down clogged streets amidst proud flags and motorcycles with flashing lights. Sandwiched between stern-looking cavalcade cars and men with black suits and glasses, President Kennedy's car was a long, dark convertible, flaunting its openness.

He wanted to be seen, I thought, *to drive down that street full of people who weren't supposed to like him, and smile and say: "Look at me. I'm right here. Close enough to touch."* People grinned, shook his hand, hung out windows, and off balconies and fire escapes to wave at him.

In the next succession of still pictures, the crowd thinned, and the cars maneuvered a sharp corner. The president clapped his hands to his throat and tilted sideways. A man in a suit launched off the cavalcade car behind the convertible and sprinted to leap onto its trunk. Just before he got there, the president's wife turned and scrambled up onto the trunk, like she was trying to escape a swarm of bees. The suited man guided her back to her seat and then shielded her and the president with his body. The car sped off.

A cold, uncomfortable quiet gripped our living room, all of us encapsulated in the shock of a twenty-year-old moment.

"What happened?" I flinched when I realized I'd been the one who broke the silence.

"He shot him," Dad croaked in disgust, heaving out of his chair and flicking off the TV set.

"And she had to live with that for the rest of her life." My mother pressed her lips together and stabbed at her half-formed toque before yanking out a row of stitches.

I wondered if that's why Mom married Dad, because he was quiet and she'd never have to worry about him drawing the wrong attention. I wanted to tell Dad that quiet was OK and sometimes you got candy for it.

That night, I lay in my bed and remembered Mrs. Kennedy in her pretty dress and hat, army crawling onto the trunk of that shiny car, and how the man in the nondescript suit protected her. I wondered if anybody remembered that man. He'd probably be happier if nobody did.

It would be smarter to be the quiet man in the suit, the one who looks like everybody else, because the man who is seen, the hero who smiles for the cameras and pulls attention to himself like a magnet, he's the one who gets shot in the head.

Days later, Miss Martin set a fresh pencil with metallic blue wrap in the groove at the top of my desk.

"Happy birthday, Daniel," she said.

I wanted to tell her there'd been some mistake. There was no Daniel in our class, but fluorescent light flickered off the iridescent pencil on my desk in turquoise and green, like a peacock's feather. I wanted it for myself. I didn't care who Daniel was. After snack, we practiced writing. I carefully transcribed the date from the blackboard into my journal with my crisp new pencil. 11/24/83. Blinking down, I rolled the digits in my head.

It is my birthday! I realized with a jolt. *I'm seven.*

I couldn't concentrate after that because I remembered once how Mom sent a cupcake in the twin's lunch on their birthday. They saved them until they got home and ate them in front of me without sharing, chocolate icing smearing their bunched cheeks as they laughed at my tears. I squirmed in my seat until the lunch bell sounded.

Flipping open the tin lid of my G.I. Joe lunch box, I scanned the contents. Salami and cheese sandwich, a bruised banana, an apple juice box, and a bag of dried out carrot sticks from yesterday. There was no cupcake. I sniffled, punched the straw into my juice box, and peeled the salami off the bread.

Maybe Mom was planning a surprise party. Excitement re-ignited in my chest. I'd go home and there'd be stacks of unfamiliar shoes littering the welcome mat because everyone in my class would be there, and they'd all yell surprise, and every one of them would have a wrapped present for me.

But no-one yelled surprise when I got home. Mom complained of a headache and paged through a magazine with JFK's face on the front cover, dabbing at tears in her eyes. We ate liver and onions, instant mashed potatoes, and green beans for supper. Jord and Jess had a food fight, and we all got sent to bed early. I lay in bed crying and hiccupping, onion still rank on my breath, and nobody asked why.

Next week an envelope with my name on it came in the mail. It was from our doctor's office. On the front, there was a picture of a black chimpanzee wearing a lab coat with a stethoscope around his neck. I hated his yellow–toothed, grimacing smile. 'Happy Birthday,' the card read, and on the inside, 'Seven years old, and still monkeying around! Just a reminder that Davis is due for his physical exam and immunization boosters.'

Mom phoned Dad, and he brought home a Sara Lee chocolate cake, and a gift bag with a coloring book, crayons and seven chocolate bars in it, one for each year. Everyone sang Happy Birthday, but Dad looked mad even when he tried to smile at me.

Mad at me or Mom? I couldn't tell.

That's when I knew something was wrong with me, the year my mom forgot my birthday because some president who'd been shot in the head twenty years ago was more important.

I squash the memory of JFK because it's triggering a flashback of a gun to my head. Pressing into the green couch, I rub my chest and breathe slowly against the squeezing in my throat and the erratic bass beat of my heart in my head.

Snap out of it.

I slip my hand into my pocket and hold on to the skeleton key like it's an anchor. It's cold in my palm, and, as it pulls warmth from my hand, it unspools my anxiety with it.

"You okay?"

Dad's voice makes me jump. I didn't hear him come in from the porch. Everyone else is out there, shucking a big sack of corn Mom bought at the market. I hate corn. I don't get why everyone makes such a big deal of something that comes out of you looking exactly the same as it went in. It's cow food. I'd used my invisibility to my advantage and ducked out of the ridiculous chore by simply keeping quiet.

"David, you okay?" Dad rounds the corner of the couch, frowning.

"Yeah, yeah." I nod and fake a smile, point to my head. "Headache is all. Just resting."

"Mom's got chicken salad sandwiches out there. Better grab one before they're gone."

"Thanks." I mean it. *Jesus,* for someone in my family to remember me concerning a meal hasn't happened in a long while. My brothers eat like sharks, like every meal could be their last, and every mouth is out to steal it. Tears prick my eyes, and I blink, surprised and instantly angry at the stupidity of them.

The couch jiggles as Dad sits next to me. "You sure you're ok? Is this about the army, because—"

"No, Dad," I choke. *God, no. Don't start this conversation. I don't have the energy for it.* "Just not hungry. Migraine maybe." I press one hand against my closed eyes but keep the other clenched in my pocket. *Deflect him.* "What're you guys up to today?"

Dad's eyebrows raise. "Well, your mother is hiking up to the falls, and I'm driving your brothers to the go-cart track. Stuart said if they tuned up a few of the engines, did some oil changes and swept up, he'd let them have the track to themselves after hours. You coming?"

"I don't think I could take the exhaust fumes right now." *And I can't think of anything I'd like to do less than ride around in go-carts with my jackass brothers.* "James going too?"

"Yeah, he promised to do some welding for Stuart."

"You guys have fun. I think I'm just gonna stay, try to sleep this off."

Dad zeros in on that. "David?" he asks sharply enough that I look up. His eyes are watery blue behind his glasses.

I take in his protruding Adam's apple, tanned skin and receding grey hair. *When did he get so old?* "What?"

"Have you been drinking my beer?"

"I hate beer, Dad. I think we both know where your missing beers went." I lie effortlessly, just like I do about smoking. Jord and Jess are so easy to blame, I almost feel guilty about it. Almost. "It's just a headache, honest." *God, I could use a smoke.* The tin under the front porch calls to me.

"Okay." Dad puts out his hand like he's going to pat my shoulder, but then seems to think better of it. His fingers curl, and his Adam's apple bobs. Then he stands up and goes back outside. *Breakable. He thinks you're breakable, David. That's the vibe you're putting out.*

By one p.m., my family has squeezed out of the cottage like frantic bees out of a hive, and I'm alone as silence soaks into the house, soft as sunlight. I do have a headache. I don't realize that my lie has turned into a reality until the tension at my temples eases in the newborn quiet. I stare at the crack under the door.

Where'd the dishtowel go? The question has been needling me all morning. Maybe my brothers took it, but I didn't risk asking them for fear of them breaking out into the harmonized chorus of 'Maneater' again. *Jesus,* my family has dated taste in music. In everything, really.

I slide my sock feet toward the crack in the door, but there's no draft. *Of course not. It's daytime. It only comes out at night, right...?* I smile, but it fades. *How many nights with no draft? Three? And as soon as you found the key and opened that door, it came back. Did you trigger it, whatever Everett built in there, did you start it up again? Some sort of trip wire that toggles on, what, an air conditioner?*

I pull the key out and turn it in my fingers. I've rubbed the handle so much that the word 'Pithos' is polished and black. It stains my fingers with soot and makes them smell like cast iron.

Bullshit. It was a regular guest room the next four times you opened the door. You must have imagined Bizarro world.

Maybe the draft and the key aren't connected. I'd felt the draft the first three nights here, before I discovered the key.

Maybe it's a cycle? Three days on, three off sort of thing? That is one messed up air conditioner. But you didn't see an AC unit in either version of the room—not when you hallucinated, and not in the regular bedroom afterward.

"Only one way to find out," I whisper, scrubbing my palm on the knee of my pants and standing.

Rolling my head, I shake out my shoulders and let my arms hang slack. The key tugs toward the door like a magnet. Frowning, I kneel and pin the key against the hardwood floor, under my thumb. I cup my other hand in front of it, half-expecting it to jitter across the hardwood when I release it, but the key doesn't move.

Of course it doesn't move, idiot.

I straighten and look down at it lying between my feet. My fingers twitch. They're fidgety, like they get when I take a long inhale of second-hand smoke. My fingers get desperate to cradle rolled paper between them.

You can get a smoke later. The key wants you to open the door.

And damn, if I'm not fighting the impulse to pick it up and tuck it into the keyhole like Mom presses the last pieces of her massive jigsaw puzzles into place, with a small, satisfied sigh. She doesn't have many complete sets anymore. Random pieces have gone astray, and there's the odd puzzle piece that doesn't seem to fit in with any set.

Kind of like her kids.

Sniffing, I bob down, clutch the key and march toward the door. The single tooth slips into its hole and turns the tumbler with a gratifying, heavy clunk. I flex my hand on the crystal knob and breathe once, twice. On the third exhale, I ease open the door just enough to see a sliver of bright green velvet.

Shit.

It's Bizarro room again. I squeeze my eyes shut, tuck my chin against my chest and clamp my teeth before refocusing, but the room remains too detailed to be an illusion. This time the couch is pristine, the pokey spring is missing and the pine floors gleam with fresh finish. It's darker in here, and when I glance through the kitchen window, it's drizzling rain outside.

Don't go in. There's something there. Something wrong.

Pressing back from the doorframe, I squint over my shoulder at our kitchen window. The sky is cobalt blue, and the lake is bright and choppy. The clock on the wall above the fridge reads 1:14. Bizarro world's kitchen doesn't have a clock at all.

I shudder and turn away, disoriented.

OK, go in for a minute. Try the door. Go outside. If it's some set up, some sort of elaborate diorama box around the window, then the fake front door will open to the trees out back.

Retreating to our front entry, I slip into my sandals and return to the five-panel, crossing the threshold from worn planks to freshly varnished ones.

As if it's not messed up enough, I'm friggin' time travelling now? Jesus, this is bigger than my imagination could scrape together. My toes curl, and my inhalations perch high in my chest, puffy and insubstantial, like birds.

Count your fingers. Dad made me do that when I was younger, and crying would grip me until I turned blue in the face. *Count your fingers, David.* I tap my thumb against my index, middle, ring, pinky and back again until I can breathe without panting.

I don't want to close the door but am horrified by the idea of leaving it open, like this room will leak into ours and muddy everything up if I don't keep it contained.

Besides, if Dad comes back early, and sees it open, what then? I shut the door and lock it from my side.

It feels safer locked. Like something here is watching me, waiting to slip around me and rush onto my side. Something with sinister intent. I slide the key out, press it back in and unlock it. I don't know how many times I practice the mundane task before I pocket the key and turn back to face the room. The door calls to me.

*Everything else in here could be procured and set up, a mock set, a big joke, but the window and the door...*I can't grasp the realness of them.

Edging past the kitchen, I stand before the front door and peer out onto a convincing porch and beyond, the lake, choppy and slate grey. Pressing my fingers against the glass, I draw them down, searching for the distorted pixilation trail a screen would produce, but it looks and feels like normal glass.

Just open it. I yank the front door open and cold air that smells of ozone tingles against my cheeks.

"Shit," I murmur. "Holy shit, what is this?"

Mist curls off the lake, and my breath puffs out of me with the urgent tempo of a stoked steam engine. *You're being ridiculous. You can't figure this out if you can't calm down.* Hadn't Dad used that line too?

I sit on the rocking chair for a good ten minutes, trying to ratchet my breathing down, rubbing the back of my neck as it prickles. I don't see another human being the entire time. Birds, yes. Squirrels, check. It's all real—too real—to be a hallucination. I can even vouch for fish jumping. No people. No Angus or Evie or Veronica, shame really. Nobody.

The silence laps at me like ripples on the grey lake. Rain blows in waves through a line of trees shorter than the ones I know. Chilled, I retreat to the house and keep my wet sandals on, tracking water across the floor.

Mom will murder me for this.

I open the fridge and a glass jug of milk rattles in the door slot. Wax paper parcels and glass casserole dishes line the wire shelves. A row of stubby beer bottles crowd toward the back behind a covered butter dish. The old Philco's compressor is quieter than I've ever heard it. Pressing the door shut, I stare up at the loft and remember the out-of-place dictionary on the bed yesterday. This loft seems empty. There's no cot. No beanbag chair. I climb the ladder to find a thin mattress on a rug, made up with a patchwork quilt and lace-edged pillow. Behind it is a bookshelf. Only a few dozen books all hard covers, and the dictionary stands out among them like a giant.

I crawl over the lumpy mattress and pull the heavy book into my lap. The cover smells of new leather and the gold-leaf glints brightly. I open it. Someone has written over the original printing in tidy cursive, rows and rows of it, each letter and swirl in broad, dark lead, like the writer had pressed hard enough to imprint three copies of carbon paper invoices.

The rules are different here. I can't keep track without writing them out, and I can't afford to mess this up anymore. I've got to fix it. Annie already thinks I'm crazy. I'm not sure she's wrong. Who could blame her? How could I explain any of this? I can't even figure it out myself. Things I know for sure:

The key is the gateway, not the door. I don't know what kind of brand name Pithos is, but it must be old, because I can't find any information on it. The key churned up with the clay when I was drilling the pile holes for the addition. How in God's name would a skeleton key get buried so far down, in clay no less? I drilled those pile holes six feet deep. That's when the key spun off the auger bit and hit me in the shin. God, how I wish I never saw it. I should have buried it as deep as the poor bastard before me must have done, but I didn't. As far as I can tell, the only thing special about the closet door is that the key happened to fit and I was tickled when it did. No surprise there, though. These old tumbler sets are pretty standard. Last week I bought five other keys at the flea market, and two of them fit. If someone is reading this, if you found the damned key, get rid of it. Throw it as far into the lake as you can. That's my advice.

This one is damned important, so perk up. You can't leave anything behind here. It would have been nice to know this one beforehand. See, with just the key, the signal comes in patchy, like a bad radio station. Some days this wretched place tunes in, and others I just sit locked in the empty guest room I built instead. I tell Annie I'm varnishing the floor. Anyways. My tobacco tin. I must have left it here on the counter one day because I can't find it anywhere on the other side, and now the hellhounds have locked onto it like a scent, and they want through. Badly. I haven't seen my guest room in a long time, just layers and layers of purgatory. I'm sorry, Annie. I'm sorry I opened the door and lied about this place. I'm sorry I ever picked up the key. What kind of man opens a gate to hell? One who's got a penance to pay, I suppose. I'm here. I hate this empty, soulless place. It's eating away at me, but I'm here, do you hear me? I'm trying to set things right again.

"Jesus Christ," I exhale and turn the page, but it's just a blank copyright page for Merriam-Webster.

I thumb through the dictionary twice but can't find any more handwritten pages. When I stop at the 'G' thumb tab, there are no crayon markings around the word Gulf. Turning back to the first page, I trace the thick lead with my finger, reading the passage again, carefully.

This is Everett. Has to be. Jesus, if he saw it too, it's real. I'm not hallucinating, not crazy. He found the same key.

Straightening, I peer out the kitchen window as rain ribbons down the glass. My gaze wanders to the wall above the fridge.

"Shit!" I slam the book closed and ram it back onto the shelf. *How long have I been in here? Half an hour?*

Dad would be back by now. I plunge down the ladder two rungs at a time and skid when I get to the door, listening for movement on the other side. Dropping to my belly, I press my cheek onto the smooth hardwood and peer under the crack but see nothing but more hardwood.

"Screw it." *I need to get out of here.*

Pressing to my feet, I slip the key into the hole and ease the door unlocked, squeezing through. It's empty on my side. Exhaling, I lock the door and jam the key back into the safety of my pocket. My eyes dart to the clock above the fridge.

1:14. Holy-C.S. Lewis, not one second past the moment I left.

Everett must have hacked up that Goddamned wardrobe and re-purposed it into a door. I smile, but it's not funny, really.

He said the door wasn't the gateway.

My hand clamps around the key so hard its blunt tooth bites into my palm. The metal is still cool, no matter how tightly I grip it. I reach behind me and jiggle the crystal knob, double-checking that it's locked.

The old guy thinks it's a gate to hell. Either you're both crazy or there's something seriously messed up in that room. Regardless, I feel safer with it locked before heading out the front door into the real world.

This time I find Angus in his office, crammed behind an impossibly small metal desk with a pencil behind his ear, a pen in his hand and a large, yellowed ledger opened before him.

"Hey, Angus!" I offer in an overly cheery voice, but he doesn't look up. I step closer. "Excuse me, Mr. Tyler?"

He jumps at that, glares at me for a second before his eyes clear and so does his throat. "I help you with somethin'?"

No Sir Rawlingson for me. "Yeah, actually. Just curious, really. You said Everett was the name of the guy who built the addition on our cottage?"

"Which cottage?" Angus squinted and clicked the pen against his teeth.

The one with the gate to hell, apparently. "Ours," I answer stupidly. "My-my dad. David Rawlingson."

"Oh!" Angus brightens. "You find the key?"

My throat twitches and I shake my head, hand pressed deep into my pocket. "No, no, sorry. No key. The guy's name is Everett, right? And his wife was..."

"Annie, if ya need to know." Angus leans forward and his chair squeaks. "Why?"

"I just found a book that belongs to him. Them. Her name is in the front. I thought he might want it back, maybe?"

Mr. Tyler doesn't look like he believes me. He drums his fingers on the worn particle board desktop and stares at me for a long moment before sighing. "I s'pose you can bring it round an I'll hold it for him, how's that sound?"

"Great. Yeah, great, I'll do that." I nod and grab a pepperoni stick.

"That'll be ten cents." Angus says and I walk back to the cottage as, dusty, shirtless kids on bikes stream past.

It's him, Everett, and he thinks he broke into hell somehow. He said sometimes it's just a normal room and sometimes it's purgatory.

Obviously he didn't find his tobacco tin and seal off the other world before his wife got sick, did he? A thought clicks in my mind, one that dries my throat and brings me to a stop in the middle of the dirt road. I choke on the pepperoni and swallow hard to get it down. *The dishtowel. The strawberry dishtowel is gone, the one I stuffed under the door.*

Sprinting back to the house, I sag at the sight of the old Econoline bellied up to the cottage. *Dad's back.*

Although I can't tear the place apart, I spend the rest of the afternoon surreptitiously searching the cottage for a dishtowel. There's plenty of them here, but not one with strawberries printed on the front. It's gone. The coincidence of reading about Everett's missing tobacco tin and losing the towel I stuffed under the door to stop the draft freaks me out.

What if something pulled it under? What if it's more than just a cold draft?

That night I lie sideways on the sofa with the support bar digging into my hip and my gaze pinned to the crack in the door. I wait for the cold draft. Somewhere around 10 p.m., it wafts through turning the skin on my arms to gooseflesh. Even though I'm braced for it, I shudder, stand and yank the blanket off the back of the armchair, layering it over the one already on the hide-a-bed.

You're gutless, David. This is all just some insane old man's room, some sort of smoke and mirrors twisted prank. I shovel a few more wedges of firewood into the woodstove and watch the sparks. *Or art. Yeah, maybe Everett dabbled in modern art and turned the closet into 'Cottage: A Study in Desolation'. Sure.* I nearly convince myself. Settling back onto the foldout couch, I nearly flush out my irrational fear with a solid, improbable rationale, and then the hand comes under the door.

CHAPTER SEVEN

It happens so fast, I nearly miss it. One second, I'm dozing. The next, my eyes roll open, and I glance toward the closet door. This black, hairless, four-fingered hand eases through the gap, drums its thick claws against the bottom edge of the door and then bites hard into the wood. Paint chips and the door creaks. Tendons stand out on the back of the hand as it yanks back hard. Everything rattles.

I pull my bare feet up onto the safe island of the couch and scream my ever-loving head off. By the time I get a hold of myself, lights are flicking on and my family is pouring into the living room in their underwear. James careens down the loft ladder brandishing an honest-to-god candlestick.

"What on earth, David?" Dad's voice is even, but he's frowning.

"You okay?" James grabs my shoulder, spinning me toward him, and I flinch, pull out of his grip and refocus on the door.

Four parallel gouges trail down to the bottom left corner.

I point at them and stutter, "A-ah hand. A hand came under the door."

"Ah, Jesus," Jord sighs. "The haunted door again? What are you, four years old?"

Adrenalin seeps out of me like hot sap, leaving nothing but prickling limbs in its wake. I blink and swallow hard because tears are welling up in my eyes like I *am* four years old. I keep my gaze on the door for longer than I should because the collective, dissecting gaze of my family is settling on my back, and I hate the heaviness of their attention on me all at once. It's suffocating.

"No. Look." James stumbles past me toward the door.

I want to reach out and stop him, but my arm is too sluggish, and he's past me before I can react.

"There's scratches. Look at them! Those weren't there before." James traces his fingers down the ragged grooves.

Jesus, James. Get away from it. I want to say, but my throat is so tight my breathing is coming out in sick, whistling exhales. An awful pressure grips my chest. Everyone is staring at me. *You've been loud, David. You pulled all the attention in, and now you have to pay.*

Mom, of all people, saves me. "James, get away from there. Raccoons have rabies."

"Raccoons?" Jess hoots.

Mom smoothes down her hair and tightens her housecoat over her chest. "Vera—you know Vera from three houses down?— she said that Angus's been trapping them this winter, they've been so bad. He sent one away for testing. Rabies, the whole lot of them down here have it, and I'm not leaving early if you get bitten by one of the filthy things, James."

"Rabid raccoons. You friggin' serious?" Jess grins.

The air unclogs around me as the attention in the room shifts. I can't stop staring at the black crack under the door, and James's hand so close to it.

He shifts toward me. "What'd it look like, David?"

I latch onto Mom's theory like a lifeline, even though it's absolute bullshit. "It was black. Could have been a raccoon, yeah." I know the difference between a raccoon paw and a claw the size of my bloody head.

Hellhounds. Everett called them hellhounds. Jesus, he wasn't crazy. I'm not crazy. There's something on the other side and it stole the bloody dishtowel.

Jord snaps his fingers and starts humming the chorus of Maneater.

"Shut your mouth, Jord." Dad orders.

A pot of coffee and Bailey's Irish Cream later, we settle on the comfortable family verdict that the hand was indeed a raccoon who'd found some hole in the floorboards of Everett's windowless room.

"Well, perfect reason to bust the door open then." Jord raises his coffee cup like he's making a toast. "Rabid raccoon exterminators! Angus'll thank us."

I cringe at the thought of anybody breaking the door down. Without the key locking the other world away, the draft and whatever that hand belonged to could access my world unimpeded. I know little about dimensions or science shit like that, but mixing two worlds together willy-nilly seems like what causes black holes or a future full of mutant humans.

"No-one is busting anything." Dad smacks his mug down like it's a judge's gavel. "*I* pay for this place. *I* pay the damage deposit. I'll speak to Angus in the morning about setting up a trap out back, and Jord, if you want to do something productive, you and Jess drive to the hardware store in the morning and pick up some steel wool. We can find whatever hole it's coming in through and stuff it full of that. Mice hate the feel of it between their teeth. I imagine raccoons would be the same."

I sink further into the hard kitchen chair and grip the skeleton key. When Mom had started the coffee, I'd slipped into my jeans to keep the key close. I knew the conversation would swing toward opening the door.

Throw the key into the lake, that's what Everett said to do. But it's too late for that. I let one of the maneaters pull a dishtowel through the crack. My fault. *And if Everett is right, my brothers won't need a key to get into Bizarro world now. The dimension locked onto ours now because of a Goddamned strawberry dishtowel.*

We finish the pot, our cups filled more with Bailey's than coffee. The alcohol and the warmth bleed tension from my shoulders and I relax, shrugging and wholeheartedly backing the raccoon theory, even though it's bound to ensure a merciless bout of teasing from my brothers. They'll forget soon enough and move onto something else. They never pay attention for long.

I don't want them in there. I don't want my family anywhere near the black-hole evil that wafts from under the door. The hand had seemed sentient, alien, and hungry, like it would have pulled me under if it could, like that undistilled maliciousness that makes up the molecules of childhood bogeymen. That as-yet-undiscovered black matter we somehow lose sense of in adulthood. Yet it still exists in stale midnight corners and behind the eyes of Sam Ren as he kicks the life out of you in a fast food parking lot.

I don't want to go back through the door. I don't want to be the idiot who sees the blackness coming and doesn't run, but I have to do it. *I* dialed in Bizarro world with that Goddamned dishtowel. My fault. *I* built this bridge.

A sour half-smile twitches my lips. *"You ever thought about building bridges, David?"* MacNeill had said that, hadn't he? *The first day we met when I was sixteen. Bloody ironic.*

By the time I turned sixteen, I thought I knew which bridges to maintain and which to burn to slip through the cracks of life with minimal turbulence. I wore hand-me-down clothes as bland as white bread, even though I could afford to buy new if I wanted to. I landed an after-school job at Dairy Queen. By the end of the first day, I'd mastered the signature curl that topped the soft ice cream cones, but still listened to my manager drone about how curling a cone was all in the wrists for another week and a half after that. He called me Darryl the whole time, even though my name tag clearly read David. Darryl wasn't such a bad name.

My co-workers seemed to register my presence only when a job came up they didn't want to do like inventory in the freezer room, cleaning toilets, sanitizing the soft serve machine. I didn't mind those jobs. They were tedious, but nobody yelled at you about their cold burger if you weren't manning a till.

At home, James, the twins, and I were the only kids left. Jeremiah was married with a kid on the way. Justine was travelling abroad. Julie had moved in with her boyfriend, and Mom hadn't talked to her since. Jord and Jess were loud enough for the four of us. My parents saddled them with all the household chores and they were currently paying rent because Dad caught them smoking in the backyard. Idiots. I'd been smoking since fifteen, but no-one had caught me yet. There were perks to being the invisible one, but there was always the guilt to contend with too, because I wasn't *completely* invisible. Eventually, I moved too fast, or spoke too loud, and became visible.

I once tagged along when James drove the twins halfway across the city to their rugby practice. We piled out of the Econoline in the parking lot, and James yelped and jumped as an orange-striped cat dove out from behind the wheel well on the driver's side and froze before him. Cold, pale eyes measured my brother, who stared back in shock. God knows how long that cat had been along for the ride, clinging onto the undercarriage, without us knowing.

That's how people stared at me when they actually *saw* me, like James gaped at that cat. First came the shock of my sudden presence, then the slow guilt as it sunk in, the realization that I'd been along for the ride the whole time, beneath their attention, and they hadn't known I was there. After that usually came anger. Most people didn't particularly like sudden surprises, and no-one enjoyed being guilted. James, after a dazed second or two, cursed and kicked at the cat.

My parents, and teachers, after several disconcerting rediscoveries of the existence of David, joined forces and sentenced me to a month of twice-weekly meetings with my school guidance counselor, because, apparently, I was 'withdrawn' and 'overly quiet'.

At first, I thought the joke was on them, because the guidance counselor was a bit of an airhead. Every time I answered one of her questions she'd frown, bite her bottom lip, and nod her head so vigorously her ponytail bobbed. After my second visit, she consistently forgot her appointments with me, and I figured smugly, *Problem solved.* How was I to know that Airhead would lose her job for allegedly fondling a student—I didn't think she had it in her—and her temp replacement, Elliot, would be so gung-ho on organizing a school job fair that he'd use me as free labor during our appointments? It wasn't so bad. I mostly photocopied and folded brochures. *Very* therapeutic. The day of the job fair, Elliot lent his office to his brother, an army recruitment officer named Jim Mac-Neill, who locked me in his sights ASAP.

"What're you in for?" he asked, like we were jail buddies or something. We sat across from each other, me in a hard molded plastic chair and him in his brother's seat. I watched as he lined up a stack of pristine white business cards on the edge of the desk.

Picking one up, I squinted at the name. "Well, Jim. My parents seem concerned about my lack of peer-driven, teenaged rebellion."

"Seem to be doing fine in the sarcasm department." A hard smile cracked his face as I set the business card crookedly back on his desk. He kept his gaze pinned to it for a moment, but didn't

move to realign it. "Elliot says you're socially isolated, and you pre-
fer dodging conflict as opposed to facing it head on."

I tipped my chair back on two legs. "Elliot's breaching student
confidentiality then, isn't he, Sir?" I hoped the 'Sir' would get a rise
out of him, but Sergeant MacNeill didn't take the bait.

Instead, he leaned back in his chair until it creaked, smoothed
his fatigues over his rounded belly and squinted at me, like he saw
me, like I didn't surprise him at all.

I wonder if Jim owns a cat? The thought struck me out of nowhere.

"You ever thought about building bridges, David?"

My chair slammed back onto its front legs, and I snorted. "I
didn't peg you as the psychological type, Jim."

"Shit, kid. I meant literally." He shook his head, swiveled his
chair away from me to heave a thin, faded brown briefcase onto the
desk. Rifling inside, he tugged out a brochure and handed it to me.

I frowned down at a glossy pamphlet with a red seal around a
golden beaver in the corner. The title read: 'Combat Engineer'.

"Sapper. Build bridges to connect the good guys and blow
up the one's the bad guys want to come across." Sergeant MacNeill
explained.

I skimmed over first few lines.

We serve:

*By clearing routes, constructing fighting positions and bridges to
aid combat operations.*

*By placing, detecting, and detonating explosives to prevent ene-
my movement.*

"Jesus, you don't waste your time, do you?"

"I'm not one for bullshit." Jim shrugged. "We both know why
I'm here today. I was a sapper for three tours and there's not a job
out there like it. All set for a job in civil engineering, construction,
or building inspection if you decide, down the road, that the army

isn't your cup of tea. Elliot says you've got the math grades for it, and, to be honest, you're the right type. Flying under the radar is a key skill when you're the soldier *in front* of the front lines."

I nodded dumbly, folded the brochure and held it out over the desk, but the Sergeant waved me off.

"Keep it. Think about it." He handed me the business card I'd discarded. "And we can talk about it more if you're interested."

I threw out the pamphlet, but that night, I remembered JFK and the men in suits, the quiet ones who all looked the same, who blended into the background and shed attention with practiced ease. I wanted to be important like them. Just once, I wanted somebody to look at me and say, 'David, thank God you're here!', but that had always seemed impossible without stepping into the centre of attention.

I could build bridges. I could connect stranded people. Damn, I'd look good in camouflage.

For the next two weeks, I ditched my guidance counselor and visited Sergeant Jim MacNeill at his office in the recruitment centre after school instead. It was on my way home, and my parents worked late and never missed me anyways. Sergeant MacNeill and I talked of route reconnaissance, road construction, and Bailey bridges, and I left with an invigorating sense of belonging and purpose. He coached me on the steps to enlisting.

"Now, you're sixteen, so you need parental permission. Give them some time to warm up to the idea, and you're welcome to bring them in any time to meet with me."

I didn't know how to broach the subject with my parents. Mom would cry, guaranteed. Everything triggered crying with her, but Dad, he was a man of quiet discipline who kept his hair as neatly trimmed as his yard. He ironed his jeans for Christ's sake. Surely he'd back me if I stated my plans to join the military logically. So I started planting recruiting pamphlets around the house, but it was ages until my mother found one and delivered it to my father.

He cleared his throat three times as he tapped the brochure on his thigh. "What is this, David?" he asked with quiet precision. "Is this yours?"

I nodded and squared my shoulders, feeling six years old again. *Be loud, David.* "I think it'd be a great career choice with a lot of opport—"

"NO!" Dad bellowed, shot out of his chair and chopped the pamphlet through the air like an axe. He stared at me with a strange desperation in his eyes. I don't know what he saw in mine, but he shook his head violently, and balled his hands in his thinning hair. "Jesus Fucking Christ, David. No!"

That was the first time in sixteen years I ever heard my dad yell, take the Lord's name in vain, or swear.

It floored me, but a niggling, sardonic thought crept through my shock. *Well. Two years to warm them up to the idea.* I could be persistent as hell when I needed to be.

I lie in the dark, curled as far away from the five-panel as I can get. The metal edge of the foldout couch bites into my shoulder blade and I let it. I stare at the cottage ceiling and review the last year in my head. I feel older than seventeen. Tired. Except for the door, there's nothing else pulling me forward anymore. I'm pretty sure seventeen is too young to lose momentum, but I have. I don't sleep. I keep waiting for the draft to come back.

"You look like shit, Skippy. Get any sleep?" James says as he stomps down the loft ladder the next morning. Mom's clattering in the kitchen like she's lost something. Pancakes are burning in the cast-iron pan.

When I don't answer, James ducks around Mom with ease, flips the blackened pancakes onto a plate, and spoons four more circles of lumpy batter into the pan. He eyes me the entire time. "You know what? We should switch."

"What?" I heave on the foldout couch and the mattress accordions into the depths.

"Switch beds." James pokes at the pan and Mom glances up. "Yeah, I just about turfed her off the loft last night after we all went back to bed. Woke up with my toes hanging over the edge, arms wind-milling. I must have been sleepwalking again. Think it might be safer for me down here."

Bullshit. I give him the side-eye as I stuff green couch cushions into place. I know he slept soundly last night. He didn't move at all.

"And the cot up there is more comfortable. What'dya say?"

"I think it's a good idea." Mom chirps and I blink, shocked for a moment that she's involved in this conversation at all. She pulls the milk from the fridge, sniffs the container, and pours a glass for James. "You still sleepwalk? I thought maybe you'd grown out of it."

For a single moment, I thought you might be worried about my welfare, Mom. Thanks.

"Grow out of what?" Jess stumbles in from the bunkroom, hair pasted to the side of his head and eyes squinty with sleep.

"James is sleepwalking again. He's going to switch beds with David so he doesn't fall out of the loft and break his neck." Mom frowns at me, as if just saying my name brings on the guilt.

Jess zombie-walks to the kitchen and swipes one of the burned pancakes. He rolls it and stuffs the whole thing into his mouth before Mom slaps him.

I rake my teeth over a loose flap of skin on my lower lip, but can't figure out how to change James's mind without looking like a jerk. *Goddamnit. He cornered you. He's curious about the door and knows you're hiding something.*

"Gonna protect widdle David from the man-eating raccoons, are ya?" Crumbs spray from Jess's mouth as he elbows James.

James grins, unfazed. "I'm gonna get in. I'm gonna see what's behind door number one."

Shit. Don't encourage them, James! My fist clenches and the key pinches me, like it heard, like it knows.

"Bullcrap!" Jess stabs a finger at our older brother. "Not before me and Jord!"

"Don't talk with food in your mouth, Jessie." Mom beckons him to the table, peeling plastic wrap off a big bowl of fruit salad. "Sit down, both of you. I'm cooking." She goes to the cupboard and sets two plates out. Just two. One for Jess and one for James.

The twins have left for the hardware store and Dad has strolled to Angus's office to discuss raccoon traps by the time I grab a plate and sift through the spoils of breakfast for something salvageable. James is up to his elbows at the sink, scrubbing plates. Now and then he looks over his shoulder, frowning. Something's eating at him. As I pick chunks of watermelon out of my runny fruit salad, he finally speaks.

"Why don't you ever eat with the rest of us?"

Not this again. "I'm eating." I shrug.

I know James. He's bringing this up as a lead into talking about something else, because we've broached the subject of my invisibility many times over the years, and both of us know it's not something cured by a simple conversation. Mom makes lame excuses whenever James broaches the conversation with her. Dad clams up. I've long believed I'm irreparable, but still indulge my older brother when he brings it up, because I can tell it frustrates him, the fact that I'm the only one who acknowledges my invisibility.

"You didn't sit down with us this morning, or yesterday."

"Jesus, James. You know how it is." I soak a dry stack of pancakes in blueberry syrup. "All elbows, stabbing forks, and reaching arms. I like eating without someone's armpit in my face, that's all."

He shakes his head. "Mom doesn't set out a plate for you."

I shrug again. "I'm a big boy and I know where to find the plates. Besides, I like the quiet. Dad takes his plate out to the porch, I don't see anybody hassling him."

"Mom sets out his plate."

"James, come on." I stab the pancakes with a fork and cut into them so hard my plate jiggles. "I'm not some stray dog you have to look after, alright? I eat. I'm eating, see?" I cram a wedge of pancakes into my mouth and chew slowly to buy some time. He's going to bring up the door, that's what this is leading to, and I don't know how to divert him.

"See, that's what's wrong!" James shakes out his hands and turns to face me, jaw twitching and cheeks flushed. "A stray dog. That's exactly how Mom treats you. The twins too, and I don't know what's wrong with them. It's messed up. I'd join the bloody army too, David, just to get away from it. I don't know how you do it."

Bingo. I know how to keep James away from the door today. "About that. The army. I've been meaning to ask for your advice." I scrub the back of my neck while he watches me. "Can we walk? Maybe take a lap around the lake in a bit? I just need to get some stuff off my chest." My chest tightens in disagreement. Of course, I don't want to talk about the army. I don't need advice because I've already decided. I'm not joining, but James doesn't know that, and it's the only thing that's going to pull him away from the door today. Something big and sincere. Some explanation of why I changed my mind. The idea of opening up makes my throat close. Nobody knows why I changed my mind. I've told no-one about the gun. It's not a bridge I've cared to cross until now.

CHAPTER EIGHT

Dad's confrontation over the army pamphlet, and his subsequent blow out, shook me, but didn't defeat my enthusiasm. Over the next year, Sergeant MacNeill and I combined our efforts to present the advantages of a military career. I tallied the cost of what four years of education at local civilian and private universities would be. I even made a bloody chart, trying to appeal to my father's financial sensibilities.

"A free secondary education," I said.

"Not free, David." My father's lips pinched tight.

I rarely spoke to my mother, but I cornered her one quiet afternoon, and bit the inside of my cheek until the pain brought convincing tears to my eyes. Then, I blurted out how much I wanted this, a chance to contribute, going on about how I craved a disciplined environment, how I thought it would really help me with the social problems I'd been having, the camaraderie I'd have.

Mom nodded at all the right spots, but she kept her arms crossed tightly, and the guilt just kept growing in her eyes until my tears dried up, and so did our conversation.

I even invited Jim to supper so we could press our case together.

He showed up at our front door in a pressed shirt, thin tie and slacks. Dad thought he was a door-to-door insurance salesman until he introduced himself. When recognition dawned in Dad's eyes, he gripped the door hard and whispered, "I don't want you talking to my son anymore, understand? I'm prepared to get a restraining order, and I intend to go as far up as required to get your brain-washing ass away from kids his age." He slammed the door before Sergeant MacNeill could respond.

I snorted and shook my head. *Hippy.* I couldn't believe it. *My Dad's a Goddamned hippy.*

"Not much more you can do but wait it out, David." Jim shrugged and clicked his briefcase shut on his freshly cleared desk. Only a week had passed since Dad's front door threat, and it didn't seem like a coincidence that Jim was transferring to another city. There were other schools chocked full of impressionable teenagers for Sergeant MacNeill to mold into recruits.

The military's very own Mary Poppins.

"The army will still be there when you're eighteen." He smiled grimly.

Thanks for nothing, Jim. If I couldn't convince them with you, I've got no chance on my own.

I started lifting weights at the gym after school, and picked up an extra shift at Dairy Queen, anything to avoid my parents. During slow times, I'd write sample Canadian Forces Aptitude Tests in the back room where An Mei, a tiny Cantonese woman with deep smile lines, iced all our cakes.

"What all that for?" She prodded a frosting tip toward my stack of papers before piping out a delicate orange flower.

"Tests. Entry exams for the army."

"Army?" She pushed the band of her hairnet up with her wrist and leaned over the cake intently. "Why you want to get shot at?"

"Well…" I said. "If I do it right, I won't get shot at."

"I move here so my boy never have to fight in war. Here, they put up hands to go. You not stupid, David."

"My most notable accomplishment is fastest soft-serve machine sanitizer, Mei. If that's not stupid, I don't know what is."

"You good boy." She swapped out icing bags and pulled a notepad closer to her, carefully sounding out the words jotted in blocky marker, before transcribing them in blue gel. I thought the conversation was over, but she straightened and squinted at me. "Smart, too. You want to be Rambo or something?"

"Something," I chuckled, crossed out an answer and circled another. "Not Rambo, but something."

An Mei shook her head, pointed her gnarled fingers at me like a machine gun, and pursed her lips. "Bap-bap-bap. You no Rambo, David. Better than that." Then she gestured around us. "Better than this too."

"God, I hope so," I sighed.

Because she didn't drive, Mei's son, Ren Shun—he called himself Sam Ren—picked her up after every shift. Usually, he waited in the parking lot, slouched in his Porsche. I'd never seen a more thoroughly used-up car that was still drivable. The thing was all cracked upholstery, missing trim, and pitted paint.

I guessed Sam was my age, but had never seen him at school or chumming around with anyone else. In fact, the only time I'd ever seen Sam outside of his car, he'd been obsessively polishing a hopelessly faded fender. So it stunned me when, halfway through our shift during my smoke break, the battered Porsche peeled into the parking lot with three heads bobbing inside.

Sam Ren heaved the driver's door open. He strode toward the kitchen's back door, eyes cold and mouth hard.

"Hey, Sam." I pressed up from my milk crate and flicked my cigarette aside, exhaling slowly, but Sam yanked the door open without looking my way, spouting a torrent of sharp words in Cantonese.

Mei looked up from her cake, shook her head and scolded Sam in a high, clipped voice. He gripped her elbow and hauled her toward the door so hard the icing bag spun out of her hand and hit the floor with an explosive splat.

"Hey!" I straightened. "Easy, man. What's the hurry?"

He shouldered by me, slapped the exit bar, and shoved Mei out ahead of him.

"Easy, man! That's your mom." I tripped, looked down and recognized Mei's sandal.

She stumbled and gasped as her son marched her toward his car, heedless of her small bare foot slapping against asphalt.

"Sam, stop. Jesus." I scooped up the sandal. "She's not even done her shift yet. You'll get her in trou—"

An Mei's sharp yelp cut off my words. Both of Sam's sunglass-wearing associates had exited his car and stood, chests puffed out to display the bright flash of their silk ties, watching as Ren stuffed his mother unceremoniously into one of the rear seats.

Mei must have banged her head on the car's low roof because she had her rubber-gloved hand pressed to her forehead. A trickle of blood wormed into the creases at the corner of her eye as she turned to face me, gaze sharp with fear.

Help her, David. Don't just stand there. Be loud. I clenched my teeth. "Sam," I hollered. "Stop. That how you treat your own mother?" *Shut up, David. If you know what's good for you, shut the hell up.*

Ren turned toward me slowly, eyes flickering through an ever-familiar succession of emotion: mild surprise, guilt, anger.

He sees you now. I licked my lips and held out the sandal. *Build a bridge, David. Fix this.* "Can we just calm things down a bit here?"

Sam flexed his fingers against the edge of the open car door, and nodded sharply. His thin moustache twitched as he spoke. "Oh,

I'm calm, Gweilo. I'm real calm, and you know what? It's none of your damned business how I treat my mother."

"There's no need to be so rough is all I'm saying." I looked down at the tiny, dirty sandal in my fist.

"David, go inside," Mei trilled from inside the back of the car.

Sam smiled, and it reminded me of one of my neighbor's dogs, the one who curled its lip and bared its yellow teeth every time I walked by. "Yeah, David, why don't you go back inside."

No-one would talk to Sergeant Jim MacNeill like that, even with his fat paunch. The odd thought struck me, and I heard the words tumbling out of me before I could stop them. "You know there's a surveillance camera up there." I pointed to the light post behind me. "Elder abuse, that's a hot topic on the news right now, ever since that old guy on ninetieth got beaten and robbed."

Ren's wingmen broke into motion, lurching toward me like gargoyles come to life. Sam held up a hand without looking back, and they stopped obediently. He sneered, let go of the car door and edged toward me, loose-limbed. "Yeah, I read about him. Real shame, that was."

I didn't see the punch coming. Sam's fist hooked upward just under my ribcage on the right side, and it felt like electricity arcing through me. Air barked out of me, explosively. I wasn't aware of twisting or falling until my face met asphalt and I dropped Mei's sandal. Leather shoes scuffed around me. I rolled away from them, but another set corralled me in, caught me hard in the ribs. My mouth gaped open, and my stomach sucked in, but I couldn't inhale.

Somebody screamed and a peculiar thought gripped me. *You dropped the sandal. You better find it and pick it up.*

My hands swept the hot pavement around me, but a shadow passed overhead and another foot buried itself deep into my stomach, folding me in half. My elbows pinned to my sides. I don't remember how many kicks came after that because a strange heat started radiating from my core.

You're bleeding. You're bleeding internally. But the smell of ammonia filled my nostrils as Sam and his lackeys laid into me with strange and steady patience. *No, you pissed yourself. That's what it is.* A memory of Jord in the gas station bathroom swamped me.

Sam Ren gripped my shoulder and rolled me onto my back, and all I could see was blue sky, careless clouds cruising, and a gun. Ren held a pistol, aimed at my face.

I'd heard of hold-up victims describing the barrel of the gun as this dark, expanding hole, sucking them in, swallowing them up. That's bullshit. The gun looked like a Goddamned gun. Sam Ren's eyes were the pits, black, cold and bottomless. Deep hollows.

I breathed in the smell of urine and hot tar and waited.

"Don't be stupid!" An Mei's voice. I couldn't tell if she directed it at me or at her son, but Sam's awful eyes snapped back into focus and blinked.

He curled the gun away from me, looped a finger through a belt-hole, and grinned at my soggy crotch. "See you round, Gweilo."

I blinked at a tattoo on the back of Ren's hand, three dots in a triangle, between his finger and thumb. Curling sideways, I swallowed bile. Three sets of leather shoes clacked away from me. The car door slammed with a chuff. Tires chirped as the old Porsche shuddered out of the parking lot.

I lay curled in the fetal position for three more gagging breaths before pushing to my feet, tugging at the crotch of my pants, and waddling inside. Standing in the bathroom with my legs wide apart, I swayed in front of the hand dryer, slapped the silver button and lined up the nozzle.

Jesus Christ, can you not have a pivotal, life-changing moment without pissing yourself? My shaking hands braced against cool cinderblock. *Stupid. My God, you're stupid, David. The guy had a prison tattoo, and you missed it. You let it suck you right in, walked right into the spotlight, and Mei didn't even want your help.*

Once my pants dried, I shuffled to the walk-in freezer, wedged a box of Dilly bars into the door so it couldn't lock me in, and leaned gingerly against the icy wall until the heat in my cheeks drained away. Then I unclipped my name tag, folded my apron, and left them on the back room lunch table beside Mei's melting, half-frosted ice cream cake. Nobody noticed me leaving.

I pissed blood for two days, and I never went back to Dairy Queen. To this day, my ribs still ache at the sight of a soft serve cone with a curled tip.

That summer, I quietly accompanied my parents, the twins, and James to the summer cottage, and never mentioned a word about a military career again. Until now, walking around the lake, spilling my guts to James despite every fiber in my body telling me to shut up.

"How can I, James?" I shrug, turning a flat stone in my hand before hooking a finger along its edge, and whipping it toward the water's surface. It skips twice before sinking. "How can I even imagine a job on the front lines, when I pissed my pants the first time somebody pointed a gun my way?"

"Jesus, David." James blows a long exhale. "They cornered you and beat the shit out of you. That's not your fault."

"I should have kept my mouth shut."

James stops, grabs my forearm. "Stop it. Just stop, OK? You're not like that. You care about people, man. You did the right thing."

But James doesn't get it. Doing the right thing, pressing past my invisibility and yanking at strands of attention to change people's courses, it always bites back. Every time I show the world who I am, it takes a shot at me, like JFK in his showy car. Now I've opened a door to hell, as Everett so aptly put it.

What's my penance for that? How do I set things right where Everett failed? The answer lies on the other side of the door, pulling at me. I need to get back in there, but I need to divert my brothers first.

The van is back when we round Sweet Bee Circle. Dad and Angus wave at James from the side of the house.

"Well, Sir Rawlingson." Angus mops his forehead with his red hankie, and then dusts off the knees of his coveralls. There's cobweb stuck in his beard. "If there's anythin' under there, we should have it trapped by mornin'. Come by the office if somethin' trips it, an I'll come fish it out."

"Will do, Angus." Dad nods.

I follow James into the house and freeze at the sight of the twins crouching in front of the five-panel.

"Hey, Dumb and Dumber!" James grins.

I can't move. I want to say something smart, something to get them away from the door, but those wide-spaced, obviously-not-a-raccoon scratches down the bottom corner keep drawing my gaze away.

Jord straightens, smiling like he's stolen something. "Look what we found at the hardware store!" He holds up what looks like a bent screwdriver with a hooked end.

"What?" James closes the distance between them and grabs it while Jess bends, still intent on the doorknob.

"It's a pick set! Told you we'd get into the door before you."

Shit. I run my fingers through my hair. *Shit. Shit. Shit. Just what I need. Dumb and Dumber road trip to hell.*

James chuckles. "You guys are morons." He holds up the pick, scoops another off the floor and turns it in his hands. "This is a mechanic's pick set, to pry off gaskets, stuff like that, not a lock pick set. You think you can just walk into any corner store and buy a lock pick set? It's illegal to sell them to idiots who don't have a locksmith license."

"Shut up. It's working." Jess jiggles one of the picks in the keyhole, and twists another one in beside it. My stomach spasms like he's jabbing me instead of the door.

"Guys..." I start lamely, and, of course, they don't hear me. *Be loud, David. For Christ's sake, don't let them through that door. Think. Something big.* My mind scrambles and then latches onto the only sure thing guaranteed to waylay any hale teenage boy's mind. "I saw Veronica topless at the lake."

Three heads turn immediately.

"What did you say?" James snorts.

I straighten, clear my throat and paste a cocksure grin onto my face. "I said I saw Veronica topless at the lake, while you dicks were racing go-carts. I think she's got fake tits."

"Liar." Jord shakes his head, but I can tell he's imagining it.

"No skin off my back if you don't believe me. I know where their skinny-dipping spot is. You know what? Why don't you three stay here and play with the closet door? I've got some birding to do. Two rare species of Tyler big breasts around these parts. Gorgeous. And very social this time of year, I hear." My mouth feels dirty for talking about the twins like they're nothing but tits. *Like I've ever gone birding in my life. I'm ten times more invisible than any other prospective charmer out there.*

One of the picks falls from the keyhole and Jess doesn't bend to pick it up.

Bingo.

I keep them out of the house all day. We don't find the Tyler sisters half-naked at my alleged skinny-dipping cove, but we run into them during one of their firewood deliveries. Jord stares at Veronica's chest long past the point when she starts to look really uncomfortable.

Jesus. Perv.

"Any chance we can help out?" James offers an effervescent smile to both sisters and elbows Jord in the ribs, hard enough that air punches out of him, and the surrounding tension disintegrates as the girls laugh nervously.

We sit on the back of the trailer, feet dangling, as the girls double-up on their quad and pull us house to house to ferry firewood inside. At around the third driveway, as I stand with my arms extended and my shirt already prickly with splinters and bark, Veronica stacks split logs against my chest, a small smile teasing her chapped lips. She leans toward me conspiratorially. "Your name's David, right?"

My throat goes dry and my palms prickle. A girl like Veronica Tyler speaking to me and actually getting my name right is akin to a normal teenage boy getting asked to go to prom by a supermodel college freshman.

Nod. Christ, do something. I manage a head waggle, and I convince myself that the heat at my cheeks is only exertion.

"Evie said it was Dan, but I knew she was wrong." She flashes me a bright grin before plunking a last piece of firewood under my chin and turning to her sister to shout, "Evie, you owe me five bucks. It's David."

I do my best not to sag under the weight of my armload, keep my chest puffed out like a bloody firewood-toting peacock until I round the back of the house and stumble toward the battered metal woodshed.

On my next load, Veronica winks at me and flicks a sweaty strand of hair away from my forehead. Her nose crinkles when she smiles, and I can't stop staring at the contrast of her blue eyes against her pale eyelashes. I'm standing there like a raccoon frozen in the middle of a headlight-flooded road when she says, "You're cute."

You're pretty damned fine yourself, Miss Tyler.

Of course, I don't say it. Instead, a laugh that sounds like a whinny peels past my lips. I do my best to maintain eye contact instead of appreciating the way Veronica's shirt clings to her oh-so-very-real breasts, and I float between the house and trailer with my next two firewood deliveries. This might not be such a bad summer after all.

I'm doing my best surreptitious biceps flex when Veronica's gaze darts around us, checking that everyone else is out of earshot. White blond hair feathers around her face and brushes my cheek as she tilts her head to whisper in my ear. She smells like vanilla. "Can I ask you a favor, David?" She's blushing. Actually blushing.

Holy shit. My ears are burning. Suddenly, I've got wood concerns that have nothing to do with the bundle in my arms. "Sure," I croak.

"Can you tell your brother James to meet me at the docks tonight and bring his smokes? I'd ask him myself, but the guy's such a showstopper, I clam up every time I get near him, ya know? Would you put in a good word for me, David?"

Of course. More than just my shoulders sag. I swallow, lick my lips and offer Veronica a dry smile as she backs away. "Of course," I squeak.

We load up the Tyler sisters' trailer three more times, and Veronica doesn't spare me another glance after that. We probably move three cords of wood by the end of the day, which is good, because I'm almost too tired to feel stupid anymore.

You know better, David. Seventeen years old, and you get snowed every time. When has a girl ever wanted you as anything more than an errand boy?

When we pour back into the cottage, sweating, Mom informs us that Vera—from three doors down who knows everything about rabid raccoons—has invited the family over for dinner and an evening of cribbage. I'd rather stab my eye with one of the twins' new picks. My head's already pounding and my mouth is dry from Veronica, and the effort of distracting my brothers all day. Tension pinches at my neck and my shoulders ache from all the firewood, but I go because I'm afraid if I stay, James will too, or Dad.

Vera's laugh is shrill enough to break glass. She sounds like a horse on helium. I devour two of her soggy cabbage rolls and duck out of crib tournament after the second round, bury my face in a damned *Cottage Country* magazine for the rest of the evening. By the time we retire home, I'm well-versed on whether my style trends toward Shabby Chic, Coastal, or French Country.

Dad checks the live trap under the addition, but it's empty.

James has unfolded and claimed the green couch by the time I'm done taking a piss and brushing my teeth. I want to argue with him. I stand behind the couch, staring at the spring poking out for several long seconds, but my dehydrated mind is dim.

"David, go to bed." James flops over and covers his head with his pillow. "You're creeping me out standing back there."

I'm not going to sleep. I pin my gaze to the crack under the door, curl my toes and turn to reach for the ladder. My knees wobble, loose and unreliable. *I'll stay sitting up, and if the draft comes, and James wakes up, I'll just convince him to go outside. He's logical. He'll want to search for the source outside. We'll check the raccoon trap under the skirting, and maybe there'll even be something in it by then. I can keep him away from the door. I can do this.*

I crack my head hard on the loft's low ceiling. Profanity whistles out of me in a low hiss, and I grab my head, fold over and crab-walk past the bean bag.

I won't sleep.

I sit on the edge of the cot, eyes watering, skull pounding. My wandering gaze focuses on the dictionary on the shelf across from me. Even though it's too dark to read, I pull it onto my lap, open it up to the 'G' tab and stare down at the dim grey pages until my eyes dry out.

I won't sleep.

Something that sounds like a dog scrabbling across hardwood jolts me awake. I focus on a low wooden ceiling and struggle to place my surroundings. My legs tingle under a heavy weight, and when I push away what I assume is a blanket, the dictionary slides off my knees and falls to the floor with a thud. The busy scratching intensifies, reminds me of mice running through our hollow walls back home, or cockroaches.

That sounds bigger than cockroaches. I frown."Shit!" I whisper, scrambling to the edge of the loft, and blinking into the darkness below.

James is standing in front of the couch. A wedge of pale moonlight from the kitchen window ribbons across his back, and his shoulders shudder. He's shivering. A moving shadow ahead of him catches my gaze. It's a black hand extending under the door, elongated fingers splayed, claws scrabbling for purchase on the worn planks as it reaches for James's ankle.

"James!" I yelp.

He shuffles closer to the five-panel, oblivious to my call, but the maneater hears it and rattles the door violently.

"James, stop!" I plunge down the ladder and my feet hit the floor so hard my ankles twinge. Spinning, I grip the couch as I round it, grasping for my brother's shoulder. I miss, barely raking his back as he shuffles ahead with his hand reaching for the crystal doorknob glinting in the moonlight. "James!"

The black questing hand snags around his ankle and yanks hard.

James's chin snaps against his chest as the rest of him rag-dolls backward. A thick smack reverberates through the floor as his head ricochets off hardwood.

I scream and jump over him.

The claw twists James's foot sideways and jerks back, mashing my brother's heel against the bottom of the shuddering door, deaf to his waking, harrowing wail.

Blood trickles down his foot.

I trip on the ash bin, sending plumes of grey dust churning around our feet, curdling in the icy draft. My hand closes on the handle of the ash shovel leaning against the wall. I grasp it in both hands, raise it overhead, and slam its sharp edge down as hard as I can into the corded black wrist. Metal clanks against bone.

The maneater screeches and the door bucks. It lets go of James's leg, but I hack at it again as it retreats, shovel catching two fingers and neatly severing them at the knuckle.

My head fills with screams. Mine. James's and the maneater's all mash together. Lights cut on and blind me. I raise the shovel overhead like a shield.

"James?" For a second, I can't hear past the rushing in my head.

My family pours into the room.

"What the hell is going on?" Dad shouts.

"James!" Mom skids to her knees and pulls my brother's hand away from the back of his head.

He curls in the fetal position, moaning.

The twins stand tensed behind the couch, mouths open like fish.

Something brushes the side of my bare foot. I flinch and look down. One of the dismembered fingers flexes and curls against my white skin. A jagged, oozing trail of jellying blood trails through the ashes behind it.

I scream again and kick both the black, twitching fingers. They roll like crayon stubs under the crack in the door. *Jesus, did anyone else see that?*

James shudders and makes this horrible keening sound.

"David!" Dad lunges toward me, and I recoil as he snatches the shovel out of my hand.

"Did you hit him, David?" Mom's eyes bulge as she pulls her hand away from James's head, her palm smeared with blood.

Oh God, Oh Jesus. It tried to pull him under. My stomach turns. "J-James, are you okay?"

He's curling in on himself, feet twitching and face wrenched tight. "My head." His words sound wet and gurgling.

"David! Did you hit him?" Dad's gaze flits from the bloody shovel back to me.

"I don't know. I-I don't think so." *It tried to come under.* I can't stop gulping for air and staring at the twin ribbons of blood smearing toward the crack under the door, waiting for the fingers to wriggle back through.

"Look at me!" Dad throws aside the shovel. Everyone in the room jumps as it clatters to the floor. "What did you do?"

"I-I don't know." Pins and needles fire through my limbs and bile burns my throat. *I fell asleep. I let it get James. My fault.*

"He's bleeding! His foot too." Mom hunches over James, pulls him away from me as he tries to sit up. She turns and stabs a finger at Jord and Jess. "You two! Get the first aid kit. Under the sink. Now!"

The twins stumble over each other.

"Breathe, David." Dad's voice is quiet again, like he's talking to a horse that's ready to bolt, and I realize I'm hyperventilating. The room is swimming, and I'm gulping air like I'm drowning.

He holds a hand out and steps toward me.

"Don't." I wheeze between breaths and stumble backward into the door. The crystal knob digs into my back. *Don't let them near it. The hellhounds want through. They're real. Don't let them.*

"Just tell us what happened." He edges closer.

My bare feet stick to the floor as I shift them, smearing blood and ash.

Dad's gaze shifts down toward the crack, and my throat closes completely.

Save them. Get them all away from the door. Now.

I pitch forward, crashing into Dad. The back of his knees hit the hide-a-bed and we both crumble into it. I try to speak, but my throat feels like I'm breathing through a drinking straw and all that comes out is this high-pitched wail.

Cry, David. Cry baby. Be loud. Pull all the attention to you. I draw a loud, hiccupping breath and blubber, "I didn't know it was him!"

Mom rifles through the first aid kit, tears open a pad of gauze and presses it to the back of James's head, shaking her head and pursing her lips.

Tears brim in my eyes, and my cheeks flush with heat. "I swear, I didn't. I heard this bumping around down here, and I looked down and someone was standing over the couch, like they were going to do something to James. I didn't know it was him. I thought someone was in the house."

"So you hit him with a shovel? Jesus, David." Jord snorts.

"You cut his leg. Look at that." Mom stares at me coldly, voice quivering. She points to the gouge in James's ankle. "That's going to need stitches!"

I blink down at the oozing wound. *It grabbed him. It was real, and it tried to pull him under the door.*

The entire room is quiet. Feet shifting. Frowning, waiting for me to explain myself. The weight of it is suffocating, but I shoulder it and mumble, "I'm sorry."

James opens his eyes and looks around the room, confused. When he finally focuses on me, there's mistrust behind his gaze. That guts me. James and Dad, they're the only ones who see me.

Aw Christ, James, I didn't hit you. I swear. That's what I'm thinking, but what I say is, "I'm sorry, James."

He looks back like he doesn't know me, like he's trying to place me.

"What were you thinking, David?" Dad sighs and sags back, scrubbing his forehead. "You could have killed someone."

"I'm sorry," I repeat stupidly. "I'm just tired. I didn't..." Adrenaline leeches out of me and I can't even finish my sentence. I've used every ounce of energy to pull their attention away from the door.

"David's tired." Jess smirks. "Raccoons under the door, giving widdle David nightmares."

Jesus, Jess.

"That door!" Dad snaps. He straightens and glares at the five-panel. "That's what it is! You're all so bloody wound up over that door."

Shit. My whole family is staring at the gouge marks now, the blood and the ashes and the scratches on the hardwood, and I can't pull them back. *Jess, you stupid asshole.* I'm crying now, literally bawling, and it's not enough to pull their attention away.

"You know what?" Dad shoots to his feet. "Enough! I've had enough of it. Jess," he pins my brother with a withering gaze, "get the hammer. Top drawer. Right now. There's a can of nails beside the boot rack in the front closet. Jord." He spins to my other brother. "Take the flashlight and bring me the wood from under the addition. I saw a stack of it there when we set the trap. I won't hear another word about what's behind that Goddamned door!"

James slouches at the kitchen table, pressing a cold cloth against the back of his head, his leg propped up on a chair while Mom bends over his foot, dabbing his cleaned wound with hydrogen peroxide. He winces every time the hammer thuds against the wall, and so do I.

The twins press a slab of siding against the five-panel while Dad, his lips pursed around a row of nails, frenetically pounds each piece into place. There are only six lengths of wood, but Dad anchors each one to the door frame and the door, finishing by capping off the crack beneath with the last chunk of siding.

I hold my breath the entire time he's kneeling and don't exhale until he stands and steps away, head tilted to examine his work, hammer hanging slack in his hand.

"There." He jabs the hammer at the boarded-up door. "Next person who mentions the closet door is spending the rest of the summer helping Angus suck out septic tanks. Am I clear?"

"Crystal." Jord nods.

"Jess, sweep this up." Dad waves his hand at the ashes we've tracked all over the living room floor. "I'm going back to bed."

Jess juts his jaw out but says nothing.

"I'll do it." I volunteer from my perch on the couch, but I'm not sure if anyone hears me.

"You good?" Dad grips James's shoulder on the way by the kitchen table.

"Yeah," he croaks.

"He'll need stitches." Mom insists.

"I'll survive until morning, Mom." James feigns a yawn and stretches.

"Jord, clear off a bunk." Dad points to the bunk room. "James needs to put his foot up and the beds are bigger in there."

Nobody tells me where to sleep and no-one asks if I'm alright. One by one, my family wander out of the living room. Jess leaves the ashes for me to clean and flicks off the lights behind him, like he doesn't even know I'm there.

I sit on the foldout couch in the dark for a long time, head cocked and listening to the breathing coming from the bedrooms, feet planted on the gritty floor, waiting for the cold draft. When I don't feel it, when I'm sure everyone else is sleeping, I stand, flick on the kitchen light and sweep up the floor. I scrub away the caked smears in front of the five-panel as quickly as I can, throw the dirty rag in the trash, and set the can of nails back inside the front closet, but I don't put the hammer away. I tuck it into the hollow between the hide-a-bed mattress and the couch frame. Then I climb into the loft, put the dictionary away and fish the skeleton key out of my jeans pocket. My thumb nail clicks over the letters on the handle as I stare at the boarded-up door.

I did it. A small thread of relief holds me together. *Everyone thinks I clobbered James, but the door's barred now, and nothing can get through, right? Jesus, I hope not.*

Back on the main floor, I sit on the mattress with the key clasped in one hand and the hammer within reach of the other, and I stare at the crystal doorknob poking between two slats of weathered wood. The keyhole is covered, and the crack at the bottom of the door is too, but I can't shake the dread curling within me.

You were loud, David, really loud. Something will come for you now, hungry like a magpie, ready to hollow out all your soft parts. And you can't stop it.

Chapter Nine

I hang my hand, the one holding the key, over the edge of the mattress. Whenever I get groggy enough to lose my grip on it, the clang of metal hitting the floor wakes me with a start, and I bolt upright, throat dry, gaze darting to the crack beneath the door that's boarded up now. Several times the draft slithers through anyway, unimpeded by Dad's hastily tacked boards, and the door starts rattling, like a train is coming, or something else equally substantial and unstoppable.

I grip the hammer and pull my feet onto the couch and pray, actually friggin' pray. *Does it count if you're a late bloomer? God's supposed to be forgiving and all, but would he really save a douche who ignored him for seventeen years, opened a door to hell, and let his own brother suffer the consequences? Probably not.*

I pray anyway.

I lose track of the number of times the hammer thuds to the floor, but I don't sleep. The draft retreats under the door just as dawn scrubs the sky. My family wakes up and hurries through breakfast.

Mom unwraps James's foot and hisses through her teeth. "It's wide open. That's not going to close itself. Besides, it was so dirty. All that ash. A good flushing and stitches, that's what it needs." She glances up at the clock. "Two-hour drive to the urgent care. We'd better get going if we don't want to eat up the whole day."

Guilt eats at my stomach, and I slouch further into the couch.

"Mom." James draws the word out. "It's fine."

"Listen to your mother." Dad orders. "I'll not have it getting infected out here in the middle of nowhere. You've got to get back to school, have to be able to drive. Better safe than sorry."

"Well, we'll have the van for the better part of the day. You and the twins staying or coming? We drop you somewhere after?"

"I'll come." Dad says. "I've got to buy a cabin filter for the van anyways, if you're headed to the city. It smelled stale on the ride up here, didn't it?"

"I didn't notice." Mom returned. "How about you, boys?"

"Mall is good," Jord answers.

"Yeah, mall." Jess adds.

"David, you coming?" Dad asks.

I flinch. *Jesus Christ, Dad.* My chest tightens like I'm wrapped up in a net and the cords are cutting in. *This is what makes it so bad. Not the forgetting, but the odd bloody time they remember me. If he'd just give up on it, like Mom has, it wouldn't hurt so bad.*

"David?"

"I'll stay."

"You sure?"

Don't. Just don't. Stop trying to make me fit in. "I'm sure."

"Well, okay, then." Dad sighs. He seems relieved to be off the hook.

Dishes clatter into the sink. Bowls with clotting cereal and yellowing milk. The Philco fridge opens and then sucks closed like an airlock.

"If you're staying, you may as well do the dishes." Mom quips, voice cold.

Love you too, Mom. "Yep." I press my head against the back of the couch and squeeze the key in my pocket until my hand aches.

James says nothing. My family shepherd him out the door in a flurry of jingling keys and scuffing shoes. The front door slams behind them and feet clunk across the front porch. The van turns over with a squeal of fan belts, and I count the doors closing, the ones up front with a creak and a thunk, the sliding door rumbling like thunder, before chuffing shut. And then they're gone.

I exhale and fold in half, cradling my aching head between my knees. *I'm sorry, James, okay?* He'll think I'm crazy now. I told him about the gun. He took that all in stride. He wanted me to open up, and now he'll think I've lost it. Beat the piss out of him with a shovel. *Come on, James. You have to know I wouldn't do that to you. I'm not crazy. I'm not crazy.*

"So fix this." I mutter out loud. I press up and pull the hammer out from under a couch cushion. My hand shakes, so I grip harder. *You cocked it up. You opened the door. Make it right. Find the dishtowel.* Everett's diary in the dictionary said that an object on their side locked the hellhounds into a world. All I need to do is get the towel back onto the right side. I stand, feet wide apart, like some idiotic comic book hero with a hammer in one hand and a key in the other.

About then, I realize I'm still in my underwear. Pretty sure, even in Bizarro world, it's bad social etiquette to wander around with your ball sack hanging out. Retreating to the bathroom, I set the hammer and the skeleton key on the washing machine. I don't want to let go of them, but I have to piss, and I'm not doing it with a key in my hand. Turning, I lift the toilet seat, relieve myself and shake off. Wash my hands with Mom's lavender soap and pull a fresh pair of jeans out of the dryer. I frog hop into them and scoop up the hammer and key. They feel unbalanced in my hands, the key heavier than it should be and the hammer lighter. *Now you're just wasting time. Get back to the door.*

I pad back to the living room and slip into my sandals. Back in front of the five-panel, my knees are still loose and jellied. Every time my gaze wanders down to the corner with the raked claw marks, I swear I see a shadow moving down there, and my head fills with the picture of that black claw clamping shut around James's ankle like a bear trap.

"Jesus." I whisper, shaking my head and licking my lips. *It's daytime. They only come out at night. Don't be such a wuss.*

Jaw clenched with resolve, I stride toward the door, and clunk the end of the hammer against it a few times. It's quiet on the other side. I heft the hammer and smack the board below the doorknob, hard enough that a nearby nail head pops out. Easing the claws under it, I lever back and the nail curls out of the hole with a screech that makes my neck prickle. I pull nails until they're scattered around my feet like dead metal worms, and then I pry the boards off. I peel the bottom one off last, and I drop the hammer twice because my fingers are fumbling.

Daylight shines through the crack under the door.

I back away, brace the hammer on the ground and lie on my belly a safe distance away from the scratches in the hardwood. No ashes. No blood and no fingers.

"Good." I press to my feet, stack the last piece of siding against the wall, and glance at the clock above the Philco fridge. *Just past nine. Took you five minutes to pull off all the boards. What if someone comes in while you're on the other side and sees the door unbarred?*

"They won't." Time stood still last time I went in. I suspect it'll do the same now. I'll go in for ten minutes and test it to make sure. If the clock stays the same, I can look for the dishtowel on the other side for as long as I want, and when I come back through, I'll have plenty of time to board the door up again with no one being the wiser.

Stop stalling and get on with it.

I press the key into the lock, turn it, and pull open the door with the hammer raised to strike. The musty smell of small, dead things clots around me. The green couch lies like a disemboweled thing, bald fabric shredded, wood skeleton peeking through vast hollows, wads of stuffing strewn everywhere.

"Jesus." I clap a hand over my mouth and inch into the room. Under my feet the floorboards shift to warped grey wood with splotched water stains. Dust motes dance within a single shaft of sunlight, and I'm drawn, as always, to the window. The lace curtains hang frayed, like wisps of white hair on either side of it. One of the glass panes is missing, and the others are cracked, clouded, and spotted with fly specks. It's windy, and white caps curl over the lake through the tiny open square.

Close the Goddamned door. What if the maneater is still here? It'll escape onto your side.

I turn back and press the five-panel closed, lock it, hold onto the key for dear life, and take in the stale, silent cottage around me. For some reason, the Philco fridge's door is missing. It looks like a coffin, or a safe. Two of its wire shelves have spilled out and lie bent and coated in dust on the floor. A dented can of condensed milk lies in the middle of the kitchen floor.

Why milk and nothing else?

Mice droppings pepper the planks around me, and my feet leave a trail in the dust as I shuffle across the floor. There's no knob at all in the front door, just a hole where it used to be, and a splintered, busted door frame. I step out onto the porch and leaves crackle under my feet. Gobs of them gather in the corners. My heel sinks into a spongy plank, and I backtrack before edging around it.

Holy crap.

The trees are taller. Taller and thicker than I've ever seen them. Near the overgrown parking pad, mounds of half-rotten fruit surround the crab apple tree. Its trunk is thicker than my waist. I squint out at the lake and take in a riot of fall colors. Nearly-fluorescent yellows stand out against bands of red. Dotting the banks are the pale remains of other cottages, windows dark sockets in weathered white wood, doors tilted open like broken teeth. Pieces of plastic lawn furniture scattered everywhere.

Jesus, what happened here? How far in the future am I?

The wind curls leaves around my feet. When a few of them brush bare skin, I jump, remembering the maneater and the fingers. I stalk around the perimeter of the cottage several times, in widening circles, squeezing the hammer hard, but there's no sign of whatever tried to pull James under last night. I go back inside. The warped floor on this side doesn't show any claw marks at all.

The skin on my neck prickles, and I spin toward the loft. *It could be hiding up there.*

The loft tilts, and the ladder is missing a rung. Backing toward the woodstove, I can see everything except for the back half of the floor up there. I side-step back to the kitchen, pick up the can of condensed milk and lob it over the railing.

It lands with a crack and a bounce, rolling to a stop against something. Dust sieves down through the floorboards as I listen past the pounding of my heart for sounds of scuffling. Nothing.

I gingerly climb the ladder, half-expecting a black form to plummet down and crash into me. My foot slips.

Stop it. Concentrate. The rungs creak as I grip harder. No need to wonder what would happen if I fell, if I hit my head. *They'd eat you alive, that's what would happen. The sun would set and the maneaters would tear you apart.*

Wincing, I peek into the loft. It's unoccupied. I belly-crawl through dust and cobwebs. The mattress up here has melted into the floor. It smells overwhelmingly of piss. Large cracks of daylight peek through the collapsed ceiling where the remains of a huge branch still rests. The bookshelf is warped, but still upright. The dictionary's cover is missing, but the book is still there. When I reach for it, a few pages crumble in my hand.

"Shit." I regret speaking immediately.

Startled by my voice, a mouse wriggles out of the innards of the mattress, scurries along the line of the wall and leaps into the ceiling. Using both hands, I ease the stack of loosely-bound papers to the floor in front of me, and gingerly start turning pages. I'm into the 'C's before I come across a wrinkled page filled with faded pencil scribbling.

Everett! I lean closer, squinting.

Dante's Hell had nine layers, I believe. There're hundreds of them here. If you come through often enough, you get to the end of the circuit, and it starts all over again, like a Rolodex.

What the hell's a Rolodex? I shift onto my elbows.

This time through, I'm going to write down all the dates, see if I can find some pattern in it. The Gulf station usually has newspapers in the dimensions where there is a Gulf station. Sometimes it's too far back, or too far ahead for that. But the apple tree has been here since '64, near as I can tell. Most times, if I can't get to the gas station, or there isn't one, I cut down the tree and count the rings to figure out what year I'm in. Mind you, that only works if there's a tree at all. Not that it matters where I am, when I am. I can't make it stop.

I've scoured through a hundred damned versions of hell, and I can't figure out how to piece things back together to the way they were. Outside isn't much better.

I built this damned room for Annie, like she asked. That's what started all this. She figured John and Evelyn would come once they had the baby, if only we had a room with a crib. I tried to tell her grandbabies don't cure everything. They don't erase the years that a son hasn't spoken to his mother. But Annie was just so hopeful, with the cottage bigger. She got pictures of fat baby legs at the beach running through her pretty head. It sustained her for a while. I built the room, and they still didn't come. Annie must have phoned John twenty times, and he never picked up, damn him. Don't tell her, but I always took John for a bit of a horse's ass, and he is.

She's so damned lonely. I'm not enough to fill it all in our old age. That's Hell in itself, that is. And I'm only making it worse. A husband who keeps locking himself in the perpetually empty guest room. Never mind that it's only seconds for her. In Annie's eyes, I come out the door right after I've stepped in, and she cocks her head and gets this odd look on her face, asks if I've forgotten something. She thinks I'm getting Alzheimer's.

Never mind that it's only seconds. I'm no longer present when I'm on the other side with her. I'm always thinking about this damned place and how to fix it. I clam up, and I leave her alone with her thoughts. Small talk makes me angry. Tell me again why I'm supposed to give a rat's ass about Ruth White's stomach ulcer, anyway? Point is, I snap at her and I shouldn't. She doesn't know. She thinks the room is empty. She thinks I'd rather be somewhere else than with her. She has no idea.

It's gutting me, I'll tell you that much. I feel like dried fruit in here, like the very air is scouring my insides and stealing pieces of me. I don't belong here. Lord Jesus, I don't belong in Hell. This is some sort of mistake. That's what every soul in Hell says, I suppose. And they're all looking for a way out of it, aren't they? All of us running from the hounds.

That's it. I turn the page hoping for more, but like before, it's just the one page of writing. There's a column of numbers running down the right side of the diary entry.

1970
20?? – tree too thick to cut
1962 – Feb
1998

It goes on and on down the page. *Dates. They're dates he's come through on.* The printing gets smaller and smaller toward the bottom, creating the illusion that the whole column of numbers is receding, getting sucked into the dictionary.

"Jesus." I sniff and read the entry again, following it with my finger. "Everett, you're a ray of friggin' sunshine."

I squint at the pale grey sky winking through the crack in the ceiling. It's actually not so bad here.

Bit of a Texas Chainsaw Massacre vibe, and I've probably got Hantavirus, but not bad otherwise. I wriggle backward over the creaking planks, settle my foot on the closest ladder wrung, and ease my way back to the main floor.

Futilely, I wipe my palms on my thighs. My jeans are dusty as hell. *If I carry dust from this world back to mine, what does that do? Objects left on this side draw the maneaters, lock in the bridge. If I carry anything back, does that make it even stronger? Shit, how big does it have to be to make a difference? If I left dust behind from my side, would the bloody dishtowel have even made a difference, or was the damage already done?*

Self-consciously, I bat at my shirt and slap my knees, holding my breath the whole time. *No, the draft didn't become permanent again until the maneaters sucked the towel under. They must have. It's nowhere on my side. The object has to be dishtowel or tobacco-tin sized at least.*

"Listen to yourself," I sigh. *Working out the rules of this place, like it's supposed to make sense. Everett's probably Albert Einstein compared to you. He's visited hundreds of times and he still hasn't bloody figured it out.*

I wonder if Angus will let me use the phone, give me Everett's number. If I could just call the guy and ask...

"Yeah, right." I snort. Angus charged me double for a God-damned pepperoni stick last time I went to the office. He looked at me like I was the useless 'X' in his scrabble game. He's not going to just let me dial Everett up.

It's probably been ten minutes. Check the clock.

I do. I open the door to my side and the clock still reads 9:02.

All the time in the world. Figure it out. As I stare back at the layers of dilapidation, an idea strikes me. *Is it a different world, every single time I open the door? I could read everything Everett's ever written in one morning.*

Brightening, I step carefully past the crooked nails on my side, and shut the door on rotting Bizarro world. Lock it. I count to thirty in my head, like I know how long it takes for dimensions to switch gears. But when I open the door again, it's still mouse shit and a doorless fridge. I double-check the dictionary and find the same diary entry. Sighing, I grab a pad of paper and a pencil from my side, and I re-lock myself into Bizarro side. The key is warm and steady in my hand. I don't want to let go of it, but I pocket it anyway.

You're smart, David. An Mei had said that, right? Before her son shoved a gun in my face. *Keep it simple, then.*

I climb back into the loft a third time, dutifully transcribe Everett's rambling, and the dates onto the notepad. When the pencil lead shears off, I pick up the broken piece and I put it in my pocket with the pencil and the pad.

I'm not taking any chances, not leaving anything else behind.

With my shirt pulled over my nose, I turn every drawer in the place upside down, looking for the strawberry dishtowel. I flip mattresses, look under beds, even crack open the woodstove burner-plate and peer into the ashes and rust. By the time I give up, I'm filthy, and defeat has implanted firmly in my mind.

You're not going to find the towel. The maneaters didn't stow it in the cottage, like a dog hiding a toy. It could be anywhere, anytime. You'll never find it. They don't want you to. It chokes me. The ache behind my eyeballs ramps up, and my arms hang heavy. I'm tired, and I don't have it in me this morning to figure it out. *Everett hasn't given up. Neither should you.* The old man's name sparks an idea in my mind that catches like kindling.

I could phone Everett. Angus won't give me his phone number on my side, but the office and the Quonset are right outside this door too. I saw them in my nervous tour around the cottage earlier. That Quonset sagging like a hard-ridden horse, but still standing. And I have all the time in the world to sift through old papers.

Chapter Ten

Gravel crunches under my feet as I creep up the road still holding the hammer like it's a weapon. The rusty sign for Sweet Bee Circle hangs, rattling against its post with each fresh gust of wind. I give a wide berth to the cottages with yawning, busted windows, searching for movement beyond their jagged sills, but I'm eased by the sound of chattering, small life from the treetops beyond.

Small animals get quiet when there's a predator around, right? I ease my grip on the hammer and inhale deeply, counting to three before I exhale.

Corrugated metal has peeled away in strips from the Quonset front, like giant hangnails. The wood sheeting beneath is dark and oily, and the metal door to the office hangs wide open on rusted hinges. Its square of plexiglass is intact, but milky and scuffed with age.

I can see Angus's metal desk from here. The wind has scoured everything off its water-swollen, delaminated top except for a heavy binder, the tall jar that used to bristle with pepperoni sticks, and a plastic bin. Pacing outside the door, I scan as far into the room as I can see. The only blind spots are the front corner to the right of the door, and behind the desk, but the skeleton of a swivel chair leaves little room for anything else. I try to remember how big the area of the front corner is, picturing a maneater hunched there, black hands clutching around the dual candy dispenser with its glass reservoirs of stale peanuts and rainbow jellybeans.

Bending down, I sift through the small rocks between my feet, select one of the larger ones, and toss it over the desk. It bounces off the office chair and clacks to the floor. A formation of ducks sails overhead, banking toward the lakes, their wings whistling with each frantic beat while I stand poised, hammer ready, on the weed-tufted gravel road.

What the hell do you expect, David? A hellhound won't come leaping out to attack a thrown rock. They seemed smarter than that.

Twisting the hammer in my hands so I can strike with the clawed side if needed, I edge toward the door frame, step over the grey tongues of curled vinyl tile, and sidestep quickly to clear the front corner. It's clogged with mats of moldering leaves. The shelled peanuts and the bright jellybeans sit preserved behind cobwebbed glass like time capsules, unspoiled. I exhale and turn to peer over the desk, jabbing the bare plastic back of the chair. It tilts back with a protesting squeak. Shuffling back, I kneel to peek under the desk. Nothing there but gobs of dust.

I pull the corner of the binder toward me, open it and flip through the mold-spattered, wrinkled yellow pages. Ledgers, inventory lists and sign-in sheets, covered in Mr. Tyler's blocky, smudged writing. No phone numbers. Coming around the desk, I ease open its drawers, cringing at the squeal they make as they scrape over ancient runners. There's a local phone book in the top drawer.

No good to me. I need an address book. Something with more than local numbers. I don't even know Everett's last name.

The bottom drawer contains pink invoice duplicates, a white first aid tin and little else. Not bothering to close the drawers, I glance at the plastic bin at the corner of the desk. A greasy layer of dust coats its clamshell top. There's some sort of dial on its side, and a hint of lettering on the front, peeking through the dust. I set down the hammer and smudge my thumb over the word.

Rolodex.

Tipping open the clamshell lid reveals battered letter tabs sandwiching index cards on a spindle track. A faint smile pulls at my lips as I turn the dial and the cards advance on their circular track.

"Rolodex," I whisper, shaking my head, a sudden memory pricking my mind. *My principal had one of these. I didn't know what they were called.*

Letter tabs emerge from the belly of the bin and chug toward the back, clicking as they go. T, U, V. Bending forward, I crank the dial faster. I'm into the 'B' section when the access door to the Quonset on my left smashes open.

Splinters sting my cheek and lodge in my hair. I scream as the wooden door crashes into the open desk drawer, rebounds, and closes.

Fuck!

Raking the hammer off the desk, I leap over the office chair. My heel slips out of my sandal as I round the desk. Icy air pounds into my back.

Maneater.

I'm skidding over loose tiles when the door flies open again, and something shoulders past it, sending the heavy desk lurching across the uneven floor into my hip. I twist sideways and slip through the gap just before the desk bucks and hurtles against the wall. Wind-milling, I cross the floor in two strides, catch myself on the edge of the metal door and throw it closed, but its corner catches the toe of my sandal as it goes by and sends me sprawling into the gravel.

Oh God! I curl. The hammer jabs my ribs as I roll over it. My wrist twinges and I gasp, horrified as my only weapon twists out of my hand and I ragdoll to a skidding stop in the billowing dust. *Get it back! Leave nothing behind.*

Flipping to my stomach, I scramble across the gravel, my gaze locked on the wooden handle a few feet before me. Icy air blasts across my arm as I grip the hammer, roll away and heave to a stand. I spare one glance behind me as I sprint away, but that's enough to make me falter.

The metal door is open. It didn't latch when I closed it and now, it's hanging ajar in its frame, shuddering.

Shit.

Turning away, I pound back to the cottage, sandals slapping dirt as I go, lungs burning, ribs cramping. I don't stop until I'm on my side of the door. Only when it's locked, do I lean back against it, throat raw and breath wheezing in and out of me. The image of James's bloody heel mashing against the door last night swamps me. I scuttle away, tripping on loose boards. Bent nails skitter across the hardwood.

I didn't get the phone number. I sag into the couch and stare hard at the crack under the five-panel door. *And I let the maneaters out, Oh Christ!*

Leaping back up, I slap one board still prickling with nails over the door and start hammering. But by the time I've secured it, there's no scuffing on the other side. In fact, I have all the boards tacked up with fresh nails before I realize that the monsters I released from Angus's Quonset aren't coming.

They'd be here by now. You'd feel the cold air at least.

I wipe sweat away from my temple with the back of my wrist while my other hand clamps the key in my pocket. Resettling on the couch, I stare down at the freshly barricaded door.

You didn't let them out. The office door was already open, and it didn't latch when you ran.

The bloody things were fast enough to smash the Quonset

door and throw the desk across the room before I could even get out of there, but they didn't take me when I tripped and went back for the hammer. With the door open, surely they saw me, but they didn't come. They didn't chase me to the cottage, and they're not here now.

"They only come out at night," I whisper hoarsely. There're no windows in the Quonset, and only the small plexiglass square in the office.

What if they can't come out like friggin' vampires? I snort at that thought, but it won't stop niggling at me.

The longer I sit with the hammer across my knees, picking tufts of green velvet off couch cushions, the more convinced I become. The draft came with them, and it's only ever come through the door at night. They must be nocturnal or something or have sensitive eyes. One or more maneaters could have holed up in Angus's Quonset like a den. It was the only place nearby with no windows. All the cottages boasted large spans of glass to take full advantage of the lake view.

My breath settles. I get up, stretch, and go to the bathroom to take a piss.

You didn't get Everett's phone number. It's still in Angus's apocalyptic future office, and there's no way I'm going back to get it now, but a horrible curiosity urges me to re-open the door.

The world resets when you come back over. They won't be in the office yet, and if you're quiet enough...

"Screw that," I whisper, scrubbing my hands with lavender soap.

Why the hell would I go back? It's like *Alien* back there and I don't want to be the idiot who gets his face peeled off because he just can't steer clear of desolate, brooding buildings. *They tried to pull James under. Everett calls them hellhounds. Yeah, thanks but no, Bizarro world.*

But as the clock ticks above the Philco fridge, and I think about the awful gash on James's foot and the hungry snarls that rolled under the door as the black claw grappled for purchase, guilt sours my throat.

You opened this door. James slept on the couch because of you. All of this is your fault.

Without Everett's phone number, all I have is the dictionary, and it only contains Everett's diary entries on the other side. I've checked the Merriam-Webster on my side multiple times now. Nausea tugs at my stomach as I realize I'm cornered. I have to go back if I want the slightest chance of figuring this all out. I have to face Bizarro world, study Everett's entries, find out how this connection between worlds works. It's my problem to fix.

And you can't fix anything if you're jumping at every bloody shadow over there. They only come out at night. Prove it. Prove that's how the rules work there. Go back and verify. You need to know for sure when it's safe over there and when it isn't. I swallow hard and let go of the skeleton key, withdrawing my hand from my pocket and shaking out my wrist. *A soldier that operates in front of the front lines, isn't that what you wanted to be, David?* Soldiers reconnoiter. They gather intel on their enemies. They don't sit pissing their entire mission away because they're scared of a noise in the dark. They act. *You still got it in you, David? Prove it.*

I rummage through the kitchen drawers until I find the biggest knife we have. Then I duct tape it to the broom handle. After inspecting my work, I press the junk drawer flashlight against the blade's wrapped handle and tape that on. The whole thing looks like the worst cosplay weapon ever made.

Knives and sharp sticks. When has that ever gone wrong? A weak grin twitches my lips.

Pulling the boards back off the five-panel, I turn the key. The musty room is almost exactly as I left it. Only my harried, streaked footsteps are missing. An undisturbed layer of dust rests on the warped grey floor and the can of condensed milk lies in the middle of the kitchen floor. The world here has reset.

Sure enough, as I pad toward the derelict Quonset, Angus's office door hangs wide open. My muscles jitter, and heat rolls through me in waves as I stand there on the balls of my feet, armed with a bayonet broom and a hammer.

What are you doing, David? What the hell are you doing? Taking a deep breath, I flick on the flashlight and slink past the metal doorway with its candy dispensers. Tucking the hammer into a loop of my jeans, I ease the Rolodex off the desk and cradle it under one arm. My gaze flicks to the Quonset door. *OK, do it.*

Gritting my teeth, I mouth the words. One. Two. Three.

I lean over the desk and smack the side of my bayonet against the door as hard as I can. Twice. The flashlight flickers and dims. *Just like a Goddamned horror movie.* I backpedal away, hammer smacking my thigh.

The door explodes open with a resounding crack, sheering off its hinges and toppling the office chair. A massive body shoulders through on all fours, a blur of black, hairless skin and impossibly long piranha teeth.

I spin, clattering my bayonet against the wall before I twist it enough to avoid clotheslining myself on the door frame. Surging outside, I slam the door, squeeze the Rolodex against my ribs and sprint straight for the cottage. I only stop to look over my shoulder when I'm certain I hear nothing coming.

The gravel road behind me is empty. Overhead, a formation of ducks sails by and bank toward the lake. A few hundred feet away, Mr. Tyler's office door hangs open, but I can't see or hear anything beyond that.

This is it, David. Let's see if you've got any balls left at all.

I set the Rolodex down in the middle of the road and twist

the top of the flashlight until the light snaps back on. Easing the hammer from the loop of my jeans, I crouch and stalk back toward the sagging Quonset, aiming my bayonet at the door.

The dull rush of blood in my head drowns out the sound of waves on the lake. I clench my toes to prevent my sandals from slapping, and I'm five steps from the door before the cold air reaches me. It wafts over my feet, and I can't help but shudder. The office is too quiet, and I'm ashamed of how much the beam of my flashlight trembles as I tip the broom toward the door and press the tip of the knife against its metal edge.

I've nearly pressed the door completely closed when the knife-tip slips across it with a squeal. I wince and jump back. The maneater howls and shifts inside the office.

This was a mistake. I scrabble backward but keep my light pinned to the crack in the door as glass smashes and jellybeans spill out onto the gravel.

Nothing happens.

I hold my breath, the hair on my arms prickling as cold air blasts past the door and frost crawls up the metal panel. The maneater huffs and snorts. It sounds like it's pacing. My teeth clack as something large crashes in the office, the file cabinet, or the desk. The office door doesn't move at all.

It's not coming out. It sounds pissed, but it's not coming out.

Gulping, I edge forward and cram my bayonet against the clouded plexiglass window. Claws scrabble and a crescendoing screech drills into my ears as my flashlight illuminates the office. I only catch sight of its bony back and a quivering mane of appendages that look like tree roots growing out of its spine. It's tall enough that it brushes the doorway as it retreats.

Holy shit.

The cold air recedes like a vacuum. The thuds and hissing lower to a resonating growl from somewhere deep within the Quonset.

It is pissed. It can't get out. It hates the light.

I smile and stand there like an idiot for the longest time, holding a broomstick against Angus Tyler's office door window, like I'm plugging a hole in a dam. When my arms get tired, I sneak back to the Rolodex, and retreat to my front porch where I have an unobstructed view should anything come up the road.

I flick through the Rolodex, but there's no Everett in the 'E' section.

It's probably under his last name.

Sitting down on the front porch steps, I tear index cards off the spindle one by one, scanning the names and setting them aside. When I'm done, the Rolodex is empty, and I haven't found Everett's name at all. I should feel exhausted, defeated, but instead I feel invigorated and excited, and I can't pinpoint why.

For a while, I stand on the front porch and let the wind whip my hair and scatter the cards, watch the waves surf across the lake and crash savagely into the shore. At one point a cyclone of leaves swirl down what's left of Sweet Bee Circle, like red and yellow confetti. The air smells fresher here, like I'm the only one in the whole world breathing it. The woods seem wilder too. I can't shake the feeling that I'm Christopher Columbus, that no-one else has seen this place, set foot on this porch.

Everett has.

I stand on the front porch for a long time with the dumbest smile pasted across my face, and I shouldn't be smiling—I can't find the Goddamned towel or Everett's phone number, and there's an infuriated maneater in the Quonset up the road—but I am smiling because a song is running through my head.

They only come out at night...

When I get back to my side, I pick up all the bent nails and throw them in the trash. Then I tack the boards back into place, strip out of my filthy clothes, and shower. I stand there until the hot water runs out, watching debris from another world run down the drain between my wriggling toes.

Once I'm toweled off, I pluck the key from the top of the dryer, shovel my clothes into the washing machine, dress, and return to the living room. I do the dishes, and I eat a slab of apple pie for lunch—Horse-laugh-Vera sent it home with us. Then I settle on the green couch with the notepad in my hand, and I write out Everett's first diary entry as best as I can remember it. I fall asleep, and it's a glorious nap. The door doesn't rattle once, and the cottage cradles me in soft silence.

My family seems pissed when they get home. They must have fought in the van, or more likely, Jord and Jess did something stupid. Dad goes straight to the bathroom and stays there. Mom dumps a whole chicken and a bag of frozen vegetables into the black roaster, slams it into the oven, and cranks the dial. She pours herself a large glass of wine and retreats to the rocker out on the front porch, arms crossed.

A storm is blowing in off the lake.

I retreat onto the edge of the sofa as James eases onto it with a grimace, stretching one leg out across all the cushions.

My gaze focuses on his bandaged foot and the tips of his pale toes. "How'd it go?"

He raises his eyebrows and then frowns down at the glossy soft-cover book in his hands, picking at the rolled edge of a '40% Off' sticker. It's a new John Grisham. *Christ,* that man can pump out novels.

Jord and Jess drag two chairs away from the kitchen table, letting the legs scrape loudly across the floor. *Ignorant, as always. The pair of them, ignorant to the world.*

I peek over the back of the couch as Jord shuffles and deals cards to Jess.

"How many stitches?" I try again. "Your head alright?"

James scratches the back of his neck, opens his book to a dog-eared page midway through, and starts reading intently.

"I'm sorry, ok?" I pick at the edge of the couch. Green fuzz snags on the rough edge of my fingernail. God, I wish I could tell James about today, that the thing that attacked him was real, how I found out it hated the light.

"You dick!" Jess laughs, and for a second I bristle, thinking he's talking to me. "You didn't shuffle the cards good enough. War! First bloody set."

"I shuffled fine," Jord says. "Aces low or high?"

"Always high, man." Jess sings back. "I win."

I lean closer to James. "Look, I didn't mean to hit you. I freaked out. It looked like someone was attacking you, and I lost it, ok?"

Jord slams his fist onto the kitchen table, and I jump. "Jokers are automatic war."

"Since when?" Jess whines.

"Since always."

I tuck my chin into my chest, take a deep inhale, and whisper my next words as clearly as I can. "I appreciate you being there for me, man. The walk at the lake. I needed that shit. I didn't think I needed to talk, but I did. And I can't do that with a lot of people, James. Open up, you know? I wanted to thank you. I want to fix this." I gnaw at my fingernail because James is just sitting there, gaze riveted to the pages. "Tell me what I can do to fix this, James."

"Ah-hah! I'm blowing you out of the water," Jord crows.

"Dickhead."

"James!" I bark and the entire room folds into silence as my older brother casually drops his book onto his chest and squints over at me, confusion pasting his face.

"David?" He pronounces my name like he's never heard it before. "I'm sorry, what was that?"

Christ's sake, James. I deflate, mouth gaping like a windsock. *Not you.* I don't expect it to hurt so much. After all, my normal state tends toward invisible. I should be used to it, one more person ignoring my existence, but *James...* Goddamn, it hurts that it's James.

At supper, Mom doesn't set me a plate. *No surprise there,* but I'm floored when I have to ask Dad to pass the chicken three times before he complies. Afterward, Jess closes the front door in my face when I follow him out onto the porch to bum a smoke.

The pair of them would have bought a pack at the mall, guaranteed. I stand there swallowing anger and staring through the glass for a long time. *What the hell? It was an accident! I didn't mean to hurt James.* Do they think that? Does my whole bloody family think I intentionally attacked my brother? *This is the other shoe dropping, David. This is what you get for that cock-up last night, and the shit you pulled today.*

I exhale, rake my hands through my hair, and return, defeated, to the couch. *Just what I need. My family thinks I'm a certifiable asshole because I'm too damned scared to tell them about the monsters behind the door.*

James limps around the kitchen despite Mom telling him to sit. "You sit, Mom. I'll make us some coffee. Whipped cream and Baileys. How's that sound?" He hobbles past me, scoops the percolator off the woodstove and fills it at the sink.

Fix it, David. There are some bridges you can't let burn.

James and Dad are the only people who really see me. Sometimes, I forget how tenuous our small connection is, how much I need it. Christ, I'm terrified of what will happen if it breaks. The gulf will yawn between us, and I'll never find my way back to their side.

Maybe you could tell them the truth about the maneaters...

I can't. Of course, I can't. They'll think I'm certifiably insane then. *Hell, I think I'm insane.* I page through James's discarded book while the cottage fills with the smell of fresh coffee.

"God, James, that's decadent!" Mom wipes whipped cream off her top lip and grins at my brother over her cup. She loves being pandered to.

"Just what the doctor ordered, yeah?" James returns the smile.

The twins pour in from the front porch, followed by Dad. "The raccoon has eluded us again. Trap's empty." My father smiles ruefully.

"Come. Conciliatory coffee." Mom raises her mug.

"Smells good." Dad kicks off his shoes and crosses to the kitchen. "Want some, David?" he asks over his shoulder.

Just like that. Cold Goddamned shoulder all night, and then, *Want some coffee, David?* I clear my throat and press my heels against the floor hard, blinking at the sudden swing in sentiment.

"Coffee keeps widdle David up at night." Jess squeaks.

"Leave off him, Jess, or none for you." James returns playfully.

"Well?" Dad probes, holding up a mug. "Going once, David. Going twice..."

"Sure." I choke the word out. *What the hell is going on?*

We have coffee together like nothing ever happened. James tells me all about the new book he's reading. Mom thanks me for tidying up earlier, actually looks me in the eye and *thanks* me, and the whole family rallies around the newspaper to help Dad finish the crossword puzzle he couldn't start this morning. I'm like a cornered rat. Like those conditioned ones they train to push buttons in laboratory cages, only I've got no idea which button zaps me and which dispenses the treat. So I sit on the couch quietly.

"Forty down is A-L-E-E." James points. "Alee. The side of a ship that's sheltered from the wind."

"We'll make a yachtsman out of you yet." Mom grins.

"James is too busy polishing his mast for that." Jord sneers, Jess giggles along with him, but Dad just frowns.

"I'm going around in circles on this one. If I get it, I can wrap up the whole bottom corner."

"What is it?" Mom asks, leaning against the counter, still sipping coffee.

"Six letters. Starts with P. An ancient storage container for holding grain," Dad mumbles, shaking his head, and clicking his pen.

"Pithos," Mom chirps. "P-I-T-H-O-S."

I cough and spill coffee. Scalding liquid runs down my pants. Flinching, I stand and pull fabric away from my crotch "What?" I choke.

"Pithos, an ancient container used to store grain or liquids." Mom preens, blowing on her coffee without glancing at me. "They used them in Greece, like barrels, only they were these huge jars made of clay."

"Bullshit, Mom." Jess snorts. "How on Earth would you know that?"

Yeah, Mom. I lean ahead. *Tell all.*

Mom sours for a moment, before clicking her teeth with her mug, taking a large gulp, and jutting out her chin. "I'll have you know, I had a life before you, Jessie Aaron Rawlingson. My freshman year at college, our History prof was hot—"

"Aw, Mom!" Jess cringes.

"And he was passionate about Greek mythology."

"Can we agree that you won't ever use the word passionate in a sentence again? Ever?" Jord makes a gagging face, but Mom is unfazed.

"So I wrote a paper on Pandora."

"I hear she's got a nasty little box." Jess grins.

"Jessie, enough." Dad glares my brother into silence.

Everyone shut up. I lick my lips and slip my hand into my coffee-soaked pocket to run my fingers over the lettering on the key.

"That's the funny thing, actually." Mom continues. "It wasn't a box that she opened. Some scribe translated the word 'pithos', Greek for jar, to the Latin word 'pyxis' meaning box. It was one of those huge jars she opened to let all the evil out into the world. It wasn't a box at all."

"Well," Dad raises his eyebrows as he jots with the pen, "Pandora's Jar doesn't have quite the same ring to it, does it?"

Jesus Christ. Whipped cream and liquor curdle in my stomach. *Pithos. Someone wrote it on the key that knew this shit and then buried the thing as deep as they could dig, and you opened it all up, David. You're Pan-fucking-dora.*

By the time I fold out the hide-a-bed, I'm completely unmoored. I can't get a grip on what just happened. Lightning forks through the sky outside, and I stoke up the woodstove and stare into the orange glow for a long time, re-running the afternoon in my head.

How much time did I spend on the other side of the door today? Half an hour? No, more. Hours.

I'd spent hours messing around in Pandora's Box, poking demons and rooting through things that weren't mine, and when I came out, my whole family snubbed me, ignored me.

What if they weren't angry? What if they just literally didn't see me? I'm beating my chest in the middle of the room, and they can't see me.

Rubbing the key with the raw pad of one thumb, I recall Everett's words and fish the notepad out of my pocket, tracing my finger over my own hasty writing. *There it is.*

I'm no longer present when I'm on the other side with her. The air feels like it's stealing pieces of me.

Shit.

Did he mean literally? Like, I spend the morning in Bizarro world, and it takes the rest of the day to fight back into existence over here? *God help me.* I sag. *I don't have the energy for that.* Look at me. Praying again. That's twice in one day now, isn't it?

Chapter Eleven

When night comes, I face the draft alone again with the same dogged determination that's got me through a mostly forgotten life. I've wobbled around enough on loose-laced skates because there was no parent there to tie them. I've explained to umpteen teachers how Mom didn't forget to bring in the class snack she signed up for, she was just sick. I've forged parental signatures on field trip forms, opened backpacks with no lunches within, fished dusty change from beneath vending machines, shimmied into swimming trunks from the lost and found crate at the pool, and I've sat on sets of stairs at empty schools and waited and waited and waited. This is no different. No-one is coming to help. It's just me.

The five-panel doesn't shudder tonight. Cold air oozes past the nailed-on boards. Something scratches at the bottom gap, quietly, but insistently examining every crack and warp in the plank barricading it. I click on my flashlight and pad to the stove, shivering. The scratching stops when my weak circle of light hits the door, but as I shovel firewood into the maw of the stove, I feel the maneater is still there. This feels more like when a cat pauses before it pounces. As soon as I retreat to the couch, the scraping resumes, hurried and frustrated, despite my trusty flashlight spilling light through the cracks in the door. I get up again and flick the living room light switch on, but the scratching only hesitates for a moment, before digging in more.

It's not enough light. My stomach sinks. Paired with the sun today, my flashlight must have been just enough extra illumination to drive them back from the office. Without daylight impeding them, I bet the maneaters could crush any light I aim in their direction, no matter how bright.

I sit swaying on the foldout bed like it's a life raft in a sea of sleep. The hammer and key are anchors in my hands. Somewhere in the twilight hours, the scratching fades away, and an odd thought strikes me. I set the hammer across my lap, flick the flashlight back on, and fish the notepad from my crumpled jeans on the floor, squinting at my hurried handwriting. I count every date on the list. There are 112 of them.

"Shit." I whisper, blinking at the bottom of the five-panel and deflating against the back of the couch. *112 dates. Each one's another dimension, and there's only one dimension per day. If Everett knew the dates repeated themselves, he's been through them more than once. That means he's been trying to reset the door for over 112 days.* I tip my head back and do the math in my head.

Christ, that's more than three months. All Winter, maybe into Spring. And he didn't figure it out. How the hell do you think you're going to fix it? You're nothing. Your own family thinks you're nothing. And you only have another month and a half here. What happens if you leave without fixing it, and they get out, the maneaters get out? They're real. Look what they did to James.

"Shit." I let the notepad flop to my lap and scrub at my gritty eyes. *You've gotta fix this somehow, David.*

By the time dawn seeps into the cottage, I'm hysterically tired. My muscles are jittery and dried out, and I can't stop bouncing my knee. I want to go in, want to get to the other side and puzzle little pieces together like I'm David Duchovny in the *X-Files*.

That guy is such a loser.

But my family are sleeping around me and I'm pretty sure they won't be if I wrench off the siding tacked to the door. Besides, it's early. I look up at the clock to confirm. It's only been a few hours since the last cold draft, and I don't want to chance stepping in from stage right during the wrong scene in Bizarro world. I shudder, remembering the maneater's unearthly screams.

Hell no. I can wait.

With grey daylight cushioning the cottage, I let myself tip sideways, tuck the hammer between the back of the couch and the mattress, and doze. Some jackass has his speedboat out on the lake, though. The two-stroke winding up like an oversized mosquito needles between my ears. Pretty soon another one joins him, and squealing kids start pedaling up the drive with baseball cards strumming their wheel spokes. Someone's dog barks incessantly enough that I want to find it and kick it.

Serene, real bloody serene.

I wedge my head under my pillow, and don't pull it out, even when Jord and Jess roll out of bed and start wrestling over who'll get the first shower of the day. They pound through the cottage like bowling balls in a pinball machine.

A weight settles behind my eyes, and saliva floods my mouth, heralding a headache that won't ease with Tylenol. I get migraines when I'm tired. Bad enough to make me puke and leave me curled into a ball in a dark room with a bag of frozen peas on my face. I'm on a prescription for it, but Mom's forgotten to refill it.

Of course. Of course she'd forget. Of course, it would Goddamn floor me today. Please, not today.

I lie exceedingly still while the twins roll around on the floor, shouldering into walls hard enough to jiggle plates in the cupboards.

"What's going on out there?" Mom shrieks.

I flinch as her voice knives right through me.

The bathroom door slams, and one twin sniggers. I can't tell which.

Mom makes smoothies for breakfast, running the blender for an incessantly long time. The whining motor sounds like a jet engine spooling up for take-off. I'm aching for a cup of strong coffee and my pain meds, but every movement sets my head reeling, so I lie frozen, twisted up in the blankets of the hide-a-bed while morning unfolds around me.

Get out, just bloody get out of here already, all of you.

"Golf clubs in the van yet? Tee time is eight sharp." Dad strides out of the bedroom.

Golf tournament. That's right. The one-thousandth annual Honey Bear Hollow My-Clubs-Are-Bigger-Than-Yours tournament is today, thank Christ. They'll be gone all day, the whole family. Maybe God does answer prayers, after all.

"Jord, dear, go load them up. I'm making a thermos for the road," Mom trills.

I swallow against the crushing band of tension squeezing my forehead, tuck my chin against my chest and count my breaths. *One. They'll be gone soon. Two, they'll be gone soon. Three, they'll—*

A hand on my shoulder jerks me out of my reverie.

I jam the skeleton key beneath me and peel away from the pillow, wide-eyed.

James sits balanced on the arm of the couch. He's holding out a steaming mug. "Mornin'. You look like a bag of shit."

"Migraine," I groan.

"Here." He presses the mug toward me, and I lever up onto one elbow, key digging into my hip as I cradle the cup toward me and breathe in pure black caffeine.

Before I can say thanks, James shuffles back to the kitchen, reaches into the small cupboard above the sink, and grabs a rattling bottle of pills.

My eyes tear up, not entirely from the pounding head. *You're a bloody saint, James.* I blink as he screws open the cap and coaxes a few capsules into the palm of his hand.

"Two?" he asks.

"Three."

The coating of the pills sticks to my throat even though I swallow them with a large gulp of scalding coffee. I'm hollow inside, like the migraine is scouring me out, and I know that means it's going to be bad soon.

James returns to his perch on the edge of the couch, grinning faintly at me, smile not quite reaching his eyes. "I understand. You just don't want your ass handed to you in golf today."

"You got me," I mumble. *You do, James. You've got my back every time. Even when I least expect it. Jesus, I am so sorry about the other night. It should have been me.*

"I'll clear out the flock." James winks. "Let you get some beauty sleep."

He rises from the couch, goes straight to the unlocked bathroom, and flushes the toilet. Jess screams from inside the running shower. Dad mutters something that sounds utterly disappointed, grabs the van keys, and his paper, and heads out onto the front porch.

"Jord dear, get the golf clubs out of the bunkhouse and put them in the van. Then go check that raccoon trap for your father, would you?" Mom scurries around the kitchen.

Suddenly, I want to go. Screw the headache, screw the Goddamned door, I want to pile into the van with my family, watch Dad fill out scorecards with his immaculate printing while Mom drinks enough coolers to shed her anxiety and genuinely smile. I want to rib James lining up putts like he's a bloody physicist, while Jord and Jess do their best to get the golf cart airborne. The pair of them wear the most ridiculously tacky plaid pants when they golf, complete with white belts. Tweedledee and Tweedledum, Dad calls them.

Don't be stupid. You've got your own rabbit hole to take care of right here, Pandora. How can you think about golf?

I chug three more gulps of coffee before setting the mug down on the hardwood and retreating under my pillow. My eyes are watering, partly because it's too bright in here, but also because of James and the coffee and the Tylenol that I didn't have to get up for. I wish I knew how to stop moments like this from gutting me, but I just swallow them up. Hook, line and sinker, every time, even though I know they'll cut me to ribbons on the way out. For one second, they connect me to my family. And then the line snaps, and they're gone again, filing out the door without even looking back. I'm left to pick at a snarl of feelings I can't unravel. Most times I give up, cut out the knot, and start over. God, I'm shitty at fishing.

James gave you your very first fishing kit, right before he left for trade school. The unexpected thought pops into my mind and drags a nostalgic memory with it.

James stood behind the open hatch of his shitty old Ford Tempo. He crammed the car with ragged, mismatched suitcases, crumpled bedding, and an impressively ugly lamp.

"Here." James eased a package wrapped in fraying newspaper out of his duffle bag. "Since I won't be home for your birthday." He grinned and brushed his hand over the awkwardly shaped gift like he was dusting it off. "Wrapped it myself."

"With your feet?" I snorted.

The present crinkled as he dumped it into my hand. "Go on. Open it."

"My birthday isn't for months. Don't you want me to wait

until the big day?" *It might be the only birthday gift I get.*

"Nah." James waved his hands dismissively. "Open it now. You might need it before then."

"Ah." I popped my eyebrows and hooked a finger under one corner. "A carton of extra-large condoms. You shouldn't have, James."

"Yeah, well, the party section was all out of balloons, Skippy."

I pulled what looked like a travel kit out of its newspaper co-coon and turned it in my hands until it rested zipper side up. The smell of waxed canvas filled my nostrils. When I tugged open the tab, the clamshell top opened and spilled out two energy bars and a Swiss army knife.

"It's lame." James tried to hide his blush by scooping up the bars, while I went for the knife. "We put them together in shop class this year. Survival kits. They're supposed to be compact. Part of the assignment was deciding what we thought was most important to put in." James shrugged. "I don't know. I kept trying to picture my-self, alone and lost and thinking, 'What would I need most if there was no-one else there to help me, if it was all on me to get through this?'" James shrugged, pressing the chocolate-mint bar toward me. "I thought of you, David. You just roll with the punches, look around you, and use what you have. No matter what kind of shit life throws at you, you don't complain, you just... survive. You push through. You've always been strong like that, man."

I cleared my throat, hunching my shoulders and plucking open hinged accessories on the Swiss army knife. Despite the swelling ache in my throat, I answer, "There'd better be at least one condom in there."

James laughed, and nervousness sloughed off him only to re-turn to roost like a flock of flustered birds, pulling the smile from his face. He picked up the duffle bag and flicked the zipper tab, frowning down at it like he couldn't remember what it was for. "I just—" He pursed his lips, then raked his teeth over them, pulling in a whistling inhale. "Jesus Christ, I just don't want you to feel that way, David, while I'm gone. I want to know I can help somehow, even if I'm not here, you know?"

We fell into an awkward silence as I sifted through the contents of the kit, one by one. A compass. Fishing line and hooks. A float and a spoon lure. A Ziploc bag containing a few crumpled bills and some change. A fire-starting flint. A needle and a single condom. "Jesus," I laughed. "You put it right next to the needle."

"Well, if you don't make it, the next generation's got to survive, right?" He reached out and mussed my hair, like I was five years old.

"Thanks, James," I said, but coldness tugged at my guts. *Don't go, James,* the five-year-old inside me shrieked. *You want me to survive? Then don't go.*

By the time I pry the planks off the five-panel, the screech of the nails reverberates through my skull like I've taken the hammer to my head. A splotchy circle distorts my vision, like the soggy ring of a coffee cup on paper, bleeding colors. Tylenol won't tamp the pain now. After the auras start, there's nothing left but to ride it out. I wonder if the Philco fridge has any frozen veggie bags. I turn toward our fridge to look, but the sound of children splashing and screaming at the lake pulls me up short.

Quit wasting time. I check the clock, jot down 7:42 onto my notepad, and I go through the door.

The room on the other side gleams like a glossy picture out of horse-laugh-Vera's *Cottage Country* magazines. The floor is golden, and the beamed ceiling stained darker. There's no green couch at all. Instead, I recognize the old porch rockers, glowing oak, stuffed with cushions, and facing the Home Comfort cookstove with its enamel panels bright as whitened teeth. In the kitchen, the Philco fridge chugs away happily, but there's a hole in the cabinetry where the electric oven belongs. An unhung light fixture sits like a glass egg on the counter. The kitchen window is bare, its wood muntins unpainted, and the corner of a bed frame pokes out of the bedroom door, but there're no mattresses in sight.

I step in and the room echoes when I lock the door behind me. The smell of turpentine and sawdust envelopes me, tugging at my nausea.

It's massive in here, with no furniture.

Tucking the key in my back pocket, I press toward the sink and crank open the faucet tap. No water. Peeking into the empty cupboard below, I find the plumbing needs to be hooked up.

Whole place is still new. The day is overcast outside, but I cringe and squint as I look out the window. *Maybe the maneaters have migraines, too.* I snort gently and immediately regret it as pain stabs behind my eyes.

The lake is absolutely still. The only thing marring it is the blurry ring of my own messed up vision, pulsing in time with my heartbeat. When my lungs build pressure, I realize I'm holding my breath. My next turpentine-laced inhale induces a gag.

Get outside.

With a hand clamped over my mouth, I stumble over to one of the rockers, snag a cushion off it, and charge out onto the front porch. Cold, wet air slaps my hot cheeks. I sag to the floorboards, stuff the cushion under my head and lie curled on my side, eyes closed, drawing deep, shaky breaths until the nausea passes.

I'll barf soon. Then the headache will become blinding, and it won't go away until I sleep it off. That's the pattern. That's how it works. *Oh God, I wish I brought some ice from the freezer.*

Funny thing is, the pain starts fading. I roll onto my back. My shoulder blades press against straight boards, and I let the silence of this place absorb into me. It's uncannily still. No leaves rustling, hardly any birds, just the scuttle of small things in the undergrowth, and the occasional ruffle of water from the lake. When I open my eyes and turn to track the source of the sound, I realize it's fish. Not just the occasional plop of one jumping to feed, a massive school of them writhing under the skin of the water until it churns and froths with their passing, like a rippling bird flock.

What's it called? I search for the word, still absorbed by the flash of thick flanks, like a river of silver spoons coursing through the lake. *Murmuration? A murmuration of fish.* I've never seen so many at once. *I wish I had James's kit with me now.*

Sitting up gingerly, I realize my headache is gone. Completely dissipated. No coffee-cup ring vision, no splitting pain down one side of my skull, just a cottony lightness that catches my thoughts like flies in cobwebs.

Those pills James gave you, they must have been something stronger than Tylenol. Hook me up, man. I massage my temples and watch the undulating mass of fish along the lake's grey surface.

It's a far less populated shoreline than the one I know. The trees are short and thinned out compared to ours. More poplars and maples than anything else, and there are barely a dozen cabins dotting the shore. Some are just bare frames in mid-construction, others have long cars parked out front, sporting tail fins and bubble curves, gilded with chrome. Their paint jobs range from teal or rob-in-egg blue to bright orange and cream.

I whistle under my breath. *Christ, what did we do to cars? The crap on the roads now has nothing on these babies. Just look at them.* Even from afar, they exude substance, presence and a certain naive excitement. I'm not sure what Dad's old Ford Econoline exudes, probably something it shouldn't.

And they're all unsupervised. I totter to my feet, a half-smile itching the corners of my lips. *Not a person in sight, just like every other time you've come through and you don't have to worry about the maneaters, as long as you stay outside.* Three houses down from ours, my gaze pins to a lat 1950's Chevy Impala hardtop in Rio Red. Now, I don't know shit about cars, but I know James's favorite ride when I see it. Growing up, he pushed posters of this car in my face so many times I'm sure it burned the image into the back of my eyeballs. He recited every memorized part under its hood. Hell, James probably jerked off to wallet-sized photos of Red Impalas.

Excitement tingles in my chest. *Shit, when will you ever get the chance to get behind the wheel of a car like this again, David? Bet the doors are unlocked. Bet the keys are in the ignition too.*

Bingo.

I slide into the red and cream vinyl bench seat, wrap my hands around the huge, ridged steering wheel with the chrome, boomerang crosspiece, and I pump the gas a couple times before twisting the key. The engine shudders, turns over a few times before catching, but then settles into a deep-throated burbling idle that sounds more like a warplane than a car. The vibration of it carries through the frame and up my spine.

"Holy shit," I murmur. *OK James, I think I get it now.*

When I get it onto a straight stretch of road, it cruises like a giant sofa, purring its sleek red bulk up to speed while wrapping me in chrome and gleaming red. I try the radio, but static crawls across all the stations, and I wish more than once that I had someone to wave at out the window. This was a car to be seen in—*like JFK's convertible*—but I don't meet another soul on the road from the lake to the gas station. The sign out front still says Gulf. I shudder as I slow the Impala and ease it into the approach.

Different sign, shorter, not the one you remember. A canopy stretches upward from the tiny station over two tall narrow gas pumps with circular signs on top.

Sunday
Drive
©2022

The Impala chuffs to a stop with a small squeak. I get out and savor the small sounds of the hot engine ticking before clearing my throat and calling, "Hello?" through the open station door. It's a different building than the one Morrison-the-Walrus runs, more compact, cleaner. All windows.

People like their cars big and their buildings small here.

"Hello?" I try again, but nobody answers.

Nothing scuffs from the inside. I ease open the door and exhale slowly. It's nearly as bright in here as outside, and it's all one small room. I can see blue sky through the glass back-door, and an overhead sign says '*Washroom Access Out Back*.'

Nowhere for maneaters to hide in here.

I cruise up tiny aisles with stacked tins of oil, shelves stocked with packs of Marlboros, Camels and Pall Malls, and a fridge lined with tall glass bottles of Coca-Cola and 7UP. Beside the hulking register is a small, tidy stack of newspapers. I stare down at the first page of the *Toronto Daily Star*. There's a side profile picture of an astronaut with his visor up, revealing a wrinkled forehead. The headline pronounces in bold black letters, "ASTRONAUT GLENN IN ORBIT' Round World Once in 94 minutes' John Glenn, the first American to orbit the Earth.

I shake my head in wonder. *Jesus. Seriously, what happened to us? Bad ass cars. Men in space. Kennedy… and it all went to shit after this.*

I glance up at the date. February 20, 1962. It matches one of the dates on Everett's list, the one right after the apple tree in the 2000s that was too big to cut down. That's where I was yesterday. *So the list goes in order, like Everett said it did. Shit.* I lean against the counter, dizzy. *It's an actual, reliable list, like I thought.*

I pull out an icy bottle of Coke beaded with condensation, pry off the cap with the bottle opener on the side of the fridge, and take several large, fizzy swigs until my teeth ache and I hiccup loudly.

"This is real," I whisper out loud, eyeing up the faded poster tacked above the pretty rows of blue-stamped Camel packets. The advertisement displays a middle-aged guy with a thin black tie and an open, kind face reclining against a red background. 'MORE DOCTORS SMOKE CAMELS THAN ANY OTHER CIGA-RETTE' the title beneath him claims.

I heard about this. Their marketing team went to hospitals and asked doctors which brand they preferred to smoke. Usually, they asked right after gifting their interviewee a carton of Camels.

"Can't argue with a doctor." I snag a pack of Camels off the shelf and return to the Impala. There's a foldout chrome ashtray in the dash and an honest-to-God cigarette lighter. *I was born in the wrong decade.*

Back at the cottage, I read Everett's diary entry, sitting on the sunny front porch steps with a bottle of the best Coca-Cola I've ever sampled between my feet, and a smooth Camel dart between my lips.

It's my penance, this is, and I know what for. Annie, I was young and stupid. I was a boy when we married, still a boy when I took up with that leggy bimbo who worked at the post office. Youth is no excuse, though, and neither is stupidity. I did it. I broke faith with you, sweet Annie, and now I'm paying for it. Jesus, how I'm paying for it.

At first, I just figured they were wild things, you know, some sort of pack of oversized coyotes. I took them for simple scavengers, but they're more than that. They're purposeful. The devil himself sent them with a task, and they're keeping to it, alright. The hellhounds are not soul scavengers, they're something else.

I talked to this old Indian fellow once, back in the real world, out on the steps of Merle's Bar on Seventh. He had sad eyes and the kind of face that wanted to tell a story. I offered him a smoke, and we got talking about the weather and families. He kept telling me how family was so important. He didn't have any, see. His wife long gone, kids too. 'That's how you destroy a man' he said. 'He can survive if you take everything else from him, but he's an empty shell without his family.' Then he told me how, when the French and English got off their ships, they brought disease with them. I'd heard about that, of course, how it wiped out so many Indians at the time. 'Shame, that was,' I said. But then he said, 'No, you don't understand. They started doing it purposefully.' He described how settlers would take blankets of kids who'd survived smallpox, and they'd tuck them in with the goods at the trading posts, because they wanted to wipe out the Indians completely, not just the men, all of them. Whole families. Lord Jesus, I'd never heard of that. And his story stuck with me.

That's what the hellhounds are. They're the blankets full of smallpox, not simple scavengers, not wild things. They've been placed here purposefully. There're no people in these Hells, see? The hounds are doing it, and they're hungry to get onto our side, so damned hungry. God help us. I don't know how to stop them. I don't think I can do this.

I let the dictionary drop to my lap, take a long suck on my cigarette, and roll my neck as I exhale. Tension plucks at my shoulders, and Everett's horrible words hang behind my eyes, but both fade as I squint out at the quiet lake, the clear sky and the simple blank yard before me. No messy crab apple tree, no dirty kids on bikes, no garbage.

It's better off without people anyway, isn't it? Look at us, sending men into space while we kill each other off down here.

I pin my gaze to the horizon and squint until all the cottages on the opposite shore blur out of focus. *Maybe that's exactly why we send them to space, because it's far from everyone else. Maybe John Glenn thought the Earth looked beautiful from orbit, because you can't see any people from up there. Maybe Pandora knew what she was doing when she opened the jar.*

After I finish another cigarette, I go back to my side of the door. As soon as it's locked, even as I'm boarding it up, the headache returns to roost, like something digging its claws into the left side of my face, gouging at my eye. I drop the hammer on the couch, go to the bathroom and puke. Then I fall asleep on the foldout with a cold washcloth draped over my face. I don't wake up until late evening, when my family comes home, and Jord sits on me—literally sits on me—without seeing that I'm there.

I extract myself from under his legs when he shifts them, and stare longingly at the five-panel. *I don't belong here. I wish I was on the other side.* The thought shocks me.

I remember Sergeant MacNeill telling me once that sometimes, when soldiers got caught behind enemy lines, they'd stay there long after the war ended. Even when they weren't P.O.W.'s anymore, they wouldn't leave. They'd forget who they were. Some soldiers spent so much time on the other side, it felt like home.

Chapter Twelve

By the time my family tucks into bed, my headache has receded to a hollow echo of pain. I'm well-rested and relaxed enough to doze in between the cold drafts seeping under the door. There's no scratching tonight, just an odd tapping, like Morse code. It tempts a boyish part of me to knock back, but I'm not stupid enough to get out of bed and actually try it.

It's not Morse code, I turn the skeleton key in my hands as I listen, *it's a tap on the shoulder. 'I'm still here'.*

As if I could forget. As if I could brush Everett's words out of my mind and stop thinking about the force of destruction that lies curled up on the other side of that door, tapping its claws with tedious impatience, waiting for me to slip and hand my world to it on a platter.

"Fuck off," I whisper and roll away from the door. *I can't do this by myself. I can't stop a pack of maneaters, Jesus, I'm nothing, literally nothing. Jord sat on me.*

I wake up uncomfortably cold, and it takes a moment for comprehension to sink past my chilled nose and ears. Muted grey light fills the room like feathers as my brain thaws, and I remember why the cold should be frightening. I plunge my hand under the pillow, clamp onto the rubber grip of the hammer and scramble off the hide-a-bed, clawing at the blanket entangling me. My bare feet squeak on the freezing hardwood as I twist to focus on the five-panel in the weak light of dawn. The blanket slithers down to my ankles and something metal clinks against the floor.

The key!

I drop my hammer and burrow through the blanket until my fingers bump against warm cast iron, sending the skeleton key skittering toward the door. Diving, I slam my palm over it and grip it tightly. My gaze locks on the five-panel, but it's still sealed and barred.

No icy draft. No maneater clawing its way through. All the boards remain nailed into place as I left them. I lie on my chest, panting and blinking, before I realize what's happened and sag against the frozen hardwood.

It's cold because you let the fire go out, you idiot.

I turn my head and glance out the kitchen window at a dark, slate grey sky. Water beads the glass and harsh winds snag on the corners of the cottage, pulling mournful cries from the eaves' troughs, turning them into sad pipe organs.

Pressing to my feet, I groan, gather the hammer and blanket, and dump them in a pile on the mattress. I pad to the kitchen, shivering, and ease open the top drawer, the one with the matches in it. Along with a box of Redbird Strike Anywhere matches, dozens of mismatched pens roll around amongst the screwdrivers, scissors, white glue, and duct tape. I push aside a paint brush to reach a ball of twine behind it. I take the string, the scissors and matches over to the kitchen table and sit.

My fingers are shaking, so it takes a few tries to thread the twine through the scrolled handle of the key. I unroll a length long enough to loop over my head, cut it and knot it.

You should have done this a long time ago.

I yank on the knot to test it, then pull the key on the string over my head and tuck it under my shirt. The weight of it around my neck grounds me. I close my eyes and take a few breaths, feeling the heavy key rising and falling against my sternum.

Get up. I exhale slowly. *Start the fire. Everyone else is going to wake up soon.*

My ghost of a headache thumps to life as I stand. I ease a few pages out of Dad's newspaper and tear them into long strips. With the box of matches under my arm, I shuffle back to the cookstove, lever off the cook plate and start feeding balls of crumpled paper into the firebox. I stack a cabin of kindling around it, and drop in two lit matches, leaving the cook plate off so I can thaw in the orange glow of the eager flames.

You can't even get this right. I stare into the tongues of orange. *Can't even keep a bloody fire banked through the night, and you're gonna save the Goddamned world from a plague of maneaters?* I snort. I don't know why. It's not funny, none of it is, but all I can think is, *a kindle of kittens, a murder of crows, a plague of maneaters. David's supposed to save his family from being eaten alive by monsters but plays with collective nouns instead.*

The storm hunkers over the lake and my family hunkers over their coffees, resigned to spend the day in the cottage. Mom pulls out her recipe book and scrounges in the cupboards to make sure she's got all the ingredients for smothered pork chops. She gets the twins to peel potatoes. Dad does the crossword while James stretches out on the couch with his new book.

I wonder what the weather is like on the other side. I bet it's sunny. And it doesn't smell like B.O. and humid suffocation.

I can't breathe. Shoving into my sandals, I open the front closet, and shrug into a flannel plaid coat.

"You going out in this?" Dad asks without looking up from his crossword.

"Firewood," I answer, grabbing the umbrella.

"Want help?"

God, yes. I blink. "Nope." I slam the door behind me.

Gritty mud squelches in my sandals. Puddles shiver and writhe in the creases of the gravel road. Lonely lights of other cottages dot the shore, receding like runway markers into the grey. Streams of water pour off each prong of my umbrella. Angus's metal Quonset with its lean-to office looks like it's barely standing against the on-slaught of rain. Sheets of white pound against the corrugated roof. There's a feeble square of light filtering through the plexiglass in the office door, so I grab the handle and pull.

I snap my umbrella shut and shake it out, stomping my sandals on the welcome mat and staring down at my pale, mud-streaked feet.

When I look up, Angus is frowning at the mud I've smeared onto his mat, but I can't take my gaze from the door to his left, the wooden one that the maneaters tore open in Bizarro world.

They're not on this side. I swallow. *Not yet.*

Angus leans against the filing cabinet behind his desk with a go-cup of coffee gripped in one fist and the local news chattering through the speakers of an ancient, silver radio behind him. The announcer is explaining that Bill from Marten River has two pallets of cedar shingles—brand new—that he'd like to trade for an older golf cart, or possibly a motorcycle. Call him up at—

"Can I help ya?" Mr. Tyler asks in a tone that shows he wants to do no such thing.

"Hey, Ang—Mr. Tyler. Some weather out there, hey?" *Christ, what are you, a boy scout?*

Angus doesn't answer, just takes a long sip of coffee, and slow-ly gives me the once over.

"I was wondering if you were able to get a hold of Everett?" I blurt.

"S'cuse me?" Angus pushes off from the filing cabinet and it jiggles as he and leans over his desk, thumbing through a younger version of the thick memo book I'd paged through yesterday.

"I came in the other day. I'm David Rawlingson's boy, David." *You sound like you're stuttering.* I clear my throat and forge onward. "Everett built the addition on our place. He left a book behind with his wife's name in it, and I thought he might want it. You said you were going to call him to see?"

"Nope, didn't say that." Angus licks his dirty thumb and flips another page, setting his coffee down. "Said, I'd hang onto it for him if you brought it in. Did you bring it in?"

Shit. I swallow. "I didn't. Rain. I didn't want it to get wet."

"Well, bring it on in when it's dry, an' I'll hang onto it like I said I would."

I stare at the gleaming Rolodex on the corner of the desk, consider for half a second, and then launch right into it. "This is going to sound stupid, Mr. Tyler, but I can't stop thinking about what you said about his wife passing. I know my family doesn't even know him, but we stay in the same cottage, and he's taken such good care of it, and I don't know. We wanted to send a card, or maybe just call with our condolences. Is there any way we could get a hold of him?"

Angus sniffs. Takes his hat off and scratches at his mess of hair before pinning me with a direct glare. "You askin' me to breach customer confidentiality?"

"No." I puff out my cheeks and curl my toes. *Jesus!* "No, Mr. Tyler. We just wanted to send a card or something."

"Then bring it here." He stabs a finger at his desk. "With the book, an' I'll hold onto it for him, like I said I would."

I nod and swallow at the cold lump in my throat. Water drips off my hair and down my nose.

"You're a nosy piece of work, ain'tcha?" Angus leans toward me. "Always have been. I remember you."

I freeze and lock gazes with him. *Nobody remembers me, Angus.*

"Always behind someone like a shadow. Sneakin' around. Starin' at my daughters."

Oh, for Christ's sake. "Forget it. I don't want any trouble."

"You *are* trouble. I can smell it on some people, an' boy, you're trouble, alright. Always knew it."

"OK." I raise my hands. "Whatever." *No more pepperoni sticks for me.*

"Naw, it's not OK. You wanna know what? I did phone up Everett after you came in. Figured I'd offer my own condolences like, see how he was holdin' up without Annie, an' if he was plannin' on coming back this winter. No answer, so I left a message 'bout the book."

"Is he coming to get it?" *I could meet with him. I could take him aside, and he could help me. We could fix this togeth—*

"He's dead, boy. Passed. His son phoned back to say that Everett took a fall down the stairs at home some time ago. They didn't care about fetchin' a book or leasin' the cottage. So there ya go. You can mind your own business now, cain't ya?"

I stand there gutted. Angus sips his coffee and straightens until his stomach is looming over the desk. He stares at me for a long time while I blink back, gaping like a dripping, cloudy-eyed fish.

"Can I help ya?" he repeats, resetting our conversation, just like I reset Bizarro world by closing the door.

"Um, yeah." I flounder. "Firewood."

"How many bundles?"

"Two. Two's good."

Mr. Tyler slaps his notebook closed and shuffles through the side door to the Quonset. I back toward the office door and hold my breath until Angus returns with two tightly bound armloads of firewood.

"Thanks," I say, but he doesn't answer, and he doesn't offer to help me carry them.

My head is numb only for a while. As the morning rolls into afternoon and the twins rattle through every damned board game in the cottage, my headache pries its way back into my skull. The bottle of pills James gave me lost its label long ago, but I dry swallow three more of them, before climbing into the loft, as far from everyone as I can get. I lie on the cot and count the knots in the ceiling planks overhead. The one that looks like a horse stares down at me balefully. My eyes get watery and my mouth dries out until it feels cottony.

It's just the pills. Side effects. But I know it's not. I swipe a hand across my runny eyes and sniff loudly. *I'm fucked. He's gone, and I'm all alone. I can't do this.*

After supper, I crawl down from the loft to take up my post at the green couch. I've been doing it most evenings since the maneaters attacked James. Haunted by the thought of someone else dozing off so close to the door, I guard the hide-a-bed until my family files off to their rooms. They seem sick of each other after the rain, so I don't have to wait long. James follows the twins to the bunk room and my parents retire shortly after. The cottage groans softly in the wind, and a log in the woodstove settles with a thunk.

I'm dozing sitting up when the sound of a door creaking open startles me. My gaze snaps to the five-panel, but it's still barricaded. Feet shuffle into the kitchen behind me, and I turn my head and take in Dad's profile at the sink. He flips open a cupboard, withdraws a glass, and cranks open the kitchen faucet. Water gurgles into the cup.

I turn away, massaging my tender temples as Dad drains the cup with several loud swallows. "Can't sleep?" he asks.

"I'm good."

The glass clicks into the sink, and my father's feet scuff toward the living room. *Go to bed, Dad. I don't have the energy for small talk right now.* I clear my throat. "I was just about to set up the bed, actually."

The couch jiggles as Dad sits beside me. He frowns at the boards across the door, sags against the back of the couch and scrubs his eyes. A long exhale deflates his belly. "Look, I know this isn't the summer you were looking forward to, David."

"What?" *Ah, Christ. It's not small talk.*

"You haven't been yourself lately, and I get it. You're all set on the military, and I'm the asshole father that trapped you in a rainy cottage with your brothers instead."

"I'm not pissed about the army, Dad," I sigh. *This can't be a heartfelt father-to-son moment. I don't have time. The draft is coming soon.*

"Have I ever told you about my brother?" Dad asks with his eyes still squeezed shut and his chin jutting toward the ceiling.

"What?"

He blinks and rolls his head toward me. "My older brother. His name was Alan. We would have been about as far apart in age as you and James."

I shake my head slowly, struggling to follow the turn in our conversation. *Dad is an only child, isn't he?* "I-I don't remember you mentioning him."

"Well, I bloody worshipped him. He was good at everything he set his mind to. Didn't matter if it was school, or sports, or mucking out the neighbor's barn. Alan brought this fire to everything he did, and it was infectious. It made you excited to be there with him, like you were in some sort of special club. When you spoke to Alan, it didn't matter who you were, he dropped whatever he was doing, and faced you square, and listened like you were the most important person in the entire world. Like no-one else mattered more. You ever feel that, David?"

With James. I swallow. *And you, Dad.* The key hangs heavy around my neck as I nod. *I could tell him what's really bothering me, about the door, and he'd listen. He would.*

Dad stares up at the ceiling, rubbing a finger against his upper lip. He's waiting on something. He's one of the few people I've ever met who says more with pauses than he does with words.

He's waiting for you to contribute, to prove you're listening. He does it with the twins all the time. I lick my lips. "What happened to Alan?"

My father lifts his glasses off the bridge of his nose to rub at the dented red ovals of skin beneath. "When Alan was sixteen, he took the jar under his bed, the one with all his savings in it, and he bought a fake ID, and enlisted in the Navy." Dad clapped his hands onto his thighs, rubbed his palms down his pants, and shook his head.

"That was 1944, David. Mandatory conscription had just been re-instated, but after Pearl Harbor people were jumping at the chance to go. Eye for an eye sort of thing. My father was forty-six, and he had a heart problem. Even a kid could see the shame in his eyes. It was eating him up that he couldn't go, and it just about killed him when Alan went instead."

Dad straightens and pins me under his gaze. His eyes aren't watery anymore. Cold and clear, they peeled through every layer of my invisibility. "David, it *did* kill him when Alan didn't come home. He started drinking, and one night he went to bed and didn't wake up. Massive stroke."

"Alan, uh—" I falter, breaking from my father's gaze, heat crawling up my throat as I realize the intent of this conversation.

Get it over with, David. Get him away from the door. "Alan died?"

"We assume so. Missing in action. The Navy never found his body, and my mother refused to have a funeral for him. She still thinks he's out there somewhere overseas. She just can't process the fact that he disappeared."

Another intentional, awkward pause. When I glimpse out of the corner of my eye, Dad is gazing at me with hollow eyes. *Don't cry, Dad. Please.* "I'm sorry," I whisper.

"You're like him. You put your mind to something, and you don't let go of it until you've seen it from every angle and figured it out. I see it in you, David. It's a good quality. I'm not trying to quash that, I swear."

"I know." *Just go. I don't want to talk about this anymore. And you can't be here when the maneaters come.*

"I don't want you to disappear, David."

It's a heartfelt revelation, one that should warm me, and sure enough, I feel heat blooming in my chest, but it's the wrong kind. Before I can bite my words back, they spill out of me, sour as stomach acid. "Then maybe you should stop forgetting me everywhere, Dad."

His shoulders flinch.

Aw, Christ. Take it back, you asshole, but I can't. Anger clogs my throat and I press my chin to my chest.

The couch shifts, and Dad grunts as he presses to his feet. He leaves and I sit there feeling like my stomach is eating me from the inside out. *An eye for an eye, David. How's it feel hurting the only parent who loves you?* "I'm a shithead," I whisper shakily. *I can't get anything right. I can't fix this.*

Later, the scrabbling at the door is furious, like it sounded on the night James was attacked. Something shoulders the door hard and tries the knob. Dust swirls down from the rafter beams with every ram, and the frenzied scraping of claws freezes me on the hide-a-bed.

Jesus, why is no-one else waking up? I cringe as a heavy thud shakes the five-panel on its hinges, and this wet snuffling sounds from under the crack. *How can nobody else hear this?* I can't even look. I don't want to see it coming for me. I'm terrified to see the end. *Some soldier, you'd be.*

Eventually, the maneater stops ramming the door, and my breaths lengthen and even out. The cottage relapses to quiet snoring and firewood crackling. My family slept through it all. If they can't see me when I've been on the other side too long, can they sense the maneaters at all? Would Dad have felt the draft if he stayed on the couch? Would anyone else in this house even know if one broke through the door?

No. I don't think they would. Not until it latched onto them like it did with James. *What a bloody nightmare.*

James is the first one up the next morning. I know it's him without rolling over because his sock foot drags across the floor as he limps. I'm not the only one who notices. Mom admonishes him as she strides into the kitchen behind him. Her voice sounds as sharp and ragged as a cheese grater as she orders him to sit. "Let me see it."

"Mom. It's fine. Just a bit tender," James protests, but a kitchen chair creaks under his weight as he obeys.

I count my fingers, tapping my thumb to my index, middle, ring, pinky and back again as, I assume, Mom unwraps my brother's ankle.

"Oh, James. Shit." The fragile way those words roll out of my mother's mouth chills me.

My older brother coughs and asks in an uncertain voice, "Is it supposed to smell like that?"

Oh God, no.

"I'm getting your father." One of the kitchen chairs scrapes back briskly.

"Mom, wait."

"We're going back to the hospital." Mom's tone does not broker arguing.

The cottage tightens into a ball of commotion, the twins asking in bleary voices, "What's up?" Dad barking, "Get the first aid kit, and put on your coats." Moments later the entire family pours out the front door with frightening urgency. I'm still curled up on the foldout , throat aching, head pounding. I say an earnest prayer for James, but I don't know who I'm praying to.

You did this to James. Your fault. Don't think you can pray your way out of it.

I can't deal with the guilt today. I just can't. Peeling my sweating, stinking self off the mattress, I go in. Just roll into another world like it's a blanket, and I'll die of exposure without it. The headache is already fading as I turn the key to lock out my world and face a glowing, apricot sunrise off the lake in Bizarro world.

I head straight for the loft, noting that the cabin looks much the same as it does on my side. *What year is it supposed to be?* But I don't pull out the notepad. I clutch the dictionary off the shelf, thumb my finger into the red crayon colored 'G' tab and pull it open, start flipping pages. My throat closes, and my teeth clack when I find the page of handwriting.

Thank Christ. I blink rapidly at the ceiling. I don't know what I thought. That knowing Everett was dead would somehow erase his words? I don't know. *But they're here. They're still here. Thank you, God.* I refocus on the page, running my fingers over Everett's small, tidy script.

I'm getting sicker over here. It's hard to do much more than write with this bloody headache. It's giving me double vision. What the hell use am I over here if it's just crippling me anyways? And I know it's the Goddamned door, because as soon as I'm out of this Hell, poof! Headache gone. Just like that. Right as rain. A soul knows when it's in the wrong place, but I suppose the body takes a bit longer to figure it out. I think I die here. I think the hellhounds kill us. None of our things are here when I come over. Any of the dates I visit in the future, Annie's and my belongings are all gone. I mean, I know I pack up the cottage each season, but it's still winter when I come over here. It's Hell bloody frozen over, as they say, and all our things are gone. We're just erased, like we never even existed.

My poor Annie. We fought again. Her angina started acting up afterward, and her pills didn't kick in until halfway through the night. It's my fault, Annie. This is all my fault, and I can't fix it. Lord help me, I can't do anything at all. I'm so sorry.

I read it three times. I trace the grooves where the pencil pressed down hard and I imagine what Everett's hand looked like, decide whether Annie had a sweet smile. *I bet she baked a mean apple pie. I bet Everett had a helluva handshake.* Frowning on my fourth read through, I pause on one line.

I pack up the cottage each season, but it's still winter when I come over here.

It's summer every time I come over. The one time the leaves changed, but sometimes they change early if August is cold. I pull the notepad out of my back pocket. According to Everett's list, it's supposed to be 1998 right now. *That's only four summers from now.*

My gaze flies around the loft. The beanbag is here, but not the cot. I set the dictionary down and descend to the main floor. The green foldout has the spring poking out of the back, just like on our side.

Holy shit. Tension builds in my chest. I scramble to the bunk-room. Two of the beds are unmade. There's underwear on the floor. I kick at them, boxers. Jesus, I'm not enough of a perv to recognize my brother's underwear, but the twins have never picked a damned pair up off the floor their entire lives. *It could be them.*

The bed is tidily made in my parents' small room. I spot an empty wine glass on one nightstand, and a folded crossword puzzle on the other. My eyes tear up as I recognize Dad's printing filling the tiny white squares.

Oh Christ! Oh thank God, it's them. They're still here. It's four years from now, and they still come. I carefully replace the crossword and scour the rest of the room. Their clothes are in the dressers. Mom's hairbrush threaded with red, frizzy strands rests on the nightstand.

I stumble to the bathroom and squirt liquid soap into my hands, smelling it. *Lavender. Mom's favorite.* Dizziness grips me as I'm rinsing my hands. I sag to my knees in the middle of the bathroom and succumb to deep, gulping sobs. *They're alive. They're not dead in the future because they were just here, so I can't have killed them. I can't have failed. Everett, they live! It's four years later, and they're alive. We do this. We fix it. You and I together.*

I spend hours in the cottage turning my family's possessions in my hands like they're Ancient Egyptian treasure. The apple tree out front has been cut down. The van isn't in its parking spot, but the oil stain still marks the drive, and Angus's Quonset is still there. So is every cabin on the lake as I know it.

But I find nothing at all belonging to me, not one pair of distressed jeans, no graphic novels or random socks folded into the hide-a-bed, and the coffee tin under the front porch where I sometimes hide cigarettes is empty.

My teeth rake over my bottom lip as I do the math. *In 1998, you'd be twenty-one, right?*

"Maybe you just don't come anymore." I stare out at a stationary heron in the marshy shallows of the lake. Every cold wave feels like its lapping past the shoreline to wash over me until I'm numb. *I've come every summer since I was born. I've never missed one. Maybe I join the Army?*

A second realization hits me nearly as hard as the first.

There's none of James's things in the cottage either.

CHAPTER THIRTEEN

"You heard the doctor, David." It's just past midnight, and my mother's urgent whisper carries easily to the kitchen where I stand barefoot in front of the Philco fridge, a glass of milk clutched in my hand. She's talking to my father, not me. She sounds like she's arguing. "He asked if something bit James, something venomous. What kind of question is that?"

Jesus Christ. I wince and milk jostles in the glass, dribbling over the edge and onto my hand. The moment where that black claw snapped closed around James's ankle replays in the groove that it's worn into my mind. *The hungry way it clamped down, it seemed more like a mouth than a hand. Was it venomous? Was it biting James?*

"Madeline." My Dad sighs long and low. "It means he's a fresh-out-of-school doctor who's bored out of his mind working a small-town urgent care facility. He saw what he wanted to see, something more exciting than the everyday stitch it up and pack 'em out routine."

"No, you saw it. That doesn't look like a normal infection. It looks like *blood poisoning*." Mom's voice drops even lower on the last two words, like saying them too loudly will make it true.

Blood poisoning. I shift on my feet and taste ashes in my mouth.

Jesus, that's serious.

"Come on, Madeline. James is young. They're practically bulletproof at this age. He doesn't have a fever, he's acting himself, and they sent him home with a stronger round of antibiotics. It'll clear up in no time."

"That's not the point!" Mom hisses. "You saw David's face that night. He was lying. Covering up. He's hiding something. A mother knows when her son is lying."

The milk glass clatters as I set it on the counter to avoid dropping it, but my parents don't seem to hear. Both my shaking hands clutch the key hanging around my neck, and my cheeks flush with heat. *You don't know me, Madeline. You don't know me at all.*

"Why would he lie?" Dad comes to my defense. "He just looked scared shitless to me. You know how James walks around at night. And they'd all been working themselves up about that bloody, stupid door. He was embarrassed to admit that he thought James was some ghost, that's all."

"No, it's more than that. He's always been an odd child."

I flinch hard, like they have slapped me back until my butt hits the back of the green couch, but Dad's barely contained voice carries easily that far.

"Christ, not this again. You know what? Maybe he wouldn't be so *odd* if you didn't leave him behind every damned place like a misplaced handbag, Madeline. He's your son, not some forgotten accessory. You could *try* once in a while."

"Don't you dare talk to me about trying, David. *You* are the one who wanted to try for one more. Not me, you. And you go flit off to work, drink coffee and go for business lunches while I run a whole football team through diapers, and soccer, and college applications. *Try,* David? Trying is what got me into this mess."

"You've always had it in for David. The doctor brought him out to you, and you insisted he wasn't your baby. This isn't his fault,

Madeline. You can only let a kid slip through the cracks so many times before—"

I'm on the couch with a pillow crushed over my head. I don't know how I got here, and I think I'm hyperventilating. Every breath rails out of me faster than the last, like birds bursting out of an attic. Large, amoeba splotches bloom in my vision and my chest winds tighter with every gulping inhale, like a clockwork spring.

She never even wanted me, not from the moment I was born. My own mother. What did I ever do, Madeline? Anger and hurt clot in my lungs, leaving no room for air. *What did I ever do to you?*

I can't piece together a coherent thought or calm my breathing until the draft presses under the door. Cold air raises goosebumps on my arms and stills my breath in my throat. The mess of emotions in my head crystallizes into brittle fear as the hand on the other side of the door draws its claws down the wood like a knife scraping across a plate.

Nobody hears it, David. No-one but you.

It should have occurred to me long before now. I'm such a damned fool. The hellhounds, they lock on when there's an object on the wrong side. At first, it was my tobacco tin that drew them in. Now it's me. Goddamnit. Every single time I've come through and tried to figure out how to make things right, I've been practically calling them in. I should have known. The racket at the door is so much worse on the days I come through, and when I stay away, it calms back down. They lose the scent a bit.

I'm the bloody object on the wrong side, every time I come here! That's why it feels so wrong. Sweet Jesus, how am I supposed to fix this, if I can't even be here to do it? This is truly hell, this... setting me up to fall, making me the instrument of my own failure.

I'm not coming back here. I've got to let them lose my scent. I know it's not enough, but it's the best I can do until things calm down. I'm not coming back.

I curl over the dictionary until my forehead touches its thin pages. "Not you, Everett." *Don't you leave me too.* My eyes blur, and I sit up and slam the book closed to avoid getting tears on Everett's writing.

Everything's so messed up. Everything.

I had pulled the door planks off at dawn this morning, pounded the hammer's claws into cracks and reefed back hard, daring my family to wake up and face me, fighting the hopeless rage in my gut with noise. But when the last board screeched from the frame and clattered to the floor, the cottage fell back into stubborn silence. Nobody woke up. I slammed the hammer against the door frame in frustration and gritted my teeth against the answering pound in my head before yanking open the door and diving headlong into this world.

It's all unraveling, anyway. I've cocked it all up and I'm getting sucked into Bizarro world. The maneaters don't rattle the door when I come over. They do it when I'm gone for too long. I skipped that day, the rainy one when everyone stayed home, I didn't come in, and they tried to break down the door that same night. I sag over the closed book. *What the hell have I done? They wanted Everett gone, but they want me here. Odd child.* I shiver. *I'm screwed. I'm lost.* I wallow in that for a good long while before a small, hopeful realization tingles through me. Straightening, I wipe my nose with the back of my arm.

I can still save my family. I can stop the maneaters from breaking through to my side if I just spend enough time in Bizarro world to keep them calm. *Maybe it's me they want. Just me, the chance to nab me. On the days I come through, they barely tap at all at night. I'm like catnip. If they get enough of me, maybe they'll forget what they're here for and let the bridge collapse.*

I stay in Bizarro world until lunch, retreating to my side to inhale a fried bologna and cheese sandwich before returning for a second shift. It's easy, considering I'd rather be worlds away from Madeline, anyway.

The afternoon air on this side is soft and still except for the hollow cries of a solitary loon on the shimmering lake. It bleeds the pain out of my head and the tightness out of my chest within minutes of my crossing the threshold. I record Everett's entry into my notebook and, on a whim, add my own words to his diary entry in the dictionary.

I'm coming back.

Then, I return to my side and tuck the notebook between the cushions of the hide-a-bed. The van door slams outside and Madeline's shrill voice filters in from outside. Freezing and cocking my head, I strain to decipher my mother's words. She's scolding someone, probably the twins. I don't stay long enough to find out. Bizarro world has had enough time to reset, so I go back in. When I look in the dictionary, my words are gone. Only Everett's remains.

The echo of Madeline's voice settles in the back of my throat like sour milk. *Odd child.*

She doesn't even think you belong to her. Lunging away from the five-panel, I stomp to the kitchen and tear open the top left-hand cupboard where Madeline stores her delicate wine glasses. Snatching one out, I glare back at the door to my side, and hurl the glass to the hardwood.

It shatters like thin ice. Shards of glass skate across the smooth floor, fleeing from my sudden, suffocating rage. I grab another glass and smash it too. One by one, I clear the cupboard of stemware, punctuating each crash with an incensed curse.

When I finish with the glasses, I move onto the bowls, and then the hefty stack of plates, until I'm screaming the word, *"Bitch",* while ceramic shards explode around me, impaling into the floor and crunching under my sandals. When I'm done, my arms ache from hurling dishes, and the floor around me looks like a modern art mosaic, an ice jam of jagged glass, creaking and crushing under foot.

I feel invigorated, but unfulfilled, anger still lodging like a flickering coal behind my sternum, so I skid over the broken glass, unlock the door and walk brazenly onto my side. Madeline is still outside, yelling. Bristling, I go back to Bizarro world and break every dish in the kitchen again.

Fuck you, Madeline.

When evening closes, I inspect the soles of my sandals for stray glass shards before re-entering my world. Madeline scolds outside. I lock the door.

"Jord, just pick up a damned grocery bag, would you?" she snaps over her shoulder as she comes in.

I hammer boards back into place, watching over my shoulder as Madeline hoists two bulging plastic bags onto the counter. She doesn't even flinch as I pound the nails home. As my family takes over the kitchen, unpacking groceries, boiling pasta and brewing coffee, I scrub at my temples and retreat to the loft. They shovel spaghetti into their mouths and argue over who sang 'Hallelujah' best, Leonard Cohen or Jeff Buckley. The clock on the fridge reads just after lunch, but I've been gone for four hours. Only my returning headache prevents me from eating again.

At supper that night, my family doesn't even wonder aloud where I am, and when the draft bleeds through the door in the middle of the night, the maneaters are quiet.

The next morning, I page through the dictionary as a calm, glorious sunrise bathes the cottage in Bizarro world in ripe, peach tones. There's no letter from Everett. I search from front to back multiple times. It's just a dictionary devoid of his careful, cursive hand. I skip rocks across the lake for hours that day until my shoulder aches. The next day I come in, there's no dictionary at all. The cottage isn't even complete, just a bare frame with ribs of rafters dividing the clear sky above. Down the road, where Angus's Quonset should be, there's nothing but a bare parking pad.

Shit. My mind latches on the maneaters I startled in the office. I clutch the crystal knob behind me, ready to retreat. *Don't be an idiot. It hasn't been built yet. Angus might not even own the place.* Swallowing, I take in a lake surrounded by shrubbery and short trees. *No windowless buildings for a hellhound to hide behind.* Mist rises off the glassy water. The long grass surrounding it is pregnant with the scurry and song of birds. Clogged flocks of them rise and settle in squawking, raucous waves.

I shuffle to the edge of the plywood at the front doorway. Beyond, the front porch floor joists yawn exposed and newly installed. No stairs yet, no parking pad either. The bird calls crescendo as a mass of seagulls swarm over the middle of the lake on paper white wings, swirling and screaming.

Below them, the water breaks like it's boiling, and the birds dive and hover with wide, hungry beaks. Silver flashes wriggle in the waves.

Fish. I remember. *More than I saw before when I was lying on the front porch.*

The lake here looks absolutely infested. I edge out onto the porch joists as the massive, noisy flock gorges on hapless fish until they're too full to fly. When I jump down to the matted grass, something slips and clatters against the cottage. I whirl back and focus on a fishing rod lying in the dust beneath the porch.

Well, I've got all day. I shrug, drop to my hands and knees, and retrieve the rod. There's no tackle box, just the single, bare hook on the rod itself. *You can dig up some worms,* I reason, but I don't get the chance.

As soon as I wade into the long grass, with the rod tucked over my shoulder, clouds of mosquitoes churn into the air. The sound of them is unreal, shrill, like a ringing in my ears, and all-encompassing, as they swarm toward me and scrabble for purchase on exposed skin. I drop the rod, slap the back of my neck, and sprint back to the house, snorting and swearing while the little bastards latch onto me.

Jesus, David. Stop. What if they come through the door with you?

Grabbing a fistful of long grass, I heave until it tears free, slap at my back, and around my hair. By the time I scramble back onto the frame of the cottage, my skin is crawling, but the screeching buzz has dispersed. I slap at a few determined stragglers before unlocking the latch. Swinging the wisp of grass in a frenzied sweep, I open the door.

I leave the bundled grass on the other side but bring five mosquitoes through with me. I spend the next two minutes stumbling around the cottage, slapping at them and retrieving their tiny, smeared bodies to brush back onto Bizarro side.

Would mosquitoes make a difference? I scratch at my forearm and brush my fingers through my hair. *If a bloody dishtowel and a tobacco tin on the wrong side set the hellhounds off, I'm guessing anything living would be an even bigger trigger. Everett was. I am. Jesus, David. You've got to be more careful.*

Madeline has a Tilley hat in the front closet with sewn-in bug netting. I flip through the contents of the top shelf until I find it, and I don't go back into Bizarro world until I'm wearing a jacket, work gloves and my jeans tucked into my socks. *Socks, sandals and a Tilley hat. If only Veronica Tyler could see me now.*

The sound of the place is as overwhelming as it was the first time. Chattering birdcalls swell over the mist as I grab the fishing rod leaning up against the front porch and slog into the grass. Hordes of murmuring grey rise out of the thatch. Millions of tiny wings, pitched to the muted shriek of a dentist's drill, stir around me. Enough mosquitoes clog onto the bug netting that I have to swipe them away with my gloved hand.

As I close on the lake shore, I'm overpowered by the acrid smell of bird shit. It spatters the rocks with chalky white. Seagulls harangue from above but keep their distance. I search for a sandy spot to dig for worms, but the beach is all smeared gravel, feathers, and crushed eggshells. Finally, I shrug, and loose the bare hook from the eye of the rod.

I'm just passing time, anyway. Who cares if I catch anything?

Birds side-eye me overhead and I cast. The rod is weighted well, and the line unspools with a whiz, hook plopping into the water well away from shore. I'm shocked at the immediate, insistent yank.

A bite. Already? Snagging the rod back, I sense the undeniable weight of a hooked and struggling fish.

"No friggin' way." I alternate between hauling on the rod and reeling in the slack. Soon, the iridescent thrashing body of a thick rainbow trout ruffles the water at my feet. I don't have a net, so I reach a gloved hand into the cool water and grip the gaping fish behind its gills.

It stares at the sky with solemn, jewel eyes as I shake off my other glove, and reach my fingers into its mouth to pull the hook.

Maybe I don't suck at fishing as much as I thought. I grin as the trout spits out the hook and fans its tail to wriggle back to the depths, leaving a froth of spray in its wake.

The next five times I cast with the bare hook, a fish bites. I stop when one of them swallows the line deep enough that I can't reach the hook. Snapping the line over a sharp rock, I take the fishing rod back to the cottage.

And that's how I sustain myself without Everett's letters. I fish. I skip rocks and walk circuits around the lake. Sometimes I jack a car and speed all the way out to the Gulf station, and that blue-and-orange sign gleams in the sun, twirling on well-oiled bearings. The paper on the stand reads 1960, or 1971, and the bathroom smells like fresh paint and vinegar. I go into the stall that Jord blockaded when I was six, and I stupidly search for the graffiti I added later. I've memorized the words I scratched into the powder blue walls the year after my parents forgot me there. The same ones I found in the dictionary.

> Gulf: A deep hollow. A wide separation in status. Something that swallows us up.

Of course, the words aren't there when the gas station is new. I haven't written them yet, but I look for them every time I make the trip, regardless of the year.

The Gulf trips are not frequent. I only go if I have a car or a bike at my disposal and I run my vehicle of choice through a thorough inspection beforehand, horrified by the idea of something breaking down and stranding me miles away from the five-panel as the sun dips toward the horizon. I give myself lots of time.

Spending entire days in Bizarro world is hungry work, but the hellhounds are quietest after uninterrupted days. At first, I'm too scared to cook the fish I catch, but then I remember I smoked here once, drank a Coke, and took the residue of both back to the wrong side of the door. Stupid. Thoughtless, but I can't remember any ill effects from it. The first fish I cook over a campfire tastes like flaky butter. Plump fall-apart fillets with oily, crisp skin melt in my mouth, and there are no brothers to fight off. I can eat as much as I like.

On several occasions, I arrive to the crab apple tree, still felled in the front yard, and I know its Everett who cut it down but can't figure out why his changes stick in this world and mine don't. I get into the habit of counting the annual rings in the stump like he did. A few times, I step through the closet door into the crumbled, mossy outline of the long dead cottage, with a huge, gnarled apple tree bowed over it like a mourner at a grave.

The water's warmer in those future years. I can wade for hours without worrying about jet skis or motorboats swamping me with their waves. There's hardly any fish, and I can't hike far because the weather is unpredictable and swings wildly. There is snow once. Snow in summer.

One time, and it only happens once, the room on the other side of the closet is identical to mine. *Identical.* My balled-up sock and plaid blanket puddled on the floor. Left-over triangle of french toast leaning precariously off the edge of the kitchen counter. When I get outside, the Ford Econoline is bellied up to the log parking stop like a beached whale. The dent in the front corner panel is there, the one I added this spring, and Dad's pack of Trident is baking on the dash. Everything here, as I know it. Except my family.

I belong here. I'm feeling that strange sensation. Belonging. *To what? To nothing? Nobody? To a deserted version of my world?* I don't know. It's not deserted. Sometimes I find pots that have boiled dry on the stove. Spears of uncooked spaghetti poke out of a crusted black mess at the bottom, and the burner is still on. Sometimes, I re-cradle the nozzle on the pump at the Gulf station because someone left it filling their car.

I'm not alone here. I know that. I'm just a little late, that's all. Having a pretty good idea about what distracted these people from their pasta and their Unleaded, you'd think I'd be terrified, scared out of my mind. But I'm not. I own this place. Between the hours of dawn and dusk, the maneaters cower and scuff in dark buildings with no windows. As long as I stay in the light.

I've never felt more at home than in this place. It's filling me up.

CHAPTER FOURTEEN

It's disconcerting, after spending a complete day on the Bizarro side, to cross back over to the same time I left. Sometimes, I shut the door, reset the world, and just go back in. The evening world I just left reverts to the current time, and I get to relive the entire day again. I do that often, especially when there are shiny cars on the other side with easily accessible keys and ashtrays and cigarettes. I can only repeat so many times, though, before I need to sleep, and it's not safe to doze in Bizarro world.

God forbid, your nap went a little long. Those maneaters in the Quonset would love to sink their teeth deep into you.

When I go back to my side, the familiar headache uncurls in my skull like a caterpillar sensing the change of seasons, ready to eat my brain. I nap in the loft to avoid being sat on again. James doesn't pass me the butter at supper, even if I ask him three times. Madeline, reliably, doesn't set out a plate for me. I trip Jord as he exits the bathroom, and he swears and looks at me for a long second before really seeing me. Then he smiles wistfully and says, "Oh hey... David." There's always a hell of a long pause now before he says David.

I smile.

No ribbing from the twins, no hassling Madeline, and I don't have to listen to James pushing me to be more, while Dad squashes every major decision I make. A guy could get used to this.

At nights, the cold drafts come, but they're hardly more than a whisper, a breath, just this undeniably terrifying but patient presence on the other side of the five-panel. No scratching, no ramming at the door. Sometimes I doze right through it.

It's working. I can keep the maneaters on their own side, and soon it'll fade, like it did before. One morning I'll wake up and open the door, and there'll just be a plain guest room with a crib, like I saw that first day I found the key.

That's the plan. That's the best Everett and I can come up with, just spend my every waking moment in Bizarro world buying time for my side and praying that the maneaters lose scent of the place and let the bridge collapse. It's an admittedly shitty plan.

After a stormy day under a leaky cottage roof in Bizarro world, I shuffle back to our side one morning to see James sprawled on the green couch before me, but I'm not alarmed. That's where I left him. He doesn't see me anymore, and he doesn't hear me when I pound the nails back into place to board up the five-panel.

I could scream into my brother's face, and he might flinch for a second, but I've been putting in too much time on the other side to garner much more of a reaction than that. There's a balance. The more whole I feel on that side, the more insubstantial I become on this one. Not a ghost, I can't walk through people. My hands still reliably grip and manipulate objects on this side without sinking into them. I'm just entirely forgettable now.

It's only one step further than you ever were. That's a settling feeling. *It shouldn't be, should it?* But it is.

I ease onto the edge of the sofa by James's feet, run my hand through my soggy hair and smile wistfully at his frowning face as his gaze flicks across the pages of his paperback. *Second time through the John Grisham, I think. Maybe a third.*

He lets the book flop onto his chest, and winces as he lifts his bandaged foot from its pillowed perch. His toes are an unhealthy grey with pale moons of nails. I frown, lean forward, and fold the cushion in half before he rests his heel on it again.

"You know what I'm thinking of doing?" he asks.

Jerking back, I pin my gaze to him, mouth hanging open and throat too dry to respond, but James isn't looking at me and he's projecting his voice.

"What?" Madeline's muffled voice calls back from the other room.

I sag back into my seat. *You're stupid, David. You know what the rules are and what you have to give up to save them.* Glancing at James's warm face as he contemplates the ceiling, the hopeful thought grips me. *He'll see you again when this is all over. Fix this first, and then everything will be good with James again.*

"I'm bored to death hobbling around here, and I went and talked to Angus at the office yesterday," James continues.

"Did you?" Madeline ambles out of the bedroom, hooking an earring into one lobe. She's wearing a fifties-style pencil dress that looks ridiculous on her.

She and Dad must be going out today.

"And what did Sir Angus have to say?" She flashes a lipsticked smile at James.

"He said he could use some extra help if I wanted to, nothing really physical, paperwork in the office, that sort of thing. The odd welding job." James sits up. "Know what else he said?"

"Hmm?"

"He said that the guy that built the addition, Evan, I think it was?"

Everett! I straighten and square up to James. "What did he say about Everett, James?"

"He said that the guy croaked, and his family is done with this place. Angus was going to wait until fall to knock out the wall and open this place up, but he said to ask you guys what you thought about doing it now."

The words roll into me like an avalanche. *Oh no.* I sag. *Oh God.*

"It wouldn't take long. Maybe an afternoon? And I told him I could help out. What do you think?"

"James, no!" I lunge ahead and grab his shoulders to shake him, but he's as solid as concrete and doesn't respond to my grip.

"We'll ask your father." Madeline kisses James's head like he's five years old. "Might be just the project you two need. The pair of you have been moping around here all week."

I try to bat Madeline away, but she just waves her hand in front of her face like she's swatting a fly.

"James, NO!" I scream.

I lean into him and grab both his cheeks, but he lifts the paperback and the edges of the book slam into my forearms, jarring them to the bone. I lose my grip on James. On everything. "Listen to me," I sob. "You can't open it up. James? You hear? JAMES! You can't open it up!"

I flee to the other side, just turn and run, claw the boards down, tear the door open, lock myself in, and stumble down to the lake. The wind whips my hair as I kneel on the rocky shore. I splash cold water over my face until the molten pain at my temples cools like crackling wax.

Oh God. Can't breathe.

Forcing myself to sit up straight, I open my mouth wide, panting and rocking back and forth while spray dances across the lake and scours me until I can draw in a proper, sustaining inhalation.

I'm done. This is it. Finished. If Angus and James tear down the wall, the door doesn't bloody well matter, does it? And neither does the key. I'm clutching it again, pulling the twine pendant hard. *Shit. Shit, there'll just be this gaping hole between the worlds. Everything from one side just bleeding into the other. Maneaters spilling out every-where in the dark. No putting them back. No setting things right. Jesus Christ, I should have told someone about the door while they could still hear me. James would have listened. He'd have thought I was crazy, but he would have listened. I can't do this. I can't fix this alone. I'm broken. Madeline was right. Odd child. The world will get eaten alive, and it's the odd child's fault.*

"No." My denial comes out as a whimper. A magpie caws in the distance, and I flinch and scan the treetops for the source of the sound.

Don't give up on this. Not on James and Dad. You need to fix this for them. Be loud, David. Beat your chest. I let go of the key and it thuds against my chest as I swipe my hand down my face and shake the moisture off my fingers. *You have time, right? Just keep resetting today. You've only been here once, and God knows, you're not tired now, just keep resetting until you figure something out.*

It takes my frantic brain another day-and-a-half to come up with a passable plan. By the time I work out the kinks and lock away Bizarro world, James is still paging through his novel on the couch, and Madeline is putting her other earring on. I stride past them, out the front door and turn toward Angus's office at the end of Sweet Bee Circle.

Four kids careen out of a driveway on rattling bikes.

I shout and dive out of the way, but not in time. The first kid clips me, catches my hip with his handlebars and sends me sprawl-ing. I hit the gravel on my side hard. Breath explodes out of me, and I can't suck it back in. Rolling onto my stomach, I raise my head, whistle in a thread of an inhale, and flinch as the other three jackasses roll by, their tires inches away from crushing my fingers. The first bike isn't even wobbling from our impact.

"Slow down, assholes!" I try to holler, but it comes out as an old man wheeze.

The kids pump their pedals, curl against their frames, and leave dust in their wakes. Not one of them looks back.

I press my arm against my ribs and inventory my other injuries. Scraped elbow, bruised hip. The ribs are the worst of it, but my breath is coming back, and there's no sharp pain when I inhale.

Assholes.

The memory of a different beating wraps around my mind and tugs me toward its anxious depths. Hot asphalt, the ever-present smell of greasy french fries, and Sam Ren's gun in my face. The stench of ammonia. I try to blink it away, but my chest tightens, and I can't break out of the recollection until the crunch and pop of gravel filters into my ears.

Car tires.

I remember the present, the collision with the bike, and I'm brought wide awake by the thought of a car flattening me without even slowing as it bounces over. I roll off the edge of the road onto someone's front lawn, like some sort of shameful daytime drunk.

Is this what being homeless feels like? People just pretend you don't exist because you're that glitch in the surroundings, that flaw they'd rather not see? And they keep doing it until they really don't see you. I groan as I sit up, brush gravel off my raw arm, and push to my feet.

Limping to the Quonset, I open Angus's office door and don't close it behind me.

Mr. Tyler is leaning back from his desk, picking his nose, and scrutinizing the contents on the end of his finger before wiping them onto his handkerchief. I smirk and ease past him to stand before the Quonset door, and then I freeze.

Go in, idiot. No maneaters on this side. Come on. Easing the brass knob open, I blink into the gloom. Naked overhead lights limn neat bundles of firewood with pasty light. *See! It's not even dark.*

Curls of bark and splinters of wood crumble under my feet as I pad across the oily cement floor and peruse a yawning, arched shop filled with greasy car parts, broken soda machines, dented hot water tanks, faded orange life preserver rings, and two dusty golf carts. Toward the back wall, I find what I'm looking for, a metal shelving unit stacked with paint-streaked tins, spray cans and industrial cleaners. I pluck a can of black spray paint, and one of army green, give both a test shake, and nod, satisfied at the weight of them and the rattle of the ball bearing within. Then I pull two fat bristle brushes from a jar of turpentine and wipe them on a shop rag before tucking them into my back pocket.

Angus has left his desk and is peering out the open office door when I come back in. I wait as he looks both ways down the gravel drive, shakes his head, and closes the door. When he lowers back into his creaking chair with a whistling groan, I tuck one aerosol can under my arm and help myself to a fistful of pepperoni sticks.

"Thanks, Sir Tyler." I nod and salute as I back out the door, but Angus blows on his coffee and shows no sign that he's heard me.

Back at the cottage, I set my supplies behind the woodstove and gnaw on a pepperoni stick as I navigate around a fluttering Madeline in the kitchen. As she finishes with the dirty dishes and efficiently wraps breakfast leftovers, I rummage through cupboards, pulling out icing sugar, flour, and cornstarch.

There's a full bottle of white glue in the junk drawer. I add it, along with all my other absconded supplies, from the kitchen to my stash behind the stove.

All set. That's everything I need, I think.

The headache stretches within my skull. I've been awake for more than two days, but less than twenty minutes have passed on this side. Stumbling back to the kitchen, I side-step around Madeline one last time, grab the bottle of pills with no label and a can of Coke out of the fridge. Tucking them into my shirt, I clamber into the loft.

I flop onto the cot, toss three waxy capsules into my mouth, and chase them with a fizzy gulp that stings my throat. Belching loudly, I peer down at my brother on the couch.

It's okay, James. I'm going to fix this, I swear. A faint smile crosses my lips as my brother stretches until his shoulders pop.

He punches the couch pillows behind him and settles back in.

That's the last thing I remember. I sleep right through until it's dark. Even then, I only wake to make sure that James isn't still on the couch. When I peer down into the dark, the green foldout is empty. He must have moved to the bunkroom.

I hobble down the ladder, back stiff from the cot. I settle onto the couch without even unfolding it. I press my cheek to the scratchy, crushed velvet when the cold draft flutters my eyelashes, as soft and quiet as a fall breeze.

The maneaters are happy. Do they know? Do they think they've won? Bastards. Don't count me out yet.

CHAPTER FIFTEEN

Dad's sense of humor has always been as quiet as he is. I like it because it's one of the few things he's unapologetic about, and he doesn't bring it out often. It's rare, and as a child, it felt like finding treasure when Dad could make me laugh.

One weekend, back when I was seven or eight, Madeline caught a stomach flu that one of us must have brought home from school. She spent the day stumbling between her bed and the bathroom, and showed no signs of improving by evening, so Dad called the Registry Office where he worked, and left a message saying he'd be taking Monday off. Both of us giggled in the kitchen after he hung up the phone. The daily tear-off calendar on the counter read March 31, and the pair of us were bagging lunches for school tomorrow, while trading epic prank ideas.

I suggested farting into Jord and Jess's lunch bags, but Dad eventually won me over with his April Fools' idea. He spooned some icing sugar and cornstarch into a bowl and let me add in alternating drops of green and blue food coloring. We toyed with ratios until our mixture transformed into a powdery grey-green with a chalky texture. Then we sprinkled it liberally onto everyone's sandwiches before bagging them.

I stared through the Ziploc bag at a salami and cheese on rye marred with dark, splotchy blooms of powder. "It looks exactly like mold," I grinned.

"Of course it does." Dad frowned, sliding another tampered sandwich into its crisp brown bag. Then he winked. "Not my first time, David."

On Halloween we used the idea again, this time on a larger scale. Dad wanted to dress up our old plastic skeleton, Mr. Skinny Bones. I had my heart set on a zombie. He agreed, but only under the condition that it had to be something special, something different. We settled on fungus zombie skeleton.

First, we propped Mr. Skinny Bones so that it looked like he was belly-crawling across our front lawn. Jord kicked his head off, and I cried, but after Dad yelled at him and banished him inside, we got everything re-attached and started peppering the skeleton with our secret mold powder. Dad added some fake spider webs across the ribs, and we spray-painted them dark green. Then I plucked some mushrooms from the front lawn and stuffed them into each eye socket. It was perfect. Mr. Zombie Fungus Skinny Bones remains, to this day, the best Halloween decoration of all time.

I'm fairly certain I can re-create a similar effect—sans mushrooms—on the cottage addition wall. If I keep it wet enough, my artful spackling of black cornstarch, flour, and icing sugar should not only create the illusion of mold but also promote a healthy growth of the real thing in a few days. I rescue a lonely slice of stale, fuzzy bread from its crumpled bag in the garbage to use as a starter. Then I down three pills to tamp my headache, and I dive into my art.

When my family have finished breakfast, I drag one of the kitchen chairs to the living room, and use a sponge and pail to soak the top of the addition wall where it meets the ceiling. It takes more time than I thought it would. My family members keep inadvertently interrupting the process, spotting the out-of-place chair, grabbing it, and tucking it back under the Formica table.

I have to step down from it every time I notice them focusing on it, for fear they'll tip me off and I'll crack my head. I'm *that* frail now, in this world. They can sit on me or send me toppling off a chair without even feeling my weight. They don't seem to notice the out-of-place sponge or pail.

Maybe because you're holding them. Invisible by association. Experimenting, I strip off my socks and stand barefoot on the kitchen chair, and my family stops moving it after that. *It's contagious, David. Your invisibility is contagious now.*

I keep squeezing the sponge against the top edge of the panel until it warps with water stains. Old, delaminated layers of paint separate and swell into fat blisters. My arms ache from holding them overhead, but I carry on, layering on watered-down glue with one brush, while flicking on dyed powder with the other, accentuating it all with gentle circles of hazy green and black spray-paint.

The sopping wet wall feathers the paint nicely, and I admire the effect of dark stains accumulating in fresh eggshell cracks. I crumble the moldy bread in its bag and smear it into the top corners of the walls. Then I use a spray bottle to mist the whole top edge of the ceiling where it meets the addition. I don't stop until water streaks down the wall.

Stepping back behind the couch, I squint at my finished work from a wider perspective. Some stains are swimming on the wall, moving.

My vision is blurring again. My head is pounding hard enough that saliva pools in the back of my throat. *It'll have to do for now.*

I roll up the bag of flour, tuck it, the cornstarch, and icing sugar back into the cupboard. Then I bag and garbage the sticky paintbrushes and roll the spray-paint cans under the front porch skirting. I weave listlessly around Jess to get back into the house, and I drag myself to the loft.

There are four pills left in the unlabelled pill bottle. *Shit. I should have counted them before now.*

I swallow two capsules with a flat, lukewarm swig of Coke, and when I lie back on the cot, it feels like my head is melting into the pillow, my brains leaking out of my ears. Lying motionless, I pray for the nausea to recede, like that mouse hiding in the loft mattress in Bizarro world, hoping to escape the attention of the horrible presence hovering over it by freezing into perfect silence.

Sickness claws at my throat with bitter, bile-streaked claws, and I swallow and try to console myself. *Maybe, by the time I wake up, they'll have noticed it already. Black mold. No way Madeline will let them open that room then, not while she's here. Not a bloody chance. I'll wake up, and the problem will have solved itself while I slept.* It's a nice thought, but I'm not optimistic.

I can't sleep no matter how hard I try.

A square of sunlight chugs a jagged trek across the rafters and it's early afternoon when I dry swallow the last two pills in the bottle, desperate to ease my migraine. Fifteen minutes later, a horrible heat crawls up my throat and I thunder down the ladder, aiming for the bathroom, but unable to make it. I veer toward the kitchen sink and retch, puke so hard that bile burns my nostrils. The headache pounds through my skull like a bird stretching out of a cracked shell. I cling to the sink faucets, crank the cold water and let an icy stream run down the side of my face as I battle dizziness. My legs jelly, and I slide to the floor and lean against the cupboard door.

I can't make it back to the loft. If I lie here, someone will step on my head.

I crawl to the green couch and roll into its sagging softness surrounded by the sour smell of my breath. Hours later, when the front door opens, I'm unable to sit up.

My brothers pour in, all three of them by the sounds of it. I'm imagining my horrible fate, Jord or Jess's stinking ass pressing into my face and suffocating me, when blessedly, chairs scrape and my brothers settle at the kitchen table instead. The sound of beers cracking splits the air like a sonic boom. Jess's words plow through the soft mess of my brain like Evie Tyler's splitting axe.

"Garlic bread and spaghetti. Doesn't get better than that."

"You're an idiot, Jess." James snorts. "Garlic bread isn't a sandwich, and spaghetti is not soup. We're doing soup and sandwich combos, and the perfect one happens to be tomato and grilled cheese with fried onion slices in the melted cheese."

"Onions are rank." Jord pipes in. "The perfect soup and sandwich, hands down, is chicken noodle and cucumber mayo cheese."

Laughter roars across the room. "Who the hell are you, the Queen? Want us to make you high tea with that? Cut the sandwiches into little triangles with no crusts? Cucumbers! You shittin' me, man?"

"You're so creamed about grilled cheese," Jord counters, "why don't you make us some? Show us how it's done."

"My foot hurts. You want lunch? Figure out how to run a frying pan, Jord. I'm telling you, tomato soup and grilled cheese, man. You got those? You'll never starve. Teach a man to fish. Doing you a favor here."

They carry on like that, sipping beers and trading barbs. Cupboards open and pans clatter. Soon, the aroma of bread toasting and the sizzle of cheese fills the room. I think I'm going to be sick again, but I can barely move, so I press a cushion over my face to block the smell. I don't notice the silence that's settled over the room until Jord breaks it.

"We bust in now, Dad will never even know we were in there. We could just nail the boards back up after."

Shit.

I let the cushion roll off my face, and lie there, mouth gaping, vision pulsating with every excruciating heartbeat. *Not now. God-*

damnit, not now, Jord.

"Don't you need to see the other side, anyways? Check for load-bearing walls, that sort of shit, before Angus and you start swinging sledgehammers?" Jord presses.

"The wall we're knocking down is a load-bearing wall, dumbass," James answers. "We'll have to brace it with a temporary beam and jack posts while we build a permanent column. That's why Angus needs me. He wants to weld up some beam plates."

"That sounds complicated as hell," Jess says.

"All the more reason to investigate, beforehand." Jord adds brightly. "And today's the perfect day for it. Mom and Dad won't be back for hours."

I reach between the couch cushions and close my hand around the rubber grip of the hammer. Then I slither off the couch, wincing as my bruised ribs hit hardwood. *What are you doing? You going to take out your brothers with a Goddamned hammer?*

I don't know what I'm doing, but I know that if they can't find the hammer, it'll buy me some time while the Hardy Boys look for something else to pry the boards off.

Kitchen chairs scrape behind the couch.

I sit up, my head sagging like a cinderblock full of bees. Bracing my hands on the floor, I scoot backwards toward the door, dragging the hammer along with me. Over the horizon of the green couch, my brothers break into view, cradling beers and standing facing the five-panel in the classic pose of men about to attempt something incredibly stupid.

Christ's sake. You can't stop them, David. You've always been weaker than them and they can't even bloody see you now. They'll step all over you to get through, without even knowing what they're doing. They'll crush you. The heartbeat hammering in my head trips and then picks up tempo.

"Still got that pick set?" James asks.

Jord nods, takes a sip of beer and answers, "Yippee-Ki-Yay."

Oh, God. Tears prick my eyes, and I grip the hammer harder while my back presses up against the five-panel door.

"Crap!" Jess yelps, jumps, and dives for the frying pan on the stove. He jabs at it with a spatula, and black smoke mushrooms into the room.

"Aw, Jesus, Jord!" James wails. "You ruined one. Open a window."

They curl back toward the kitchen, cranking open the window over the sink, whipping dishtowels off the oven handle and flapping them around the room.

"You're eating that one, asshole!" James wrinkles his nose.

"No way." Jord sticks out his lower lip. "That black shit gives you cancer."

I sag against the door. My mind swells, like something that's boiled too long. I can't think through the mush. *Do something, David, while they're distracted.*

But how can I distract them when they can't even see me? I'm sweating, the hammer's grip squishing under one clenched hand, and the key as hot as a coal in my other. I can't come up with anything. Thoughts just keep short-circuiting in my head while I press back into the five-panel like some broken puppet sorely wishing I was on the other side.

Turns out, I don't have to do anything at all. My brothers load a fresh sandwich into the frying pan. They stir the soup, crack another round of beers, and continue their argument over which sandwich and soup should rule the world, like they've forgotten all about the door. The twins are distractible, but even they aren't so easily misled. And there's no way James would let go of the idea of opening the door so easily. He's laser-focused once he's got something in his head.

It's you.

I press a palm against the solid, old wood behind me and sit up straighter as a hopeful thought worms into my mind. *You're touching the door.* Letting go of the hammer, I twist my other arm behind my back, spreading my fingers over the boundary scroll of the bottom panel. *Maybe they really are forgetting it.* I lick my lips. *Because you're touching the door*, just like the sponge and the kitchen chair I stood on. *Holy shit.*

I don't get up. My brothers eat their lunch, and I stay glommed to the five-panel so hard that the barricade boards dig into my lower back. My headache fades and I'm pretty sure the pills have nothing to do with it.

You barfed them up.

It's the door. I'm closer to Bizarro world and it's trying to beckon me inside, calling to me. The key tugs on its twine lanyard now and then, even when my hand isn't pulling at it.

So, I friggin' live here now? That's the new plan? My chest deflates at the idea. *As soon as I have to piss, or eat, they'll be right back at this door like bloodhounds.* And besides, if I stay here, on this side, Bizarro world eventually wears off. They'll see me again, my brothers, my family, and then they'll see the door and remember how badly they want through it. *That's what the mold is for.*

I frown. *The mold.*

My brothers stared toward the five-panel for a good thirty seconds as they considered going in. They talked about a temporary beam. Surely James must have glanced at the ceiling where it met the wall when he said that?

And he didn't see the mold.

I'd surveyed it from behind the couch, from practically the same perspective, and once you faced that wall, there was no ignoring the creeping black seam of supposed death rippling along its white width. I'd made it as obvious as possible.

But no-one's said a thing.

The second realization settles heavier than the first. I gag against sudden nausea as it descends. *Oh no. The Goddamned rules of this place! You touched the ingredients, made the mold, and painted it on before you touched the door. Maybe your handiwork, anything you've moved and created, that stays unnoticeable too?* That would explain why nobody heard me reefing the boards off the door early in the mornings. *You spent all that time on it, and no-one can see the mold, not until they can see you.*

A raw ache garrotes my throat and when it eases, a long, low sob pours out of me. I let it. I sit curled against the door, crying like a baby while my brothers eat their grilled cheese sandwiches around the kitchen table, because I know now what I have to do.

The mold isn't enough.

I have to stay here. I have to stay on this side while my headache cuts my brain to ribbons and pushes my eyes from their sockets. I have to stay touching the door so that my family keeps forgetting it while I congeal back into existence on this side. It's the only way they'll see the mold at all.

How long?

I hadn't worked out specifics, but it seemed like for every hour I spent in Bizarro world, it took close to the same time to gain back visibility here. *You've been over there for nearly three days straight, Goddamnit. It's been nearly a week on this side since James went back to the hospital and you gained visibility here once since then. Dad nodded at you at the breakfast table and said, 'Morning, David'. That was three days ago. You've been in Bizarro world for three days straight.*

My mouth goes dry, and my head pounds harder. My chest compresses like someone's sitting on me.

Last time you missed one day, the maneaters went ballistic that night. Oh Jesus, the maneaters. Three days on this side! Until you and your precious mold are visible? They'll break through. They'll eat you alive before then.

CHAPTER SIXTEEN

I'm rifling through the drawers of Angus's desk with shaking hands. He stands before me, head cocked, like he's picked up an odd sound, but can't quite pin down its source. I stop, crank the volume dial on the radio above the file cabinet, cringe as the tinny sound cuts through me, and wait until Angus turns toward it with a frown. Then I claw through the contents of the next drawer.

Cough drops, pens, two squashed Baby Ruth candy bars. The first aid kit has nothing but gloves, a few crinkled band-aids, some hydrogen peroxide, and a pair of scissors.

Christ Almighty, is everyone in Honey Bear Hollow a masochist? How hard can it be to find some damned pain killers?

I tried five doors on the way here and only two cottages were unlocked. *Nobody trusts anymore.* The first one, I came up empty, and the second only had a blister packet of Advil with all but three pills already popped out. I dry swallowed all of them on my way here.

Angus stores spare life preserver rings in his workshop. Surely such a well-prepared man stocks a healthy supply of Tylenol somewhere. I just can't find where.

I slam the desk drawer and immediately regret it. Eager pain lances through my left temple and curls behind my eye. I press both hands against my head and straighten, gauging Mr. Tyler as he fiddles with the radio. There's not enough room between the file cabinet and the desk to squeeze around him, so I push his binder to one side, sit on the metal tabletop, and swing my legs over, vaulting Angus's desk.

"Thanks for nothing, man," I mumble, and snag two pepperoni sticks from the glass jar on the way by.

The smell of fatty, preserved meat nearly makes me gag, but I bite into the rubbery sticks anyway and chew slowly. Madeline always insisted that pain killers on an empty stomach caused ulcers, and it's one of her only lessons that's stuck with me. Never mind the fact that I'm mixing medications and dabbling in overdose zone. Better get some food in that belly. Don't want to get an ulcer.

They're gone today, my parents and brothers. That's the only reason I'm not camped at the door. The Boulange family from across the lake offered to take everyone out on their yacht, and Madeline dove at the chance. She is not what I'd call yachting material, despite her hasty application of a silk hair scarf and huge, tortoise rimmed sunglasses this morning. But she likes to imagine, and Dad indulges her. My brothers, like any young men, have latched onto the idea of champagne and rich, sexually frustrated upper crust girls. Even James couldn't resist the chance. No-one mentioned my absence before they filed out the front door. I'm not just invisible. It seems I'm utterly forgettable too.

Last night, every scrape on the other side of the five-panel raked through the soft spots of my mind. This morning, even though I leaned against the door, I couldn't ease the headache gripping me. I only meant to check next door for pills, but the farther I searched away from the door, the deeper the headache sunk its claws. Now, I am teetering on the point of nausea again, with little to show for my efforts. I'm like a dog on a short leash. Bizarro world keeps yanking my chain, pulling me back in so that it can swallow me whole, and the worst thing is? I want it.

Oh God, I want to go back in. I'd love to let it swallow me into its depths. I like it over there. *Odd child.*

"Just stop." I shake out my hands to ease tension as I shuffle back toward the cottage, mindful that my steps don't jar my bruised brain.

Can't I leave for one breath o fresh air? I've been cooped up in the damned cottage for nearly a month. I've been living on the other side of that Goddamned door. Can't it give me one inch? One day? It knows I'll come back, like an addict. It knows I'm hooked and can't help myself.

A mud-spattered BMX lies sprawled in a front yard halfway between Angus's office and our cottage. It looks like one from the pack that took me out the other day. I stare down at it and flex my hands.

You know who'd have pain killers? The Gulf station. Rows and rows, right beside the fireworks. My head pounds faster, as if Bizarro world has intercepted my rogue thought, and wants to flush it out with pain. The twine lanyard pinches my neck as the weight of the key makes itself known.

"Fuck off," I spit onto the gravel drive. "I'm not your dog."

I steal the bike, brace myself on the pedals, and cruise out the entrance of Honey Bear Hollow, under the burled log arch. Worry pricks me at first. This is my side, still fully populated with nosy people. Last thing I need is a forced trip to the local cop shop to put some fear into me. I'm doing just fine in the fear department already, thanks very much, and there's no way I can bear being taken that far away from the door, my headache's already shifting gears, uncoiling from behind my left eye to strike hard at the base of my skull.

I make it a mile up the road before I turf the bike on the shoulder, and bail into the ditch, retching so hard, it feels like my eyes might pop out. The puking only makes the headache worse. Dizziness fills the void, and I sway for several seconds, staring at a chewed-up gob of pepperoni stick on my sandal strap, before straightening and wiping my mouth.

"I just want a bloody Tylenol." I look up at the sky as I speak. I'm not sure why. "Leave me alone."

Pulling the bike up by its worn rubber grips, I swing my leg over and pedal toward the Gulf station like it's the last leg of the Tour-de-France.

Like many amateur racers, I break away too soon. The bike gets heavier and heavier. The pedals bog down like they're churning molasses, and finally the chain slips off the drive gear and gets bunged up in the rear wheel. I'm less than halfway to the Gulf, and Bizarro world isn't letting me get any further. I cling to the bike, my eyes watering and my vision shifting like a kaleidoscope.

"I just wanted a pill." I drop the bike in the long grass.

I weave back up the road to Honey Bear Hollow Resort, and the headache unclogs from my head like dandelion seeds in the wind. Once, I stop and peer back.

I could walk. I could walk to the Gulf, but as I think it, sunlight reflects off a car mirror in the ditch. The brightness of it slices into my eyes and rekindles the headache with a fierce heat. I don't look back again. Bizarro world will not let me get that far away from the door and I know it.

When I open the front door of the cottage, I freeze. Every ounce of heat drains out of me and cold slivers clatter down my spine.

James is sitting on the hide-a-bed, staring at the five-panel.

"What are you doing here?" I blurt, stumbling around to the front of the couch.

He's cradling a Dr. Pepper between his knees, scowling at the door, and rubbing his palm against his thigh in a desperate, wringing motion.

"I thought you went with everyone else on the boat?" My gaze trails down my brother's leg to the bandage on his foot, and the awful, waxy yellow-grey of his toes.

Jesus. He had gone with everyone else.

I'm certain of it. I kneel to James's level and try to catch his gaze, even though I know he'll keep staring blankly through me. Sweat beads on his upper lip and settles as a pale sheen on his forehead.

He's not well. "James, you feeling okay?" *Stop talking. He can't hear you.*

James sips his Dr. Pepper, massages his palm down his leg, and doesn't take his gaze off the door. He looks like some damned spaghetti western gunfighter.

I edge away from him, backing into the barred door, and pressing both hands against it as I slide down to the floor. James stares through my forehead. There's something inhuman and predatory about the hunger in his eyes. It sends a deep shudder down my spine. The clock above the fridge ticks several times before James takes a breath and breaks his gaze. I exhale loudly, sag, and let my head crack back against wood, squeezing my eyes shut and clenching my teeth against the answering pain.

He could have gone in. You just left on a spontaneous road trip, and James or anyone else could have just opened the door right up. You left your post. Some soldier you turned out to be.

A brittle rattling makes me open my eyes.

My brother reaches into his jeans and pulls out an orange prescription pill tube with a white safety cap. His gaze shifts and lingers on me.

"James?" I whisper hopefully, but he looks past my head, shakes out two pills and swallows them, before twisting to glance at the clock above the fridge. Then he lies down, maneuvering his injured foot like an old man. The stubble on his face makes his cheeks look hollow.

I wait until James's mouth is slack, and he's breathing heavily before I uncurl his hand from around the pill bottle and scan the label.

Vancomycin. An antibiotic, not a painkiller. You're an asshole for even looking, David. More concerned with your own comfort than how sick you've made your brother. Madeline's right. There's something wrong with you.

I camp out the rest of the day, leaning against the door, surrounded by wrinkled blankets, and a half-empty box of crackers. I'm waiting in line for a concert that I don't really want tickets to.

Tickets to Hell. Final tour. No refunds or exchanges.

James moans in his sleep a lot, and I can't nap at all. The floor's too hard, and I have to stay sitting up, leaning against the door if I want to doze while still maintaining contact.

Madeline and Dad are bubbly and full of champagne when they get home. They don't notice how bad James looks, but my worry eases when my older brother stretches, heaves himself off the couch and eats a sandwich before retiring to the bunk room. The twins don't come home with my parents. It's not until I've retaken my post at the green couch, well past midnight, that my brothers pour in through the front door, whispering loudly and reeking of pot.

After they close the bunkroom door, the draft billows past the five-panel like it was waiting for a full house. Something snorts a frustrated exhale. The door shivers, and the crystal knob winks with shards of moonlight. Wood creaks in complaint as something heavy leans into it and then a sharp, resounding crack pounds through the room.

"Shit!" I bolt upright and it strikes again, like a baseball bat, or a battering ram, reverberating through the ribs of the cottage.

Why didn't I reinforce the door?

I roll off the couch, landing on the balls of my feet with the hammer gripped in my hand. The hardwood is cold as ice. Something scuffles and I wince at the clattering of furniture crashing on the other side of the door.

The kitchen table?

I edge forward until I can press a hand against the five-panel. Silence settles on the other side, then claws scrabble, and the door groans as the maneater presses slowly against it. It huffs and a whistle of air bursts out of the keyhole beneath the crystal knob, so cold it burns my wrist. I jerk away.

"Fuck off," I hiss, shaking out my hand and swallowing against the sour taste in my throat.

It snorts, almost like it's laughing. Claws ease down the edge of the door and poke into the keyhole, testing.

My hand clamps around the wobbly crystal knob, holding it steady. The bolt on this lockset is hopelessly feeble. I try not to think about the brittle metal tab nested in its slot. They only ever built it to keep prying eyes out of closets, not hungry maneaters out of fatted dimensions.

Jesus, David. How did you think this would go?

I lean into the door, shoulder braced, knees locked, and I wince every time the maneater on the other side pounds against the door. Dust sifts down into my hair, and the edge of the doorframe splinters. With each smack, nails pop loose from the slabs of siding, and I pound the barricading boards back into place with the hammer.

By the time the maneater relents, my teeth ache from clamping them, my leg muscles are jittery and unreliable, and the key hangs like a brick tied around my neck. I slump down the door on loose limbs, clawing the twisted blanket over me and setting the hammer across my thighs. Dawn slips through the cracks of night, and I wait for my family to wake up. To kill time, and ease my nausea, I eat crackers from the sleeve one by one, until my mouth is too dry to swallow. I have to piss, but I don't dare leave the door. It's as fragile as a cracked egg behind my back.

Madeline is the first person to shuffle out of the bedroom, hours after dawn. Her frizzy hair floats around her head, full of static, like an electrical storm. She claws it away from her cheeks, and pads toward the kitchen, nightgown hanging off her like a wet rag. Her shoulders are hunched and tense as she levers onto her tiptoes to sift through the cupboard above the sink with lethargic determination.

Hangover. She's got a hangover.

"Mom?" I whisper, but she doesn't react. *Of course she doesn't! She's never the one who sees you first.* "Madeline." I try again, my voice cracking. "There aren't any pills left." She looks too thin from behind, no waist, narrow hips. How had this woman ever had the strength to bear seven children?

I hate her. The thought strikes me, startling because of the lack of emotion driving it. Rolling the idea around in my head, I analyze it like a kid peering into a shell at the beach.

"I hate you," I try out loud, but Madeline doesn't react, and the words don't satisfy me. They lack conviction.

Hate is an emotion, idiot. A strong one. And you feel nothing for her at all. That's not hate, that's indifference. I can't decide which one's worse.

Madeline mumbles to herself as she frantically claws through every cupboard and drawer in the kitchen. I can't make out her words, but they're barbed with anxiety and mild disgust, as always.

You feel something for her.

I squint as she props her elbows against the sink and cradles her head in her hands.

You don't want her to die. You want to protect her from the door, right?

But with Madeline it's like a duty more than anything else, like it's something I'm supposed to want. Of course, I don't want her to die. That'd wreck Dad and James. I care for Madeline in the same way that I care for the twins and most of my other siblings. They're the framework that supports the people I love. I care about them only because they're important to Dad and James.

You are a freak, then. You expect your family to see you and treat you like one of their own. You don't even love most of them. Odd child.

James emerges next and my throat closes at the pasty tone of his skin, and his sunken eyes. "James!" I exclaim at the same time as Madeline. *You have to see me today, James. We have to get you away from here.*

"You look terrible!" Madeline searches his eyes before her gaze drops to his foot. "Is it worse?"

My brother pastes a grin on his face that doesn't reach his eyes. "It's fine. You don't look so hot yourself. Want coffee?" He limps toward the old enamel percolator.

"Don't lie, James." I raise my voice. "Don't lie to her. Madeline, don't believe him. Jesus, can't you see through this bullshit? Take him to the hospital." *Take him away.*

James measures out heaping scoops of coffee into the percolator basket while Madeline hobbles over to the table and slumps into one of the chairs.

"How was the yacht?" he asks. He knows how to distract her. Ask her about herself and Madeline will readily drop any other subject.

Her eyes light up and she puts a hand over her chest. "Oh James, you should have been there. It was beautiful." And she launches into the details of her day, settled by the distraction of it. *Selfish bitch.*

"Are you serious?" I yell and point a finger at James. "Jesus Christ, are you kidding me? Look at him! Forget yourself for one second and look at him."

But James has her hooked. He sits across from her, dabbing sweat from his top lip while Madeline beams and chatters on about hauling halyards, and tacking, and how polished the brass in the main salon was. She's launched into her own orbit, and is happily circling there.

How on Earth has she raised so many children without killing one of us with her ignorance?

The twins come out next. They tell James that he looks like a cat's asshole before launching into retells of their supposed conquests last night. I expected that much from them. They're bloody clueless at the best of times. All three of them, Madeline and the twins, actually sit there and let James limp around the kitchen making them coffee.

Anger coils through my ribs like a live wire. "Stop this." I shake my head and pant. "You can't ignore him and make it go away. He's sick. Take him to the hospital. Convince him to go. He's ignoring it too." Nobody hears me. *Two Goddamned days and nobody hears me, Jesus Christ.*

I pin my hopes on Dad. James is sick, but Dad *will* see me if I'm loud enough. I desperately want to storm into his room and shake him awake, but I can't risk leaving the door unattended, not with the entire crowd in the kitchen desperate for something to distract their attention from James's condition.

He doesn't emerge until the second pot of coffee is on, and Madeline has eased herself away from the kitchen table to fry eggs. She looks like she's ready to gag.

"Dad!" I shout his name, and he flinches, but doesn't turn. Scratching his head, he meanders toward the steaming coffee pot.

"Hey, Dad." I clap, like this is a bloody kindergarten class or something. *Jesus.* "Dad, listen to me. Look at James."

No response this time. Something hot curls its way up my gut, and I press away from the door and stride into the kitchen, stand directly in front of my father.

Be loud, David.

"Dad. It's David. Come on! They're all acting like idiots. James needs to go to the hospital!"

Dad frowns, slurps his coffee, and walks into me without seeing me. His shoulder catches mine and I fly backward like he sacked me. My teeth clack as my ass smacks into the hardwood, and my wrists twinge at the impact. I roll out of the way before Dad steps on my legs. He clamps his hand onto James's shoulder. "How you feeling today, better than yesterday?"

"Yeah, good." James nods.

"Goddamnit, James." I whisper. "He's lying!" I screech. "He's lying to you all so you don't worry about him. Can't you see that? You're all so fucking blin—" My closing throat snips off the last of my words.

James's gaze is shifting. He's frowning and focusing on the door like it's some sort of cloudy ink spot swirling into resolution. "I meant to tell you, I was talking to Angus a couple days ago."

Shit. I dive back toward the door.

"Yeah, what about?" Dad asks.

I press against the five-panel, shoulder blades jamming against sharp boards, breath whistling through my teeth. Pinning my gaze to James, I plead. "Come on. Come on." *Stupid.* "Come on, forget about it, James."

My brother frowns. His gaze falters and then drifts back to Dad. "He wants some help around the shop. The odd welding job, that sort of thing. I think I'll take him up on it."

I sag against the door, relief and anxiety pooling together into a coagulating mess in my belly.

"You guys are all fucked! Do you hear me?" I shout, fists balled-up in my hair. Something surging and unstoppable rises in my throat and I scream, "Are you listening? I'm right here! I'm right in front of you, and you're fucked! Get out of here! GET OUT!" I keep screaming until my voice gives out and I dissolve into a fit of coughing.

My family eats their breakfast and neatly ignores my existence.

I stay pressed against the door until they go out for lunch. It gives me enough time to sprint to Angus's shop. I steal a jar of deck screws, a drill, and three two-by-four planks. I screw every piece of wood I can find across the five-panel. When I'm done, there's only a small strip of panel showing through the barricade at doorknob level, wide enough that I can press my palms against it. I mist my wall of mold until it's suitably damp.

When my family comes back, I shout at them. I bark with all the longevity of a lonely backyard dog, but it isn't enough. They can't hear me, and they don't notice the mold.

Well done, asshole. You're spending another night with the door.

The thought breaks me.

Once, when I was little, I had a nightmare where Dad was at the top of the stairs asking me something, and I shouted back my response. He got so angry that I'd yelled at him. I tried to explain, I'd only done it so that he could hear my answer, but he ignored my excuse and barreled down the stairs, bellowing and furious, and so much bigger than I ever remembered seeing him. I flinched as he clutched my arm and coldly informed me, "We have to give you up for adoption now, David". He pressed me toward the front door of the house, and I screamed and fought him, but I wasn't strong enough. Dad shoved me outside, and slammed the door, and that's when I startled awake, shrieking and babbling, "I want to go home."

Dad charged into my bedroom, sat on my bed, and folded me into his powerful arms. I breathed in the smell of him as he whispered, "Hey bud. Bad dream? I'm here now. It's OK. I'm here." He stroked my hair, kissed the top of my head, and wiped tears from my cheeks before saying, "It's not until tomorrow. We don't have to give you up for adoption until tomorrow."

Breath caught like cobwebs in my throat.

Dad smiled, mussed up my hair and shrugged. "That's what happens when you're loud, David. We can't keep you anymore."

It took an agonizingly long time for that to sink in, the horrible, gutting realization that this was still a dream. I hadn't woken up at all. I'd just rolled into another dimension of nightmares. The whole terrifying scene just repeated itself over and over again, all night.

On the third night beside the door, I try to move the green couch to barricade the five-panel. I figure if I do it right, I can sleep with my back against the door. Clutching onto its threadbare armrests, I heave backward, and the couch scuffs a few inches across the floor but refuses to budge further. I don't remember it being so heavy.

You're weak. Just put your back into it.

Gritting my teeth, I settle into a squat and groan as I heave backward, but the hide-a-bed holds its ground like a horse with its feet planted, pulling back on a harness. So I give up. I crumble onto the couch and fall asleep where I lie.

I'm dreaming about black hands clutching me, tearing at my skin, eating James's foot, when this thunderous noise pounds through my chest. I fall off the green couch and jolt awake. The cottage fills with the sound of crashing and wood splintering. I scream, scrambling toward the door in the pitch black. My hands smack against shuddering planks and slivers stab into my feet. A body hurtles against the other side of the door and the explosive concussion of it thrums through every hollow organ in my body.

It's huge. Oh God, it's enormous and it's coming through. Pain lances up the arch of my foot as I shift to brace against the door and drive a splinter deeper. *Where's the hammer? You forgot the hammer.*

Another punch, and the sound of wood crumbling.

"Shit!" I scream as something sharp rakes across my foot. *Bottom corner, where the hand came through the first time.* I leap sideways, shin smashing into the ash bin. It clatters away in the dark like a bolting animal.

Find the shovel.

I dive away from the door, arms outspread. My splayed fingers jar against the side of the cold woodstove.

Another crack slams against the door and the cottage answers with a chorus of jiggling dishes and creaking wood. I fumble behind the woodstove until my fingers bang into something metal. I grip the short, familiar handle of the ash shovel and spin back toward the door, hacking blindly at its base. The first few swings ping loudly off the hardwood, but the third sinks deep into something soft.

A scream rips through my ears. Icy air rolls over my ankles, scalding them, and I keep hacking and gulping.

It'll stop now. You hurt it.

But the maneater doesn't stop, or if it does, another one clogs in to take its place, snorting and screeching, smashing itself against the door with incredible force. Something clamps onto the shovel and hauls back, nearly yanking it out of my sweaty hand.

"No!" I kick out and my heel skitters off something scale-encrusted and sinewy.

It drops the shovel, goes for my foot, and I fall backward, screeching as claws bite into my ankle. The maneater jerks me toward the door.

"Help!" I gurgle, curling upward and gripping the shovel with both hands, hammering at the limb clamped onto my foot until it shivers and lets go. I scuttle backwards, foot throbbing and adrenaline surging over my heartbeat. "Help me!" I bellow.

Teeth clack and frustrated screams answer me in a terrible chorus from the other side of the door. I dive back toward it, chopping at limbs as they scrabble through the hole like snakes.

"Somebody help me!" I screech, but nobody answers except the maneaters, and their gleeful crows of excitement.

The door bucks in its frame and the crystal knob thuds to the floor and rolls past me. Something's burning my chest. I can't spare a hand to bat it away, and it's digging in like a red-hot coal.

The skeleton key.

The maneaters must sense it too, because the scratching moves from the floor, shifting up the door. They flop and drag their claws up the door, reaching.

Not interested in your ankles anymore.

Grunting, I wedge myself between the door and the wood-stove and bring the shovel down like an axe, blow after blow until the reverberations sing through my wrists and the bones in my arms, and I'm slipping in the slimy gore pooling on the floor.

It's still too dark for me to see. I'm terrified of dropping the shovel and losing it. Boards are clattering loose. They chatter like wooden teeth with every ram against the door, but I can't secure them, and no-one is coming to help.

No-one is coming because you're a nobody.

The raw thought nearly makes me drop the shovel, and then, amidst the harrowing screams of the maneaters, between shovel-strikes as steady as a heartbeat, another thought creeps in.

JFK's man in a suit was a nobody too, and he didn't let that stop him. Sergeant Jim MacNeill ended up as a friggin' school recruiter after serving three tours as a sapper, and you didn't hear him whining about it, did you? They didn't care that the world couldn't see them. They just did their Goddamned jobs. Do yours, David. This is your bridge. I swing the shovel harder. *You control who crosses it.*

A scream bubbles up in my throat and I let it carry me. I drop into a wider stance, brace my foot against the base of the door, and I throw all my weight into the shovel. I keep doing it, alternating between leaning into the door, and taking great, carving swings. It's like a sort of dance, like I'm rowing across a cold lake, and the sounds of the maneaters are nothing more than ripples in my wake.

I don't stop. Long after the sounds of the maneaters fade away, and the door stops jiggling, I keep swinging the shovel.

Dawn clots into the room before I blink and straighten. My hands are sticky. Bloody fingerprints spackle the shovel's handle. I've carved a ragged pit into the hardwood in front of the door and it stands out in stark contrast to the black, congealing streaks of blood, and gobbets of flesh surrounding it. Several planks of wood with snapped screws have fallen to the side, and a ragged, chewed-up hole the size of my head yawns where the bottom corner of the door used to be. I take a deep breath of air that smells like sour sweat and old meat. Then I limp to the couch and grab all three cushions off. I stack them over the hole and the mess on the floor, and I collapse onto the pile.

They're gone. I gulp, wipe my dirty hand down my face, and let the shovel clatter to the floor.

The square of sky in the kitchen window lightens, and birds start singing outside.

They only come out at night. You made it through. Oh thank Christ, you did it, David.

My hands uncurl in my lap, and my head flops back against the barricaded door. A rushing wave of relief floods over me, soaking me so thoroughly that I'm cold and nauseated in its wake. I know I shouldn't, but all I want to do is sleep. The only thing keeping me awake is my throbbing foot. I blink down at the angry, weeping gouges at my ankles.

Later.

I shiver and lean sideways, clawing at my discarded blanket and pulling it over me. It's covered in splinters of wood and dust, but I don't care.

I'll wrap my foot later. Let the poison bleed out for now. Those are the last thoughts I remember before sleep takes me.

CHAPTER SEVENTEEN

"Hey, David."

I jerk, and try to open my eyes, but they're glued shut.

"David?"

I recognize that voice. *Dad.*

I push the blanket off my chest, swipe at the gunk crusting my eyelids, and blink until the room swims into focus. *Please, let this not be a dream.*

My father stands behind the green couch, looking directly at me, a small frown bunching his forehead. "You look like shit. Couldn't sleep?" he asks.

That's it.

No relieved shout of, "David, thank God it's you". No agonized, "Where have you been for the last few weeks?" No "I missed you". But my father's mild words directed at me, his calm gaze studying my face without looking through me, they're still enough to undo me.

He sees me.

Hot tears wash out my vision, and roll down my cheeks, stinging them.

"David?" Dad's feet shuffle around the couch. "Are you sick?"

"Yeah," I blubber. "I think I am. Look." I hug the blanket closer, tucking my injured foot in, and I gesture overhead.

Dad's gaze shifts toward the ceiling, his eyes widening.

"Is that—?" He reaches a hand toward the ceiling, and I flinch.

"Don't touch it."

"Mold?"

Oh God. He sees it. He actually sees it. "I think so." I gulp and swipe at the tears running down my face. "I think it's making me sick." I swallow and shake my head, pausing long enough that Dad looks back down at me.

Hear this, Dad. If you hear nothing else I say, hear this. "James is sick too. I think he needs to go home."

"Jesus Christ, how have we not noticed it until now?" Dad backs away from me and the door and the mold.

Because invisibility is contagious. "I don't know. I've been sleeping here the whole time, and I didn't see it either."

"Get away from it." Dad offers a hand, and I take it. It means nothing to him, I can tell, but the fact that he *feels* me at all, that his fingers grip mine and we're both real and solid and fully in the same plane overwhelms me with relief.

He pulls me off my stack of cushions, and I drag my blanket with me to the kitchen table. Dad's gaze keeps flitting back to the ceiling over the five-panel. Each time he presses his lips together and shakes his head like he's disappointed in himself, like he should have seen it coming somehow.

"Madeline," he calls. "Wake the boys."

They serve breakfast on the front porch despite the icy wind rolling in across the lake. I'm visible now, but food still distracts my family enough to give me ample time to limp back into the house unnoticed, shower, and bandage my ankle.

As I move aside the stack of couch cushions and mop up the mess in front of the five-panel, Madeline twitters on the porch like an agitated squirrel. I glance up to see her standing with her arms crossed over her chest, glaring at an apologetic, confused-looking Mr. Tyler in our driveway. Wisps of Madeline's scolding voice press through the closed front door.

"...don't care if they'll be here next week. That's not the... a bloody week too late, Angus... expect a full refund."

Angus's deep voice carries better. "M'lady, I called up the remediation folks jest as soon as I was done talkin' to ya. Ya saw me on the phone. They's got a full schedule, but they said if we can keep the mold contained until they come clean it up, it's perfectly safe—"

"Perfectly safe!" she hisses, and her voice punches up an octave. I can hear her loud and clear now, and so can this whole side of the lake. "My sons are sick, Angus! We've been breathing this in for nearly a month, not knowing what was behind those walls. Don't you inspect your buildings? That damned addition was just slapped onto the back of the cottage, leaking the whole time. Rotting out the roof!"

"I-I'm sorry, M'lady." Angus holds out his palms. "Now, if we could jest stay calm—"

Bingo. I smile.

Madeline perfectly articulates her next words. "Oh, I'm calm, Angus. You can cut the 'M'lady' crap, and you can write us a check right now, refunding our stay this season. When I get home, I'll be on the phone with you to square up the medical bills for my children, breathing in black mold in a shithole cottage that you've neglected to maintain. Or, if you'd rather, I can have my lawyer call instead."

Madeline doesn't have a lawyer that I know of, but her voice contains enough cold authority to make Angus shit his pants, anyway.

She's got some strength left in her after all.

"Naw, no need for that." Mr. Tyler actually tips his hat. "I-I'll git my check book right away, M'La—Mrs. Rawlingson. And I'll send the girls 'round to help ya pack too."

Dad scrubs the back of his neck.

Mom straightens and nods once. "Just the check, please. No need to expose your children to this mess too, Angus."

And that's it. We start packing.

It worked. My chest tightens and my legs feel loose in their sockets as the thought pours through me and the cottage whirs into action. *My God, it worked.*

Angus waddles up the drive, cheeks flushed, with a check in one hand and a box of dust masks in the other. Mom makes everyone put one on before the twins ferry suitcases out to the van.

"Mold." Jord grumbles. He elbows Jess on the way by. "Told you it was a friggin' grow op in there. Pot. Hydroponics. Humidity messes a place right up."

"Shit." Jess laments.

Dad won't let James pack anything at all. He orders him to sit across the back bench of the van with his swollen foot propped up, and he sucks his teeth as he gingerly unwinds my brother's bandage. "Jesus, James. Why didn't you tell us? That infection is worse. Air it out on the ride home. We're stopping by the first emergency room we hit."

James groans but knows better than to talk back. Instead, he changes the subject, straightening and beckoning to get my attention. "David," he says, and my chest tightens at the sound of my name. "Wanna grab my book for me?"

Him, actually talking to me, that friendly eye-contact instead of a blank stare. It rips me up. I swallow emotion thick enough to choke me. "John Grisham?" I ask.

"That's the one." He grins. "You should read it when I'm done."

I'd love to. I'd love to read your second-hand books and share pilfered beers and talk about girls. I'd love to do all of that, James.

"Sure." I nod and smile half-heartedly, ignoring the stabbing ache in my chest.

Inside, Mom whisks by me. The elastic straps on her dust mask are pulled so tight that her eyes are reduced to squinting half-moons. She's carrying a laundry basket full of crumpled clothes, with piles of toiletries haphazardly stacked on top. "We can brush our teeth in the van," she mumbles.

I find James's book beside his bed in the bunkroom and I take it back to the kitchen. Grabbing a pen from the top drawer, I settle into one of the kitchen chairs and flick it against my teeth, watching Mom shovel Tupperware containers full of food out of the Philco fridge and into the cooler. She doesn't notice that I'm not wearing my dust mask, but she spares me a disappointed glance on her way by.

"Going to sit around all day, or help?"

She can see me when she needs help and nobody else is around. How convenient. "Sorry, Mom. What do you need next?"

"Double-check the bunk room and the loft. I'm not coming back if your brothers leave behind their wallets again."

"Yes, Ma'am." I smile and salute, despite the headache gathering force behind my left eye.

"Don't do that," Mom snaps, her voice low, but intense.

My hand sags from my forehead, smile freezing as I meet my mother's eyes and find them full of tears. "W-what?"

Setting the cooler down with a thud, her watery eyes flick to the splotched, moldy living room ceiling and blink several times. She yanks the dusk mask down below her chin and wipes her nose with the back of her wrist.

"Don't 'Yes Ma'am' anyone who treats you like shit." Mom searches my face for a long moment, eyes tired, lashes clumped with moisture. She steps over the cooler, sits on it roughly, and doesn't pull her mask back into place. Frizzy hair shifts to cloud her features as she dips her head and stares at the floor.

I wait, cold shock clotting my throat.

Mom doesn't use pauses in speech like Dad does. She's like me. I realize. She's wrapping silence around her to gather strength. I glance toward the front door while she draws several wavering breaths. *Get out. Just go outside before she says anything else. This is uncharted territory you do not want to be in,* but my feet press into the hardwood, one cold, the other bandaged and swelling with heat.

My fingers pick at the ragged pages of James's book. "You don't treat me like shit..." The lie slips into silence as Mom holds up a shaking hand. I can't see her face, but her shoulders are tight, and her back curls like a spring, like she's ready to launch from the cooler.

"I've always sucked at motherhood." She barks a humorless laugh. "We're not supposed to say that, are we? But it's bullshit. You're supposed to love your babies at first sight, and I never did, not with any of you. All eight of you looked like pissed-off little red aliens when you came out, and it took months of work to love you. It took *work*, and it was exhausting. People didn't talk about postpartum depression back then. One nurse at the hospital told me, 'Just pretend. Pretend to love your baby, and eventually you will.'"

Heat slackens the stiffness in my chest, and I swallow the words clawing up my throat. *Is that what this has been? A big act? Playing at being a mother?*

"It's no excuse." She gulps and raises her head to focus on me, as if she's heard my thoughts. "Just because I struggle with it doesn't mean I should treat you like you're unloved, because I do love—"

"Wait." I cut her off, frowning, my mind turning over her previous words like stones. "Eight?"

Mom's face bunches in confusion, eyes squinting. "Eight what?"

"You just said we looked like little aliens when we were born, all *eight* of us."

"Eight." She stretches the word into a long sigh. It sounds like the wind through the branches of the apple tree in Bizarro world, hollow, but full of sweetness at the same time.

Mom nods, and then cranes her neck toward the front door, listening for Dad or my brothers. It's quiet out there. "After the twins, your father wanted to try for one more." She leans closer, and I only narrowly control the urge to scrape my chair away from her. "After the *twins.* Can you believe it? I was done. I didn't think I could handle another pregnancy, but your father, he loved the baby stage so much. He swooped right in with all of you, you know? Diaper changes, formula feedings, middle of the night car rides. He came home from work and was never too tired for any of it.

I felt like a failure next to him, and I got it into my fool head that maybe this pregnancy could be different, like the ones I read about in magazines. I was an experienced mother now. I knew what hurdles I had to jump, and that I could stumble over them as they came. I was stupid enough to think that, after all those births, there wasn't anything I hadn't already dealt with at least once."

I rub at my chest and the key jabs against my sternum. I press harder, imagining it cracking through bone and membrane and draining away the horrible, swelling anger that's choking me.

Fuck you, Madeline. You didn't deal with me. You ignored me. You just gave up.

"It *was* a different pregnancy." She continues, oblivious to my anger, ignoring me as effortlessly as she always does. All wrapped in herself. "A girl, we found out."

A girl? I swallow, gaze snapping back to hers.

Madeline's eyes are pleading as she nods. "A healthy girl, until five months in, when my body just..." she gives a heavy, solemn shrug, "rejected her. That's how the doctor's put it. I *rejected* her.

Before she was even born, David." She ducks her head and cups her hands in her lap like she's trying to hold water, or memories. "She was so small. Her name was Jillian. She was too small to even breathe."

I set James's book down carefully, and then the pen. My eyes pin to the edge of the table where the Formica is chipping. I press my fingernail into the crack and hold my breath, wishing to be invisible, praying that Madeline can't see the heat in my cheeks, and the hurt in my eyes. The front door is only a few feet away, but I've never felt so trapped in a conversation. I can't breathe.

So that's it? She spent all her love before she got to you, the last on a miscarried baby. None left for you, David.

"I made your father get a vasectomy after that," Madeline whispers.

"What?" I blurt, mind swimming with pain.

"I told him I'd leave if he didn't, so of course he did. We booked him into the first available surgery date. And that was it. I thought we were done." She falls into silence again, but I don't have enough patience left in me to leave her there gathering strength.

"I don't understand," I say. *I don't understand why you are telling me any of this now.*

"Three months after the vasectomy, I found out I was pregnant with you." Madeline leans ahead, seeking eye contact.

Horror must be leaking through my gaping stare, because she immediately shakes her head. "I didn't cheat on your father, David."

"Then what?"

"He didn't read his post-op instructions, and I assumed once you're snipped, you're snipped. Apparently, a man's still—uh..." her gaze flutters to the ceiling and she purses her lips. "... still virile afterward, for eight weeks, and I'd already stopped taking my pills." She looks down at me and tries for a smile. Tries and fails. "Your father thought you were a miracle."

And you didn't. I swallow hard. Tears blur my vision, and I clench my jaw and press away from the table.

Madeline jumps at the sound of my squealing chair. "David, wait!" She holds out her hands. "Sit."

I want out of here. I want to go onto the other side where I belong. "Please sit."

"Why should I?" I croak, fingernails digging into my palms and headache squeezing my eyes until my vision warps.

"Because I've always meant to tell you."

"Tell me what?"

"It's not your fault."

"What's not my fault?" I bark. "My existence? Jesus Christ, you do suck at this!"

"No," she pleads. "The gap between us. The distance. It's not your fault, David. It's the same gap I felt with all your brothers and sisters, the same one I've worked so hard to hide, to cross, to pretend it never existed, until it didn't exist anymore. It's me that's broken. It always has been. I blamed you, but it's always been me. I just can't seem to get across the gap to you, and it hurts when you can't reach someone you love, David."

"Someone you're *pretending* to love. Isn't that what you mean?" I curl my lip.

"No," she deflates. "I do love you, David. I just quit reaching after a while. I quit trying. And love isn't enough, not without trying. I'd like to start trying again, if you'll let me, if it's not too late?"

I can't answer. The vague hope in Madeline's eyes crushes me. *It is too late.* Tears slip down my cheeks.

My mother stands. I let her reach out and wipe her thumb across my cheek.

"It's okay if you hate me," she whispers and shrugs, eyes full of fresh tears. "I fucked up."

"I don't hate you," I mumble. My chest feels like it's collapsing in on itself, like the start of a panic attack. *You have no idea what I've fucked up. But you're right. It's not too late to fix things... Mom.*

Feet clomp up the front porch steps, and both of us snap out of our agonized paralysis. I swipe James's book and the pen off the kitchen table, and turn toward the counter.

Mom leaps up from the cooler, snaps her dust mask back over her face, and dives toward the fridge, opening its door and staring into emptiness.

The front door opens, and Dad calls in to us, "Last load?"

"Would you grab the cooler for me?" Any emotion in Mom's voice is muffled by her mask, and the humming of the Philco fridge.

"Sure thing." Dad shuffles into the kitchen, grunts, and hauls the cooler back outside, slamming the door behind him.

"I'll check the bunk room," I choke out before Mom can say anything else.

I leave James's book on the counter and dodge past her. *Breathe, David. Count your fingers and breathe.*

My brain feels crisped, emotions popping and fizzling into nothing while my breathing scrambles higher and faster. Nausea burns my throat, so I beeline toward the bathroom instead, lock the door behind me, and count out loud until the cottage is silent and the roaring in my head dulls to white noise.

Don't think about it. Don't think about anything she just said, David. Just pack your things and go out to the van, like you planned.

I clear the loft and the bunkhouse, fish a wristwatch out from amongst the dust bunnies under one of the beds. By the time I get back to the kitchen, numbness is washing over me. I think it's shock, but I don't care. I know what I want to write in James's book now. Cracking open the novel, I scribble the hasty note onto the inside of the front cover, clamp it closed, and shoulder the backpack stuffed with my own clothes and effects. I go out the front door and close it carefully behind me.

Two Sea-Doos carve lazy figure-eights across the lake. Rooster tails of white water flare behind them. The front yard smells like apples and charcoal barbeque. Kids scream and splash in the shallow water far below. I look to our old Ford Econoline. The passenger door hangs open as Mom leans in the side door, rearranging the cargo within, like she's the loadmaster on a military transport aircraft.

"Here you go." I pass the book to James.

"Thanks, Skippy." He grins.

"Get in, Saved you the middle seat." Jord sneers.

I let my bag slide off my shoulder before straightening. "Hang on a sec." I frown. "Think I forgot something."

"Aw, Jesus," Jess whines.

And just like that, I get nostalgic. *Hold it together.* I have to turn from the van so my brothers don't see my face twisting.

"Wait for me?" I force out the words brightly, but my voice cracks, ruining the effect.

Wait for me. That's what you said at the gas station when you were six. Of course they won't wait. You know they won't. You planned it like this.

I'm surprised at the force I have to use to press up the stairs. It takes everything in me not to turn back and run to the van. Gritting my teeth, I cross the porch, open the front door, and close it behind me. I shuffle into the living room, where my family won't see me standing there like a dumbass, and I wait. An immense ache builds in my throat as I tap my thumb against my fingers and count in my head, once for every ragged beat of my pulse against the insides of my skull.

"I'd like to try again, David, if it's not too late." A fresh, horrible ache grips my chest as I remember Mom's words.

"It's not your fault, Mom. I'm forgettable," I whisper. *I'm forgettable and this will prove it.*

I flinch at the sound of the van's front passenger door closing.

It takes five more minutes before the sliding door chugs shut. The fan belt squeals as the engine turns over.

Five minutes is all it took for them to forget you. My chest seizes as the van eases back out of the driveway, and I'm pretty sure it's the last time I'll ever see it.

Jesus Christ, David. Guaranteed you are the only person in the world who's ever shed tears for a 1974 Ford Econoline. Snorting loudly, I wipe my eyes on my sleeve, exhale, and dump my backpack onto the couch. *This is it. It's done. Forget what Mom said. You're all alone now.*

I fish for the hammer hidden behind the mattress.

Every squealing nail grates through my bruised brains, as I reef off the boards barricading the five-panel. My headache ramps up with incredible intensity, as if Bizarro world can sense what's happening.

What is happening? What now?

I hadn't planned past the mold and the evacuation of my family. Hadn't Angus said that a remediation crew was coming to clean up in a week or so? If I'd heard right, and he'd actually booked them, then my problem still stands. A mold clean-up crew will strip the wall to its studs before disinfecting and rebuilding.

"Wonderful," I mumble, and the hammer hangs slack in my hand. I'm tired and I don't want to think this through right now. My head is pounding, and my bandaged foot echoes it emphatically.

It will be easier to think without the headache, so get inside. For now, you balance the scales, David. You make up the time you spent on this side and throw the maneaters off your scent. Three days there for three out here. Better make it four to be safe. My eyes ache at the impossibility of staying awake for so long. *I can do it in shifts. Come back to this side for a quick nap. Set an alarm clock.*

"It'll work." I lever off the last two boards across the five-panel.

I pull the twine lanyard over the top of my head, insert the key and twist. The tumbler unlocks with a neat snick. Searching for the crystal knob, I fit it back into place and open the door to a room that looks much the same as this side. The smell of Dad's aftershave greets me, and tears prick at my eyes again as I turn to lock myself in. The key snags in the door. I tug on it, but it remains jammed.

Stepping back, my bare heel jabs into something small and hard. It throws me off balance. Angry pain flares from the wounds at my ankle and I flail for something to hold onto. My fingers catch on the twine looped around the key, and it twangs tight before snapping and slithering to the floor.

I look down. Beside the frizzy twine is a hair elastic, the kind with two bright, oversized plastic beads looped over both ends.

That's what you stepped on. Blinking down at it, I turn to take in the surrounding room, throat aching. *My family's still here on this side.* Small socks litter the hardwood floor, along with half-naked Barbies with matted hair. *The girls are still here, Justine and Julie.* A teething ring sits half-stuffed between the cushions on the green couch.

I limp into Mom and Dad's room, and I smell their pillows, like some friggin' orphan boy. *Jesus Christ, David. Snap out of it. You can still figure this out. And they'll come back for you...* My thoughts trail off, the life bleeding out of them. Heat drains from my cheeks as I see it. Everett's dictionary sits on Dad's night-stand.

Chapter Eighteen

My legs wobble and I crash backward onto the mattress, staring at the dictionary like I'm scared it'll attack.

It's always been on the shelf in the loft. Why is it on the nightstand this time? What the hell, Everett?

I wipe my palms down my thighs, once, twice, and then I lean ahead, grasp the book with both hands and pull it onto the bed beside me. It's newer, unmarred by red crayon. When I open the cover, the pages smell like fresh ink on paper. I flip through once and find nothing, so I pull it up onto my lap, and doggedly start from the front.

There's writing in here somewhere. He wouldn't have bloody left it in a different spot if he didn't want me to find it.

Painstakingly, I thumb through each tissue-thin page, and I find it near the end, in the 'Y' section. Breath crashes out of me, as my eyes scan over the first few lines of Everett's tidy printing.

I got my ham radio license when Annie and I lived in Nebraska. It seemed the sensible thing to do. At the time, the local ham radio club operated as an early warning system for severe weather. When the phone lines went down, us hams could track a tornado in real time, and route people to the least crowded shelters. What can I say? I felt important fiddling with bandwidth and talking to people half a world away.

I think this bloody place works the same, like a radio. The Pithos key is the toggle switch that turns the whole thing on, but once it's powered up, any key that turns the tumbler can open Hell. I tried with the spare keys I bought from the flea market, and a few times they worked. But Hell transmits a fickle signal. On the radio spectrum—depending on the time of day—some waves reflect off the ionosphere back to Earth, making voices across the globe sound as close as a drinking buddy across the table. Other times, the signal just shoots off into space and the connection fizzles out.

At first, the door only opened into Hell occasionally. The rest of the time it was just the normal guest room. And then I left the damned tobacco tin behind, and the hellhounds got a hold of it. It worked like a booster antenna. So do I, amplifying the signal every time I come over, making the connection stronger and stronger, and I can't shut off the Goddamned radio. The key only turns this place on, not off. I see that now, but I didn't then. I was so stupid. I shouldn't have yelled at Annie.

She took the key.

God bless her, she was only trying to rescue me in her own sweet way, but I blew my top when I found out, horrified that Hell would suck her in too. I shook her and yelled at her to tell me where she hid the key.

Lord God, I actually laid hands on my own wife, and shook her. She cried, pressed her lips into a thin line, and looked at me like I was some sort of wild animal, which I suppose I was. It's no excuse, but I felt pent up, like a bull being pressed toward the killing chute.

I turned the whole house upside down, emptied cupboards, broke dishes, overturned chairs. She screamed at me to stop, and I roared back at her like a madman. I could tell just when it happened, the heart attack. Annie's eyes popped, the light went out of her face, and her legs just folded beneath her. I caught her before she hit her head, but I really lost my mind after that.

I got her into the car, and I drove like the hellhounds were giving chase. I didn't stop to tell Angus we were leaving, I just put on my flashers and sped to the nearest hospital, which wasn't near enough.

God save me, I should have called for an ambulance.

I shouldn't have ever yelled at her or shook her. I should have never built this room. My sweet Annie, I'm so sorry. What have I done?

She never made it out of the hospital. The last time I held my wife was in a sterile room with the curtains drawn and the warmth still draining out of her.

The doctor handed me a piece of paper telling me her cause of death, and he quietly informed me that Annie would be kept in the hospital mortuary until I made arrangements for a funeral home to pick her up. I was to collect her possessions at the nursing desk and the ladies there would give me a receipt in exchange. I don't remember doing any of those things.

I just recall standing in our doorway back at home with a plastic bag clutched in my hand. Inside were Annie's pearls, her watch, a shamrock broach, a five-dollar bill and two nickels. All I could think at the time was, two nickels? Why the hell did they even bother putting in the two nickels? Lord Jesus, all that was left of her, I held in that little bag.

I phoned John, and the mangy idiot didn't answer, of course. I had to leave him a message, desperate enough to make sure he called back. "John, it's Everett. There's been an emergency with your mother. Ring back as soon as you get this". I just couldn't say it, not over the phone, not in a Goddamned answering machine message. Annie's dead. How could I say it if I couldn't believe it?

I looked up a local funeral parlor in the Yellow pages, and I dialed them up too. It was two in the morning by this point, so I was rightly shocked when a person answered the phone instead of a machine. Apparently, these kinds of places are open twenty-four seven. Death never waits that sort of thing.

I recited the address of the hospital listed on Annie's death certificate, and once all the immediate arrangements were made, I hung up, sat by the phone, and waited for John to ring me back. It was nearly noon the next day before he did, and as gently as I tried to lay out what had happened, I couldn't keep the rage out of my voice. Goddamn him! His own mother, and he didn't get around to phoning until halfway through the next day.

I drove right back here after that. I told myself I wanted to pack up things for the season. I wanted to do it while shock still dulled my senses enough to make it somewhat bearable. All lies, of course. I came back to find the key, and to write in this damned book. At least I ticked one of those boxes off my list.

I've got no damned idea where Annie hid that cursed key, but it doesn't really matter now, because I know what I have to do. I'm just so damned scared to do it. I know very well where I'm likely to end up afterward, and I deserve it. I think I'll wait. I want to make sure she's got a proper funeral before I go. Our forty-eighth anniversary is two months from now—would have been two months from now—July 1st. How Annie loved to watch the fireworks from our front window while we enjoyed our candlelight dinner.

"Like the whole country's celebrating with us", she'd giggle, and we'd raise our cheap champagne flutes, and I'd say, "Of course the whole country is celebrating with me. I've got the best girl in the world".

There's not much left to stay for now, anyways, not if I can't find the key. I hope Annie hid it well. I pray to God that no-one else finds it. The other family doesn't come around here until July anyways.

I know I'm going to Hell, but I think I can clear my conscience a little if I can break thegateway before I go. I found the key and opened the door. I left my tobacco tin behind and locked Hell in. Surely my death will end it and stop others from following in my footsteps.

I'll light the candles, Annie, and I'll watch the fireworks for you. I think a tumble down the stairs should do the trick. They're steep and straight, and that way it'll seem like it was all an accident. Maybe it will be enough. Maybe, it'll work like atonement and get me to you again, Annie. God, I miss you so much.

"No," I squeak, and I claw through the next few pages. *There has to be more. This isn't it.* "No." The sound barks out of me louder this time. *You misunderstood it. Read it again.* My head pounds as I trace my finger below every word and mouthing Everett's words.

Our anniversary on July 1st... She loved watching the fireworks... I'll light the candles, Annie, and watch the fireworks for you. A tumble down the stairs should do the trick.

"Son of a bitch!" I gape down at the book.

Air whistles out of me and I can't suck enough back in. *What had Angus said, when I asked to phone Everett? He called him, left a message, and his son rang back and said that Everett took a bad fall.*

"Jesus Christ, Everett." I sag over the dictionary. Its corners prod my ribcage, and black inky spots bloom before my eyes.

Breathe, David. Just breathe.

But I can't.

My mind scrolls desperately back to Canada Day. We'd been here, what? Three days before that? *And all three nights, the cold draft had come under the door.* Bizarro world was locked in then. James stayed up with me that night after fireworks. We drank beer on the couch and the draft didn't come.

It didn't come because Everett... "Oh, God."

My head swims and I squeeze my eyes shut, but it doesn't get any better. *The draft didn't return until three nights later, after I found the key in the ashes where Annie buried it. After I opened the Goddamned door with it. And then it was patchy, on and off. A radio signal, just like Everett said. Sometimes it was just the guest room, until the dishtowel disappeared and amplified the signal.*

Nausea bursts up my throat. I stand and the dictionary skids off my lap and topples to the floor. Pain cinches around my ankle as I stumble to the bathroom and curl over the toilet.

He fixed it. I put it together fully between awful, choking retches. *Everett fixed his mess. He shut off the radio and you turned it right back on again. You did this. You. And there's only one way to end it. Balance, David. Everything has to be back on its own side.*

"I can't find the dishtowel." I blubber in between gags.

Then whoever touched it, whoever left their scent on the object on the wrong side, has to die. That's how Everett cut the connection, and that's how you have to do it too.

"No." I shake my head hard enough that snot pastes across my cheek. *I'm not dying for a Goddamned dishtowel. I'll find it.*

But the maneaters had a whole world over here to hide it in, and there aren't enough daylight hours for me to look that far out. I flush the toilet and belatedly realize I've now left half-digested remains of crackers on the wrong side of the door too.

Fantastic.

The air swims around me, thick with my panic. I'm drowning in the relics of my family as I stumble back to the bedroom, pick up the dictionary off the floor, and smooth out its pages, actually bloody apologize to it, to a *book*.

"I'm sorry," I sob.

My face is burning. Every breath I gulp rattles out of me before I can draw any sustenance from it.

I have to get out of here.

Hugging the dictionary to my chest. I wince as I wriggle my bare feet into my sandals and hobble out the door.

Mist peppers my face, and the lake beckons with an endless array of white caps.

I limp past the empty driveway and the crab apple tree, follow Sweet Bee Circle, and pick my way down the rocky shoreline to the lake, but I can't make it all the way down. I keep falling and dropping the dictionary. Rocks scrape my knees, and rods of hot pain fire up my bandaged ankle until I can't stand the idea of taking another step.

Through the blur of my tears, I spot a faded foldout chair, abandoned on a flat shelf of sand amongst the rocks. I hop toward it and sink into its web of plastic woven bands. Once I'm in it, I can't get back out. My limbs settle like sandbags, and a sledgehammer throb sets up a tempo at my ankle. I cradle the dictionary between my knees, flip it open to Everett's writing, and press down the pages so that the wind doesn't pick at them. I read his last note, his bloody suicide note, over and over until my eyes feel full of sand, and the frothing crash of waves against shore numbs me.

Turns out I don't die for a dishtowel. When it comes right down to it, my time in my world ends because I fall asleep in a sling-back chair at the lake.

Simple as that.

The cold feet are what wake me up. For a second, I frown down at them, expecting waves. Then I look up, blinded by the sun-set, scanning the lake for the ever-present kids in water wings, for the Tyler twins tanning on the rocks, for the bobbing, bright fishing boats, but there's nothing. It takes too many moments for that to soak in.

You are in the middle of a summer resort, on a beach, and there is no-one else here. Just you.

"Oh no," I whimper.

I'm on the wrong side of the door. I'm in Bizarro world, and its sunset. It's *sunset*.

Another curdling, cold draft rolls over my feet and I jerk them up, wincing at the grueling pain at my gouged ankle, and gripping at the plastic armrests of my chair.

The shadow of the hill across the lake rolls rapidly toward me, and behind its border, *Oh God. Oh God, OH GOD.* I'm not alone. *The maneaters.*

Long, hideous four-limbed creatures, loping along the border like spider monkeys. Hoards of them crawl over each other. They call out with hungry, keening wails reminiscent of fingernails raking a chalk board. Every time they do so, the root-like crests on their backs quiver. Thousands of flat faces focus on me.

"Fuck," I yelp, stand on my tender ankle and stumble back-wards, folding myself into the lawn chair.

The back of my head cracks into a rock. As I lie there panting and dizzy, the hellhounds howl something wordless yet unified. It sounds eerily like a soccer chant. Another wall of icy air hits me. I fight off the folding chair and press my palm to my head. It comes away sticky and red. Snags of driftwood pull at my shirt as I scramble up the rocks. It's an uphill sprint to the cottage, and I can't run, I'm limping, wall-eyed. The road keeps tilting.

Shake it off, David. Shake it off and run. Run or die.

I glance over my shoulder. The shadow of the hill surfs slowly over the lake now, and the writhing mass behind it has split. Black bodies bound effortlessly over the rocks, heads bobbing but attentive as they skirt the shoreline. I can see their mouths from here. From *halfway* across the bloody lake, almost comically oversized for their faces, and bristling with pale piranha-teeth. Like what the Joker would look like if he swallowed a porcupine.

Shit. Stop looking back. Run. Just run.

Fear swamps the pain radiating from my ankle. I pick up speed and focus on the roofline of the cottage. I've never been on a sprint team or anything, but I run hard enough to blow off a sandal halfway there. With one bare foot slapping the gravel, and sharp pain jarring up both my heels, I round the curve of Sweet Bee Circle at a dead sprint.

The black bogeymen take the corner early, shift to my right and head straight for the cottage, screaming now, laughing like hyenas, spindly back crests standing straight up. They are still behind, but the crescent shadow cuts toward me like a scythe. I look over my shoulder, and my breath catches as I digest the side profile of a hairless demon moving at the speed of light. Small things register. The sharp, human nose. The frying pan face on a long, low-slung neck. Those teeth. All those *bloody* teeth. Then my toe catches a rock, and I turf into the gravel.

Breath thuds out of me and I skid onto my face. *This is it.* The bewildered thought settles over me gently, like dust. *They eat me and it's done.* My throat clamps and I roll over to see a maneater pacing the shadow border meters away from my toes.

It has no eyes. Instead, there are twin holes, deep sockets like you'd make if you pressed your thumbs all the way through a ball of dough. But they're still looking somehow. They're staring, unblinking and utterly aware, zeroed in on me.

Like Sam Ren's eyes when he held the gun. That same universal evil. *Jesus.*

The thing snorts, and its breath hits me like dry ice. Wisps of vapor roll between its teeth. That exaggerated mouth widens into a sneer. And then it looks away. Toward the cottage. It doesn't look back at me again.

The key. The thought slams into me like a kidney punch. *You left the key in the door. They don't want you. They never wanted you. They want your entire world, and every world they can devour beyond it.*

I'm supposed to stop them. I'm supposed to hold them back from all the times and dimensions they haven't eaten yet.

Gritting my teeth, I scramble to my feet and press my burning legs past their limit. I streak toward the cottage as shadows close over the spot in the road where I fell. The maneaters howl behind me.

You never fit in on your side. That's why people look at you like you're an alien, why Mom can't close the gap and reach you. You've been on the wrong side the whole time.

Claws clatter behind me on the gravel.

I'm supposed to be here. Right here. Right now. Doing this.

Icy breaths bathe my back, and teeth snap. I press beyond all my weaknesses.

Sergeant Jim MacNeill's solid words burst incongruently into my mind. *Build bridges to connect the good guys and blow up the one's the bad guys want to come across.*

It's not too late. I can still be a sapper. *You were never meant to build the bridges, David. You're the one that destroys them.*

As I launch over the porch steps and crash through the front door, three maneaters leap up and over the steep bank and skid on the driveway.

Get to the closet. I hurdle the green couch and skid to a stop, yank on the skeleton key. It's stuck. *It's still stuck!*

The doorway blackens behind me, and the room temperature plummets. *Don't let it happen, David. Don't let anyone ever come through again.*

The green hide-a-bed crashes into my back. Stunned, sagging under the unfolding mattress, I cling to the key and keep twisting. Crank on it as hard as I can. I think I'm screaming. I think I'm crying when the key finally snaps. Gasping, I jam the broken stub between my teeth and swallow it. It tears at my throat all the way down. When I collapse, I can see through the hole in the door onto my side. Crooked nails litter the carved-up floor.

Teeth clamp onto my ankle, jerk me from under the couch, and I smile. I remember the nonsense I wrote in James's novel.

I'm David Rawlingson Junior. I'm the man in the black suit. The gulf. I'm the wide separation, the chasm, the abyss. You can't see me, but I promise I'll keep the darkness from swallowing you up.

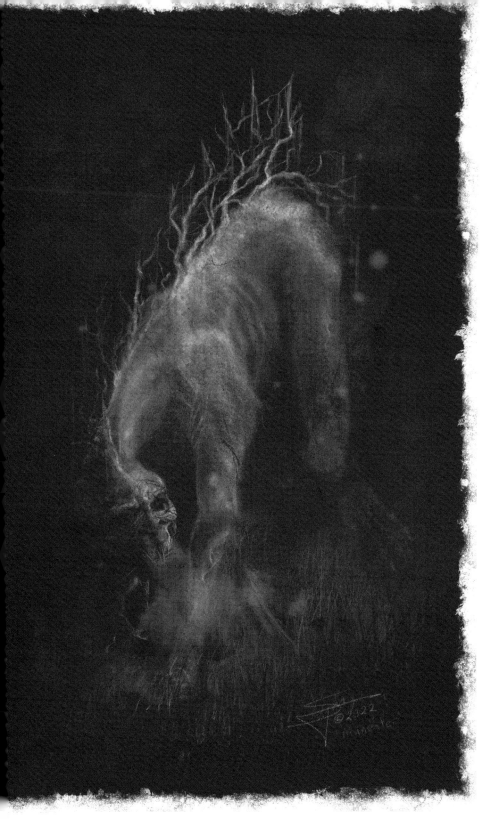

EPILOGUE

White light blinds me. I'm not talking a tunnel of light, choirs and doves or any of that shit. It's literally just blinding white light and a percussive growl pulsing through my chest. The maneater clamped on my ankle lets go and screams. I jerk my leg away and slap my hands over the ragged edges of the bite, only to yelp as something stabs into my palms, like quills or teeth.

They leave their teeth behind when they bite, oh Jesus.

Shrieks and thudding furniture ricochet across the room as I yank long thorny teeth out of my palms and brush them off my blood-slicked leg. I scramble back under the couch, shielding my face with my hands. Dark afterimages swim before my eyes before drowning in the flood of light filling the cottage.

I'm not dead. The realization seeps past the congested rumble rattling through me. *I'm still in the cottage and the maneaters haven't torn me apart. What the hell?*

Claws scrabble across the hardwood floor. The front door smashes against its frame, glass shatters, and then the roaring settles to an idle and whines to a stop. The light dims, but it's still bright enough that my eyes ache.

"You wanna come out from under the couch, Sunshine?

They're going to be back soon." A woman's voice calls, and a shadow passes in front of the light. God help me, I flinch and cower further back.

Well, at least you haven't pissed your pants yet. There's a plus.

A pair of steel-toed boots with the leather worn off and scratched silver peeking through the gap scuffs to a stop in the triangle of light at the end of the overturned couch. "They didn't gut you, did they?"

It's a person, an actual person on Bizarro side. Maybe she knows Everett. "N-no." I squint and scoot ahead past a smear of my blood, like the green velvet sofa bed is birthing me. All I can make out of the silhouette before me are curves and hands on hips, backlit by a blinding white.

"Hell of a dramatic way to close a gateway, don't you think? You stupid or a virgin because I haven't seen anyone—Ah shit!" she interrupts herself, crouching down and pressing a gloved hand below my knee. I'm overtaken by the smell of vehicle exhaust, leather, and bubblegum. "This isn't good. Stupid, then. You're stupid. My luck. You have a belt?"

I can't seem to hang onto her words. They make sense individually, but I've lost the ability to string them together into understandable sentences.

I'm not dead. The thought throbs through my head as this stranger plucks white slivers of teeth out of my leg and casts them aside. *I'm supposed to be dead, and I'm not. Shit. Shit. Oh shit! If I'm not dead, the bridge isn't broken, and I fucked it all up. The maneaters can still get through and my family—*

"Hey." A hand grips my shoulder and shakes me. "You got a belt? What's your name? Talk to me."

"D-David," I stammer and look down in muted horror as the strange woman tugs at the belt loops of my pants. *She's undressing me. Why would she—?* Then the words click. I swallow and lick my lips. "I'm not wearing a belt, but there should be one in the bedroom closet, the—

uh—one off the kitchen."

"OK. Look at me, David. Can you look at me?" Her voice has switched to that calm schoolteacher mode that means shit is real and she's trying to keep me calm.

Squinting, I nod. A dark face with pursed lips and analyzing eyes swims into focus.

"OK. I'm gonna go get that belt and you are going to hold both of your hands below your knee really tight and take some deep breaths. Think of Playboy models or puppies, whatever the hell calms you down."

"Playboy models don't calm me down." A half-grin twitches on my face as she pulls my hands down and clamps them where hers squeezed moments before.

"Puppies it is then." She smiles. "I'll be right back. Hold tight. Literally, you got it?"

I'm being poisoned. That's what's happening, why James's foot got infected. The maneater's claws and teeth are venomous, just like the doctor thought.

"David!"

My fingers spasm and clamp tight against the throbbing in my leg. "Yeah. Yes. I'll hang on. Got it."

As soon as she's gone, an immediate, visceral fear grips me and rattles me hard. *What if they come back? She said the maneaters would be back soon. What if they're just out there waiting for the poison to kick in so they can eat me alive?*

My heart pounds in my ears. "Shit. Calm down," I whisper to myself and clench my fingers tighter over my bloodied leg. It feels like it's doubled in size.

Past my white fingers, two jagged lacerations slash diagonally down my shin. They look wet and meaty, welling with dark blood.

More nauseating are the multiple tiny punctures above my ankle, nail holes surrounded with white puffy flesh. They look like giant bee stings.

They're starting to feel that way too.

Searing pain lances up my calf, spasming the muscle no matter how hard I grip the flesh below my knee.

Something thuds and rattles in the bedroom and I hope it's the girl. I don't know how old she is. Scuffing, rapid footsteps rake across the kitchen floor.

"You're in luck, David. I found two. You want black?" She holds one of my father's dress-belts up. "Or black? Who owns two black belts unless they're a martial artist?"

"My dad." A tired laugh presses past my lips. *I'm never going to see him again, am I? Him or James.*

"Your dad's a martial artist?" The woman jokes as she leans toward me, and her frizzy halo of hair brushes my face.

I catch a whiff of campfire smoke and bubblegum again. I'm about to toss back a smart reply when she cinches the belt tight around my leg. I howl instead, like a dog.

Smooth, David. Real smooth.

"Come on. We're running out of time." She grips my forearm and though I try to help her, it's mostly through her strength that I stand.

"It's bad?" I ask, embarrassed that it comes out as a whimper. *It is, and she doesn't want to say so.*

"Nah." She flashes me a smile, and it changes her whole face. Wrinkles warm her eyes, but not soon enough. There's this slight hesitation.

She's a liar. A good one. I'm dying then.

"You can tell me the truth."

"You're not dying yet, David, but you're bleeding out. That's what the venom does, it stops clotting. You're lucky. These dark walkers have eaten this entire world already, and they're still bloated from it. If you came through to an unconsumed plane, they wouldn't even wait for you to bleed out before devouring you, but they're careful when their full. They don't like losing teeth. I think it hurts them. Look, the lights will hold them off until we get you somewhere safe."

Somewhere safe. There's nowhere safe here at night. I pull back from her. "My flashlight never worked against them, the maneat— dark walkers. Artificial light didn't scare them at all when I tried. There needs to be sun too." *I don't want to leave. The whole world out there is crawling with monsters.*

She squeezes my forearm and gestures ahead of us. "Good thing my flashlight is huge and attached to a very fast KTM Duke 390."

I stare to where she points, beyond the dazzling spotlight the size of my head. Recognizable shapes emerge behind it. Handlebars, a high, gas tank hugged by a low, two-tiered seat. "Motorbike?"

"Yup. Supermoto." She grins.

"You drove a motorbike through the front door into a pack of maneaters?"

She snorts. "Is that what you call them? Would you rather I'd parked it outside and waited for them to finish?"

"How did you get it up the porch stairs?" I wonder aloud.

"Held my breath. Look, you don't have to worry about the light. I brought my own. I just clamp it to the battery of whatever I'm driving. They hate LED lights way more than incandescent. I don't know why."

My mind whirs and I'm wondering if the tourniquet is working because I can't keep track of words again. "I have no idea what you just said. Eleedee? What's that?"

"Oh, David." She pats my shoulder and steers me toward the bike. "You sweet 1980s child, you. I'll explain later. Here, I've got one for you too." She hands me helmet with a rectangular lump of plastic clipped to a thick elastic band. "Like mine." She jams her head into her own helmet before pressing a button. Three rows of blisteringly bright lights blaze from above her visor.

"A headlamp?"

"Yes. Put it on."

I pull it on and the girl—she's my age, I'm sure of it—flicks the switch on, squinting as pale light blazes over her oval face.

She shrugs something off her back. A flat, hard-sided backpack, but as it turns, it blazes with the same fiery bands of lights, like a string of pearls, but bright as stars. It's another enormous bank of lights. "Whoever rides bitch gets to wear the light pack." It dangles as she holds it out.

I step away from the five-panel to take it, but then freeze, looking back at the jammed keyhole.

Oh no. The gate. I can't go. The maneaters will claw their way in as soon as I leave because I didn't keep my end of the deal. I didn't die. I was supposed to die.

"Come on. We don't have all day." She nods to the doorway. "They're out there right now, waiting."

I know they are. My heart sags behind my ribcage. "I-I don't think I can go. I didn't finish it. I didn't break the bridge, and my family's still over there."

"Hold up, Sunshine. You finished it alright. The dark walkers would tear through both of us to get through that gate if you hadn't. Your other side is safe. What are you worried about? What's your keystone?"

"Keystone?"

She exhales impatiently and glances at the front door. "What did you leave in this world from your world that locked in the gateway?"

She knows. She knows how it all works, just like Everett did. I take a hopeful breath. "A towel. It was a dishtowel."

"Cotton?"

"I think so."

"Shit, you're lucky. That'd break down after the dark walkers ate it. It would take a few weeks, but they'd shit it out, eventually. After that, they were only after you. The man on the wrong side, am I right? Biodegradable keystone. You sure it's your first time, gatekeeping?"

I don't realize that my mouth is hanging open until I close it again. I can't even digest what she just said. "Gatekeeping?" I repeat.

"Never mind." She sweeps her hands and straddles the bike. "We can cover it all later. Put the pack on."

"Ok." I shrug into the light pack and limp toward her.

Cranking the handlebars, my rescuer walks the bike in a backward semicircle until its headlight aims out the cottage door then thumbs behind her. "Get on."

Gripping her shoulders to keep my balance, I ease my injured leg over the back fender. The motorbike roars to life beneath us, throaty and eager. When she twists the throttle, the engine growls before revving back down.

"Aw shit. I almost forgot. I need your ticket." She reaches her hand over her shoulder expectantly.

I frown. "I need a ticket to ride bitch on your motorbike?"

She cranks her head to look at me, an aggravated look pasted across her face. "Your *ticket*. Jesus! What was the artifact you used to open the gateway the first time?"

The skeleton key. Pithos. Artifact? "A key." I answer.

"Oh, that's old school! An actual key? Hand it over." She beckons impatiently.

"I broke it." I remember the rawness in my throat. "I broke it in the door and I swallowed the half on this side."

Her face drops. "Swallowed it?"

"Yeah."

"That could be a problem, David. Jesus, you really are a virgin at this aren't you?"

"Yeah. First time." I clamp my teeth as she clicks the bike into gear.

"First time for everything, I suppose. Let's get you out of here, Sunshine."

The bike lurches ahead and I scrabble and grip the girl's waist. Our helmets clack together as we plunge out into the night.

I haven't even thanked her. I squeeze my eyes closed as maneaters scream and scatter away from our circle of unapologetic noise and harsh light.

I didn't even ask her name.

BONUS NOVELETTE

The Darkness

I remember Mom closing the van door and Dad easing back out of the driveway and how wrong it was. Leaving. Watching our yellow cottage recede in the cracked windshield. It felt like leaving skin behind. I can't explain it any better. Just this sensation of ripping off a scab too early and leaving behind a crater of raw, wet pink. And it was more than end-of-summer nostalgia. At the time I thought it was just the antibiotics making me loopy. Turns out, I was going into shock.

Let's back it up a bit. See, I sleepwalk. Still. At twenty-one years old. A few weeks ago, during our family vacation at the cottage, on one of my midnight jaunts, I tipped over the ash bucket and had a falling-out with the fireplace tool-set. It came to blows, apparently. I cut my leg up pretty bad, hit my head. That's how Mom tells it, anyway. The whole family found me lying on the floor bleeding, with clouds of soot still settling around me. Scared the shit out of everybody.

My ankle got infected, and I've been fighting it off ever since. I need to come up with a better war story than that. And I really thought I was healing, honest. But when we left the cottage, my whole leg started burning, my breathing went ragged, and I couldn't stop shivering.

The twins in the bench seat ahead didn't realize anything was wrong until they snatched the book out of my hands—a John Grisham novel I had a death grip on. The pages tore, and I didn't react to their smirks. Jord's face dropped, and he turned and started hollering at Dad. Everything got hazy after that.

My bones felt full of molten metal when Dad hauled me out of the van onto a bright tarmac. There was the whoosh of automatic doors and the stale dimness of an emergency room. Lots of shouting. Someone with unicorn-print scrubs called me 'Sweetie' and told me to lie down. A doctor fired orders that could have been in another language. "...an IV in. Levophed, ten micrograms per minute, and I want serum lactate levels..."

This is the third morning I've woken up in a hospital to stare at a whiteboard across the room with *James Rawlingson* and all of my scheduled tests for the day scrawled beneath it in chunky text. Dr. Ansell, who performed my surgical debridement, will be dropping by to check on what's left of my ankle. Ruth is the registered nurse on shift this morning. My activity goal is to walk the hall three times today—on crutches. My roommate is Alma. She looks older than dirt and knits like her life depends on cranking out as many baby booties and toques as humanly possible.

A dream, so vivid seconds ago, slips like sand through the cracks in my broken brain. It feels familiar, like I've fallen into it countless times before, but I can't grip the memory.

I whip off a blanket that stinks of bleach, swing my legs out of bed, and ignore the bone-deep throbbing in my left ankle. Hanging off the IV pole like a tired stripper, I limp to the whiteboard, uncap a marker, and write in shaky printing anything I can remember about the dream. The coldness of the floor radiates through my bandaged foot. I shiver and close my eyes to shut out the clack of my roommate's knitting needles and the ping of alarm bells from the nursing station down the hall, and I hang onto the rapidly fading dream I've had for three nights running:

There's a boy. I can't focus on his face. It's like trying to stare at the sun. We're close. I keep calling him Skippy. It's his birthday soon but I'm leaving for trade school before then and he's wearing one of those smiles that doesn't quite reach his eyes. Like he's trying to look happy for me, but just can't muster it.

I push a present into his hands that I made in high school shop, and there's words all tied up in the newspaper I wrapped it with. Tangled feelings that I can't straighten out, but hope he'll understand. It's a survival kit, the gift. A handmade waxed canvas clamshell bag stuffed with supplies. Lame, I know. Before he peels off the newspaper wrapping, he jokes about hoping it's a box of condoms.

The scene keeps fizzling out like an old rabbit-ear antenna TV with touchy reception, but I absorb what I can. One thing is clear as day. When Skippy laughs, his whole face brightens and the darkness stalking him recedes. I want him to keep going. I want to be the one that makes him laugh and protects him from whatever is trying to scrub him away—because something is. Something evil is hunting him. I can't make out what it is. My mind keeps going blank when I try.

Next thing I see is the boy rummaging through the canvas bag and pulling out a compass and some fishhooks. Then he says thank you and his face goes slack. Black swallows him and I try to pull him out of it, but I'm paralyzed. I can't even blink as he melts away like a body sinking into tar. His eyes are open when he goes under, and the undiluted fear in them burns into me. But I can't help him, and I can't wake up, not until he's gone.

"Good morning, Mr. Rawlingson!"

I flinch and drop the marker. Desperation must be stamped all over my face because the nurse who just bustled in with a bright smile falters and frowns.

"How you feeling, Hon?"

"Hey, Ruth. Good." I swallow and paste on a grin. That's all you have to do around here to ease ruffled feathers and it isn't the first time I've relied on good looks and straight teeth to win people over. When you're my age, it's all anyone pays attention to. They don't even try to look deeper when I turn on the charm—like it's inconceivable that I could be decent looking and have a functioning brain too. I focus on her ridiculous printed scrubs. "Sea creatures, today. You're rocking it."

Her eyebrows rise as she scans the words I've scrawled on her whiteboard:

Skippy

Condoms

Fishhooks

"Skippy? Like the peanut butter?" She huffs. "That's an oddly specific shopping list you've got there."

"Yeah." I smile harder even though every fiber of my being wants her to leave. "Hey, could I get a pen and some paper when you have a chance?"

"Time for vitals, Hon." She moves to the bed and pats it with a placating smile. "I'll see what I can do after that."

But by the time Ruth brings me back a pad of yellow lined paper and a ballpoint pen with the forewarning, "Careful, pens grow legs around here and walk off," I've forgotten what exactly it was I wanted to write down.

Sweat plasters my hospital gown to my ribs when I wake up from my afternoon nap. My pulse stabs behind my eyes, and I sweep the nightstand beside me for the pen and paper only vaguely aware of

Mom calling my name. Something falls to the floor with a *thunk*.

Skippy. Shorter than me. I write the words so hard the paper starts to tear. *I tell him he's a survivor.*

"James?" Mom stands from the worn visitor's chair and puts her hand on my shoulder.

"Wait," I hiss. *In front of the house. My old Ford Tempo. I'm leaving and he wants me to stay. He's wearing*—Shit. I squeeze my eyes tight and slap at my temples. The details are right there. On the edge of my memory. But I can't picture what he's wearing. How the hell can he feel so real, but I can't describe him? His voice still rings in my ears. "Thanks, James," he says before the pavement liquefies and sucks him under.

"James! Honey, you're okay. You're in the hospital." Mom's frizzy hair brushes my cheek as she bends over me. "Your fever's breaking. That's good."

I squeeze the pen hard enough that it bends. "Who's Skippy?"

"What?"

"Did you ever have a nickname for any of us kids? Skippy?"

"I don't know what you're talking about. Look, you're on a lot of medication right now and some of the side effects are agitation and hallucinations. It's normal to feel edgy, but I'm here and we'll get through it together, okay?" She scoops up a book from the floor and I recognize it even with its cover torn off. It's the John Grisham novel the twins snatched on the road trip, just before they realized I was sicker than a dog on de-wormer.

"Can I have that back, please?" My voice breaks as I hold out my hand. The book means something. It's important, but I don't know why, and *Goddamnit* everything's evaporating again. My brain is crusting over like the chocolate pudding cup on my food tray, too sticky to think straight.

"How about I get you some more apple juice, hmm?" Mom asks like I'm three years old. *Yes please, apple juice in the green cup.*

Come on, James. Get her out of here.

"Sure, that'd be great." I flash a sheepish smile. It feels stiff on my face, but it must be convincing enough, because she hands me the book, pats my knee, and leaves.

A long sigh bleeds past my lips and takes the last wisps of the vision with it. My leg throbs out of sync with the thumping in my chest, like it's stuck half a second behind the rest of me. The IV in the back of my hand pinches, my throat feels like I've been sucking down welding fumes, and I have to piss, but that can all wait.

I study every word on the yellow paper until my eyes blur, but there's no epiphany between lines. I can't squeeze anything revealing from my sloppy notes, and I can't remember anything new. Wrung out, I lean back and open the novel to three pages in, where a careful inscription has been partially torn off from the twins' rough handling.

> unior. I'm the man in the black suit, the gulf. I'm the
> asm, the abyss. You can't see me, but I promise I'll keep
> the
> om swallowing you up.

"Skippy," I whisper. He wrote this. I'm one-hundred percent sure of it.

"Dad?" I puff.

I don't have the IV stand or crutches for support anymore, so my father holds my elbow as we make slow circuits in an antiseptic hallway full of garage sale artwork. Five laps today. Whatever it takes to tick the boxes and get out of here. Last night, Alma, my eighty-year-old knitting roommate died, or transferred. They won't tell me which—so it's probably the former. "You don't happen to remember where we picked up that John Grisham novel this summer, do you?"

"The one in your room?" he frowns. "Local bookstore at the mall, I believe."

"They sell used books?"

"I wish. I tried to take in a boxful from the cottage a few summers back. Those Harlequin romances your mom likes, bird identification guides. They wouldn't take any of them. Why?"

I stumble and catch my weight on my bad leg, and it feels so damned frail, like my foot might snap right off. Dad holds me steady and ignores every sour curse that whistles through my clamped teeth.

"Thanks." I finally straighten. "The, uh, binding's faulty on the Grisham book is all." I lie. "That's why it's coming apart. New book. Good thing I didn't pay full price."

He stares at me for so long, I wonder if I might have overdone it. Dad is legendary at rooting out lies. "You were thinking of going all the way back out there—a three-hour drive—to get a refund on a faulty book you've already read a dozen times?"

I choke out a laugh. "What the mind comes up with on a steady diet of Jeopardy and lime Jell-O. Am I right?" I paste on my salesman grin and gesture down the corridor full of other dogged hallway marathon walkers. "One more lap and we blow this pop stand?"

Dad clears his throat and pushes his glasses up his nose. "One step at a time."

When we get back to my room and past the stripped mattress that used to hold Alma, the yellow lined pad is lying neatly on my nightstand. The ballpoint pen is lined up above it and the first page smoothed down—not how I left it. I'd slammed it down haphazardly with four pages folded back shortly after waking up.

He read it while you were in the bathroom.

I glance at Dad, and he clears his throat and frowns at the pad, confirming it, but he's more mindful than Mom. He won't bring it up unless I do.

Here goes. I lick my lips and nod at the nightstand. "You ever have recurring nightmares?"

The hand holding my arm flinches and Dad doesn't answer me for several breaths. "Sometimes. In times of stress."

"What are they about?"

"I-I can't remember." He pauses for a beat, then: "Have you taken your meds yet?"

Dad stutters when he lies or changes the subject. *Jesus, is he dreaming about the boy too?*

"What do you do about them?" Tears prick the corners of my eyes.

He pats my arm, and his Adam's apple bobs several times. "Nothing," he croaks. "They go away on their own." And his smile is the least reassuring thing in the world.

I'm the one people lean on. When they need help, I'm the one people come to—so can I just say how Goddamned frustrating it is to be leaning on everyone else for so long? After four days, I'm discharged from the hospital. I can't drive myself home because the painkillers make me dizzy, my car is a stick shift, and my left foot still feels like it's buried in an ant hill. I'd rather be heading to the apartment I share with a rotating cast of roommates during trade school. I'd rather chew tinfoil than spend a week of recovery being coddled at my parents' place. But Mom freaked at the idea of me three hours away so soon after surgery, and you don't get to pick your destination if you can't drive, so Dad comes and picks me up in the iconic Econoline van he's been driving since the wheel was invented. I swear, he's made some sort of deal with the devil to keep that old piece of shit running. Who sells their soul for a 1974 Ford?

Mom apologizes profusely when we arrive. She talks so fast I only catch half of it. A pipe burst in the bathroom. It's Dad's fault for not updating the old copper lines, and there's water damage in my old bedroom. The carpet is all torn up. It smells like cat pee. The amount of garbage she had to clean out of the guest room to get it presentable was *unbelievable*. I assure her that I'm fine taking the spare room and bee-line there with my overnight bag just to get away from the anxiety pouring off her. She's still chirping about the certainty of supper being late when I close the door between us.

The spare room smells like vinegar. Its worn plush carpet is groomed with fresh vacuum marks and its dark wood twin bed has been so severely made that the geometric patterned coverlet is stretched as tight as a snare drum. There are far too many pillows on it. I toss a few aside and sit on a creaking mattress that has surely absorbed the farts of every single one of my five siblings in turn before they graduated to a bigger bed. It was mine at one point. Amongst its peeling glitter stickers and stylized dick graffiti, the headboard still bears a crude carved silhouette of a classic car with white-wall tires created by Yours Truly. So why do I feel like such an imposter all of a sudden? I run a thumb over the edges of the car engraving and scan the blank walls peppered with snags of Scotch tape and rectangles of unfaded paint where posters recently lived. Why does this feel like a recently dismantled memorial instead of a spare room? Maybe this is how it feels visiting your childhood house as an adult, older, jaded, and with more hangovers under your belt.

"Bullshit," I announce to no-one in particular. My voice echoes in the empty closet across from me. Naked wire hangers cluster on a wooden rod and one of the bi-fold doors hangs crooked off its tracks. I stand and limp toward it, desperate to fix something since I can't repair the wrongness perched in my chest. I reach up, press down the spring-loaded pivot, and ease the door away from its frame. Then I realign the guides in their tracks, unfold the panels and click the pivots back into their sockets.

A corner of paper pokes through the crack between the panels. I tug on it and when it doesn't come free, I peek at the backside of the door. A binder clip has been taped firmly there and dangling from it crookedly is a folded pamphlet. Someone hung it discreetly so that it was hidden between the panels of the broken door. I unclip it, shuffle back to the bed and unfold the glossy paper, smoothing it over my lap. It's a suggested weekly training program to prep for the Royal Military College Physical Performance Test.

"Jesus," I snort as I scan the chart of daily challenges, each one significantly more intense than my most grueling workouts. I flip the pamphlet over and squint at the copyright on the back. Printed in 1990. Not Jeremiah's then, as he would have been out of the house for well over a decade before this rolled off the press. Not Justine's or Julia's either. The girls don't strike me as military types. The twins then? I snort again. They're the furthest thing from soldiers that I can think of, and they wouldn't hide something like this. If they participate in any sort of physical challenge, the whole world hears about it. Jord and Jess don't do anything quietly. Dad hates anything to do with the military, and a workout this gnarly was liable to put someone his age into cardiac arrest.

"Then who?" I mumble.

At supper, I ask Jord and Jess if they're training for anything, and they smirk.

"Just working out the one arm." Jord pretends to jerk off. It's the punch line to the majority of his jokes.

Jess slaps his flabby belly and says, "Competitive eating. Up and coming athlete over here. Why, you wanna arm wrestle?"

"Not at the dinner table," Dad mutters without looking up from his plate.

I push chicken salad around on my plate and listen to the clatter of cutlery around me before asking with forced casualness, "Hey was anybody staying in the spare room before me?"

Dad perks up and pins me with a concerned frown.

"Everyone's cast-offs were." Mom dabs the corner of her mouth and shoots a hard glare at the twins. "I swear you kids have used that room as a garbage dumpster for I don't know how long. I took three garbage bags of dirty clothes out of there today. *Three.* They've been in there so long they don't even fit anyone anymore."

"Someone leave you an old sock and some hand lotion in there, James?" Jord asks.

"Not at the dinner table!" Dad snarls with uncharacteristic vitriol.

Everyone side-eyes him and startles into awkward silence.

His cheeks are flushed, and he blinks several times before speaking again. It's unlike him to let the twins rib him into losing his composure. He shovels two spoonfuls of stringy chicken into his mouth and brings his water glass to his mouth hard enough that it clicks against his teeth before turning his hard gaze on me. "Why do you think someone's been staying there?"

I shrug and fall back into my old defense: a winning smile. "Feels lived in, I guess? Mom did such a great job of getting it ready."

Mom falls for it. Her sharp face softens into a preening smile.

"Eat," Dad says slowly, shrewd eyes still examining me like I'm a witness on the stand. "Your medication says to take it with food, you need your strength, and I refuse to drive you back to school next week if you're not healthy."

"Guess I'll hitchhike." I grin like it's a big joke, even though my face feels tight, and my hands are balling into fists under the table.

I'm tired. I've had enough of my family for one summer. I can't believe I'm actually looking forward to eight weeks of third year training, back to the grind in the fabrication shop, studying for my Red Seal exam. I haven't told my parents, because they'd flip over how expensive it is, but I want to be an underwater welder. I've been working a second job, forking out for night classes at a commercial diving school, and my roommate Micah's been putting in a good word for me with his uncle who runs the underwater skills program at Seneca College.

My family's keeping secrets from me? I've got a few up my sleeve too.

It's dark and I don't know where I am, but my ankle feels like someone took a sledgehammer to it, and my mouth is full of something cold, gritty, and coarser than dirt. I bend over and retch. A black blob splats to the linoleum floor. Scraping off my tongue, I struggle to put all the pieces together.

I'm standing beside a sink. A microwave's digital clock glows to my right and reflects off the patio doors like a set of malicious green eyes peering in from the black backyard. This isn't school. I frown. I'm in the kitchen, at my old house. A used coffee filter still half full of soggy grounds lies crumpled between my feet and the filter basket has rolled under the breakfast nook.

I gag again and claw my way toward the sink.

You were sleepwalking. You ate old coffee grounds for fuck sakes.

Cranking the faucet on, I lean down into the stream, fill my mouth, and spit out several times. Then I gulp down cold water until the burning of bile eases in my throat. When I straighten, I desperately scan around me.

One time at the apartment, I woke up in the bathroom holding a bottle of toilet bowl cleaner. My throat was burning. I dropped the jug, and it ricocheted off the toilet and into the shower stall loudly enough to wake Micah and another roommate, Johnny. They lost their minds because none of us knew the number for poison control. I begged them not to call an ambulance, certain I couldn't have swallowed much before it woke me. We compromised. I chugged an entire two liter jug of milk and they stayed up all night with me to make sure I was okay. I shit blood for days. We stored all the cleaning products in a cupboard with a child lock on it after that. To this day, Micah remains convinced that it was some sort of botched suicide attempt. My constant sleep-walking spooked Johnny enough that he moved out.

Luckily, the kitchen counters are clear tonight, and Mom uses all organic, non-toxic cleaners. Coffee grounds seem to be the extent of the damage, thank Christ. I leave the lights off and grab the broom and dustpan from the pantry. While I'm staring down at the scattered mess on the floor, I'm overcome by this weird déjà vu where the floor is covered in ashes instead of coffee grounds, the linoleum has been replaced by scuffed hardwood, and there's screaming.

Breathing hard, I dump the dustpan into the trash. Nausea is still boiling in me, and it feels too hot in here. I yank the full garbage bag out of the bin, unlock the patio doors, and shuffle out onto the back deck.

Cool night air washes over my flushed face and the smell of oncoming rain fills my nostrils. I ease into Dad's slip-on sandals and mince down the steps, across the lawn, and out the gate to where the trash cans sit. The streetlight barely reaches back here and low clouds scudding across the sky choke out any moonlight, but I can see enough to navigate around the three extra bags already leaning against the fence. I open the lids to confirm the bins are both full before knotting the bag from the kitchen and setting it beside the others.

And then I stop.

"I took three trash bags of dirty clothes that don't fit anyone out of there today," Mom had said. This is what was in the spare room before I came.

I go back to the kitchen and grab a flashlight and the stool Mom uses to reach the high shelves in the cabinets. Then I hobble back out to the alley, plunk my ass down on the stool, and start tearing open bags to the sound of two cats fighting further down the alley.

The clothes are nondescript. Blank t-shirts and quarter-zip collared sweaters in muted colors. Distressed jeans. I clamp the flashlight between my teeth and rifle through a few thick graphic novels, one called *Melmoth* and another titled *High Society*. There's a book about JFK called *One Brief Shining Moment* with a stamp from our local library on it. It's long overdue judging by the slip inside. I pull out a stack of *Rolling Stone* magazines, and several posters—Nirvana, Weezer, Star Wars, Drew Barrymore. Then I open a Soundgarden CD case with a cracked cover and no disc inside. There're some hard candy wrappers that I can't identify, a pair of imitation Converse shoes that smell so bad I have to hold them at arm length, and underneath them...

I find it.

A waxed canvas clamshell bag.

The one I made in shop.

My shaking fingers struggle to undo the zipper. Inside there's a compass, fishing line and hooks, a fire-starting flint, and a needle.

"Holy shit," I whisper. "Holy fucking shit."

Skippy is real and he lived in the bedroom I'm sleeping in.

He wears distressed jeans and fake Converse shoes. His birthday must be after September if I miss it because I'm at school. He likes hard candy. Shorter than me, younger too? Wants to be in the military.

I tap on the yellow pad until the lead breaks, and then I hurl the pencil across the bedroom. It hits the door with an unsatisfying click.

"Goddamn it, come on!"

I rake my fingers through hair slick with sweat. The covers have twisted around me like a boa constrictor. I can still see his eyes as the darkness sucks him under, wide and white, but I can't pull any detail out of it. I don't even know what color they are.

"You good in there?" Mom calls from the kitchen. She's an early riser.

I prop my elbows on my knees, press my palms against my closed eyes, and take two deep breaths to steady my voice. "Yup. Fine. Be out soon."

But I don't come out soon. I swallow two Tylenol 3's that Mom left on the bedside table for me last night along with a glass of water. I don't know where she's hidden the rest of my medications. She doles them out one dose at a time, worried about me sleepwalking and taking too many—rightly so, judging from my past adventures in eating crap I shouldn't.

I grab the John Grisham novel from beside the water glass and trace the letters of the inscription with my finger over and over again. The last line, I'm sure it says, *"from swallowing you up"*. Skippy was promising to keep something from swallowing me up. He was saying something about an abyss. It's the darkness. It's the Goddamned darkness, and I let it swallow him up. This wasn't some exchange student or casual friend couch-crashing in the spare room for a few weeks. An acquaintance wouldn't write shit this deep in a book for me. They wouldn't put up posters on the walls and make the room their own. This was someone closer. Family.

I wait until Dad leaves for work. Madeline ought to be pouring her second cup of coffee by now. I can hear her still rattling around in the kitchen. It smells like she's frying eggs again. She thinks I love them over easy. Gross. Yanking a shirt on, I clamp my teeth, cross the room in two strides and whip open the door.

"James?" Madeline calls, but I head down the hallway in the opposite direction.

I barge right into her bedroom, and it feels as forbidden as it did when we were kids. But I'm not a child anymore. And she's lying to me about something, I know it.

Passing the unmade bed, I turn into a walk-in closet. On the top shelf she keeps a memory box. I know this because she hauls it down on every one of our birthdays to show us blurry ultrasound snapshots of us paired with ugly knitted beanie hats. Madeline likes to remind us how difficult our births were. Why did the woman have six damn kids if she hated delivering babies so much? Pulling a floral print shoebox down, I set it on a dresser, and peel the lid off. Then I sift through the contents, pulling out photos of Rorschach images that are supposed to be babies. I lie them in a row.

"James?" Madeline calls from the kitchen.

Fuck. Blood rises like static between my ears. *Holy fuck.* There are eight ultrasound snapshots. At first, I think some of them must be duplicates, but all the poses are different and when I scan the small print, all the dates are different too. With trembling hands, I put them in order. 1958, '59, '62, '72—that's me, '74, '75, '76. I pick up the last two. *Who the hell are 1975 and 1976?*

"What are you doing?"

I spin to see Madeline in the doorway still holding a yolk crusted spatula in one hand.

"What the hell is this?" I hold up the two extra photos.

"Language," she chides, one hand on her hip.

"What the *fuck* is this?" I step toward her, and she shrinks back. "What are you hiding?"

"Let's sit down." She sets the spatula down on the dresser like she's laying down a weapon.

"Fuck that. You tell me what's happening right now. Six kids. Eight ultrasounds. You threw out everything in his damned room."

"Don't speak to me like that. I'm your mother."

"You were his too." I hiss.

"James, you're digging into something that's none of your business." Her voice cracks.

"I wouldn't *have* to dig, if you'd tell the truth!"

"Six hats," she croaks.

"What?"

"Six knitted caps, James." She sweeps past me with tears in her eyes and flops onto the bed. "You think I'm keeping secrets from you? Mom's supposed to be an open book, huh? How many times do you think a woman can get pregnant and it all goes perfect, it all ends with a healthy, happy baby and a smiling mother?" When I don't answer, she barks, "How many, James?"

"I-I don't know."

"Take a guess." Her voice raises and I hear the muffled voice of one of the twins asking if we're alright from the basement.

"I'm sorry. I don't—"

"I miscarried. Twice." She swipes tears off her cheeks and jabs a finger at the ultrasounds. "You happy?"

I blink down at the crumpled pictures. "Did they...did they have names?" I whisper.

"The girl was Jillian, and the boy was..." Madeline's voice cracks and her face contorts. "I-I don't remember. It was so long ago."

"A boy." I latch onto that, leaning toward her. "Mom, I've been dreaming about a boy that I can't remember too."

Her chin jerks up and her eyes flash like a startled animal's.

"He's falling into the dark," she murmurs.

"Yes!" I drop the pictures and grab both her hands. "And you can't save him before you wake up."

My mother's face sweeps through a rapid-fire series of emotions, they all blur together before she settles into patronizing compassion. She brushes the sweaty hair out of my eyes and when she speaks again, her voice is low and careful, like I'm a wild animal she doesn't want to spook. "James, you're on a lot of medication."

"Bullshit." I squeeze her hands hard enough that she flinches. "We're having the same dream. Dad is too, I think. He's someone we love. There's this black cloud clinging to him except for when he smiles." I know she's seen it too, because she sucks in a sharp inhale and her eyes start tearing up again, but then they break away from me to focus over my shoulder.

"Then he, like, sinks into quicksand, right? It swallows him." Jess stands in the doorway in his boxers. "Freaky shit."

"You've been dreaming?"

"Every night that I'm not shit-faced. Jord too."

"How long?" I gulp.

"Since we dropped you at the hospital. We thought it was just a twin thing, or trauma 'cause you almost lost your foot or something."

"Holy shit," I whisper. "He's trying to tell us something."

"Who?" Madeline and Jess ask at the same time.

By the time Jord wakes up, Jess, Mom and I are a couple shots deep into a bottle of gin we found behind the baking supplies. We've discovered that the beginnings of our reoccurring dreams are all different, but they all end the same. I'm giving him an early birthday gift,

Mom is running down a road toward him in the dark, Jord is in a public washroom, and Jess is on the beach. But they all end with the boy at various ages sucked into the black.

"In the dream, I call him Skippy," I say.

"Like the kangaroo?" Jess grins.

"I think it's a nickname."

"Makes sense," Jord quips. "I'd choose a horrible death, too, if you called me that."

"Shut up." I top off the twins' shot glass and my own and hold the bottle out to Mom.

"I think we're just stressed." She holds out her glass and I fill it to the brim. "It's been a long summer and we were breathing in all that mold at the cottage. God knows what that did to us."

"Made us psychics." Jess waggles his fingers. "Forget welding, James. New career."

"Be serious for one damned second," I sigh.

"How can I? I'm scared shitless here." He pounds back his shot and makes a face.

"It's just some underlying fear we're all sharing. James, you were in bad shape. We could have lost you." Mom sips her gin and scrubs her palm down her thigh. "Probably a common dream."

"Like forgetting your pants." Jord smirks.

"Or losing all your teeth," Jess adds.

"It doesn't feel like that. Besides, I found his things. It's *his* bedroom, Mom. You threw out all his stuff. I gave him a survival kit for his birthday, the one I made in high school. I found it in the trash."

"You've been digging through the trash?" Mom wrinkles her nose. "Look, that canvas bag has been kicking around this house forever. I didn't know it meant so much to you. I told you, you've all been tossing your junk in that guest room like it's your own personal landfill. Don't get pissed at me for finally dealing with it. What are you accusing us of?" She motions around the table. "Hiding some black sheep child under the stairs like lunatics? Wiping out all evidence of his existence? And we're all in on it. Me, your father, your brothers who can't keep a secret if their lives depended on it? Are you hearing yourself, James?"

"No." I toss back my shot and wince as it burns all the way down. "The clothes he wore in the dream, they were in the trash too."

"Before or after you pulled them out of the garbage and decided you were sleeping in your estranged dead brother's bed?" Mom softens her words and reaches for my hand across the table even as I pull away. "You're manifesting, Honey. Your body is sick, and your mind is itching to be busy, and you're medicated. Jesus." She frowns and grabs the gin bottle. "We really shouldn't be drinking. Your liver," she laments.

"More for us." Jord eases the bottle out of her hands.

"Let's not tell your father about this." Mom pleads.

"About gin for breakfast, killing James' liver, or our new group vision superpowers?" Jess asks.

"All of it."

"He's having dreams too, Mom." I press.

"And who do you think wakes up beside him when he does? He doesn't want to talk about them. I've asked. If he knows we're having nightmares too, he'll worry, and then he won't sleep at all. Work is cutting staff right now. He doesn't need more stress, understood?"

When we don't answer, she uses her I'm-not-taking-any-shit voice. "Understood?"

"Yes ma'am." We answer in unison.

Maybe Madeline is the one with secret military interests. She channels her inner drill sergeant easily enough.

"Call for you." Jess walks into my room without knocking and waggles the cordless at me.

"Hello?" I cradle the phone against my shoulder and squint down at Chapter Fifteen of the Grisham novel.

"James? Shit! We're in, man."

"Who is this?" I frown.

"Who fucking is this—It's Micah. We're *in*. My uncle has openings next fall and if you can scrape together your tuition, get your journeyman license, and pass your Red Seal this year, he's holding two spots for us, man. Do you believe this shit?"

My throat dries out as I straighten in my chair. "The underwater program? I don't have enough hours. There're guys out there working garbage jobs for *years* to get their foot in the door at Seneca."

"I know. Pays to have family in high places, yeah? We're going to score offshore jobs and spend all our vacation time drinking on beaches and banging chicks with no tan lines."

"Next fall?" I croak. "I'm not going to be able to sleep if I want to get my hours in before then."

"Sleep is for the weak. Come back early, man. Put some time in at the shop before the semester starts. That's what I'm doing."

I can't drive. But I don't tell him that. "Yeah. I'll be there, man. Shit, I owe you, Micah. This is fucking huge."

"Damn right you owe me. Would it kill you to come out clubbing sometime? Help a bro out and break out the lady-killer smile when I'm around to catch a moth or two caught in your orbit?"

"Shut up."

"Get your ass down here, Loverboy. Show my uncle you're serious about this shit."

"I'm on it. Thank you. Jesus Christ, thank you, Micah," I say with my heart pounding between my ears. *This is it. My dream career plunked right into my lap. And I just have to work hard enough to prove I'm worthy of it.*

I book a bus ticket and I pack. Mom catches me and I tell her that something came up and I need to head back to school early. She panics and cries like she always does, but I'm stronger than her when I'm set in my path. I announce that I'm a freaking adult and order her to hand over my medications. Then I tell the twins not to be assholes—impossible—and I taxi to the bus station before Dad gets home from work. If he wants to have words with me about my sudden departure, he'll have to drive all the way to the apartment to do it.

Three weeks later, my ankle has mostly healed, and I've weaned Mom and Dad down to one concerned phone call a week. I'm at the fabrication shop, wedged under an aluminum trailer, flat on my back, doing some overhead TIG welding and running the pedal with the side of my knee. After I finish the bead, I shimmy back and twist to sit up. An electric pain sizzles down my back so suddenly that I groan, and my helper asks if I'm alright.

I'm not.

I have to crawl away from the trailer on my hands and knees. My eyes are watering and I'm choking down the pain for a good few minutes before I can stand up. Luckily, I've got a healthy stash of painkillers with a side of codeine back in my room. I don't have any time for some random pinched nerve to slow me down. Not with classes through the day, insane hours in the shop in the evening and working the second job at night. No time for sleep, either, other than power naps. Good news is you don't have nightmares if you don't sleep. Can't sleepwalk either.

The headaches start after that. My hands go numb when I'm welding. I can't risk my inspector seeing any sloppy beads, so I double up on the painkillers and squeeze in some yoga stretches during the slow times on the nightshift job. When the pain eases and the tingling fades, I go right back to studying hunched over my books, pretzelling into awkward positions at the fab shop, and lifting things I probably shouldn't at work.

One morning I go to bed at three a.m. and when I wake up at six, I can't get up. Can't even roll over. Every time I move, it feels like someone's clamped cables on either end of my spine and is gleefully cranking up the amperage. My fingers brush against the bottle of pills on the nightstand. It takes several swipes to tip it toward me and, by the time I uncap it, I'm panting. I dry swallow a handful of pills. I don't even count them before popping them in—it's definitely more than three. Sweat cools on my goose-pimpled skin as I wait for the agony to fade so I can get up. But it doesn't happen. Instead, I fall asleep and dream about the boy.

Maybe it's because I'm delirious with exhaustion, or it could be the pain. More likely, it's the fact that there are way too many pills dissolving in my belly, but the vision is the most lucid it's ever been.

I can smell that the old Ford Tempo is running a little rich. The duffle bag I'm holding has weight to it. Its handles pinch my fingers. Skippy is not some nebulous dream wraith. He's real and whole. He's got dark hair and light eyes, and he's wearing a baggy cable knit sweater and jeans with holes in the knees. His shoelaces are untied. One hand is stuffed deep into his pocket, and the other holds the canvas survival kit. He offers me a wry, expectant smile like we're actors who've practiced this scene to death.

I'm not watching anymore. Not remembering. This isn't a normal dream. He's waiting for me to say something, to break out of our script and improvise, so I blurt, "Look, I don't mean to be an asshole, but if you're a ghost or something, I don't have time for this shit right now. Life is fucking nuts, you know what I mean?"

His smile turns sad, but he nods and tries to hand the gift back to me.

"Nah, you keep it." I wave him off. "I made it for you. Just hang in there until I'm done with all these bloody tests, and we'll figure something out, okay?" It sounds like a cop out, like the shittiest thing in the world to say to someone who looks so lonely. I'm supposed to look after people. Guess I only do it when it suits me. Sick heat eats at my stomach like I swallowed batteries instead of pills.

Skippy meets my gaze with a steady one of his own and offers me his hand. "Take care of yourself, brother," he says, and when I grip his hand to shake it, it feels calloused and warm.

Then the road starts to suck him in, and I can't hold onto him. He knows it's happening, puts on a brave front, but, same as always, he loses it just before his face goes under. Breath whistles out of his nostrils and gurgles to a stop. His eyes widen and then roll back.

And I wake up.

Brother. He said brother. And he didn't seem like the type who was smooth enough to throw around that term casually. *He's my actual little brother, and I just fucking ditched him.*

"Wake up, man! You're late." Micah knocks on my bedroom door hard enough to rattle it.

My mouth feels dusty, but I swallow and try to sound convincing. "I'm good. Go without me. I'll be there in a minute." A lie.

I spend more than a few minutes figuring out the mechanics of crawling out of bed without crying, and an even longer time lying on the hard floor biting my bottom lip before I'm able to prop myself up, pocket my pills, and face the day. I miss most of my first class and float through the rest of the day in a medically-induced haze.

And I forget to write down the details of the dream so, reliably, it fades.

You can do anything if you take enough codeine, but only if you balance it out with a lot of stimulants. I fine-tune the dosages over the next few days until I can weld without feeling like someone's jabbing my spine with a red-hot poker and still have enough energy to stay awake with a stack of open textbooks cradled on my lap on night shift. But I have to be careful. It's easy to make stupid mistakes drugged up like this.

I skip my buoyancy check in one of my dive classes and get lectured about the dangers of an uncontrolled ascent. I forget to hand in my timesheet at work and my employer staunchly refuses to pay me for those two weeks. Micah is on my back like a bloodhound, especially when he finds the pill bottle on my bedside empty long before the refill date on the label. But I manage. I do more than manage.

I load up on over-the-counter pain meds and cough syrup with codeine and I hide my stash above a drop-ceiling panel above my bed. My welds pass every integrity inspection and I'm confident I've studied enough to pass my Red Seal exam as soon as I get enough hours in. My back pain fades, but when I cut back on the cough syrup too much, the headaches, nausea and sweats kick in, so I keep taking it.

I'll ease off tomorrow, I promise myself daily.

Other than some gnarly scars, my ankle is good as new. Things are looking good. Until I lift a SCUBA cylinder one night at dive school and *wham,* my back goes, and the pain is so fierce and fast that I'm on the floor before I know it. Other divers are standing over me and I'm trying to insist that I'm alright, but I can hardly breathe through the pain. Someone brings a scoop stretcher. I try to get up, but my dive buddy, Irwin, leans into my chest and barks at me to keep still. The instructor is on his phone, calling an ambulance, and I'm mortified that I'm heading to the hospital again.

After an x-ray and an MRI, a tired-looking ER doctor whose

name I can't remember tells me I need to cut the syrup or next time he'll call the cops. Micah comes to pick me up and they give him something called a naloxone kit. The doctor refuses to sign my discharge papers until he's trained my roommate on how to use the syringes in the kit. The painkiller prescription I'm sent home with specifies _no opioids_.

When we get back to the apartment, Micah finally stops chewing me out, and helps me to my room. He gives me two of the new painkillers and pockets the rest. Asshole. On the bright side, the medication does tamp the pain down. Enough that late that night, I'm able to hobble to the kitchenette, grab the broom, and knock the ceiling tile in my room down. Bottles of purple cough syrup rain onto my mattress. I don't care if Micah hears it. I chug back as much saccharine liquid as I can stand until every muscle in my back unwinds, euphoria settles warmly over me, and I feel blissfully detached from my exhausted, broken body.

And then I see Skippy. Right there in the room with me.

I'm still awake, leaning against my door to stay upright. He's standing beside the cramped desk, looking down at a book titled _Metallurgy - Residual Stress and Distortion_.

"What are you doing, James?" he asks.

"Surviving," I mumble.

"Bullshit." He crosses the room to stand in front of me with both hands shoved in his pockets.

He's wearing a faded ACDC t-shirt and a chunky leather wristband. The darkness under his eyes hints at a tiredness rivaling my own. I've never seen him so crisply before. His lips are moving but I can't concentrate on what he's saying because I'm trying to memorize every detail before he fades.

"You hear me?" He leans closer and I shake my head. "This isn't surviving. This is you killing yourself and hiding it behind that fucking golden boy smile. You some sort of masochist?"

"No." My legs feel soupy. I keep my knees locked and my chin up even though my words are slurring. "Am I s'posed to keep calm and carry on? You *know* it's wrong over here. You're gone and there's just this...this hole. The world keeps trying to cover it, but we can feel it—Mom, Dad, all of us. No matter how much it tries to make us forget."

Skippy's eyes shine with tears but they're not the frustrated ones I remember from when he was my kid brother. He looks relieved, like he's been hanging onto something heavy and now he can finally put it down.

His voice wobbles through his next words. "It's okay to forget. You can let me go, man. You've got to." And his feet start sinking into the floor, dirty carpet lapping around his ankles.

"No," I bark, and push off from the wall toward him. The air is as thick as my cough syrup. Walking feels like swimming. Everything is too slow. "I'm s'posed to save you."

I'm close enough to see that the *Highway to Hell* silk screen lettering on his shirt is crackling and peeling, but I can't reach him.

Fuck. I can't do this again.

His hand hits my chest like an arc crossing the void. Breath pounds out of me too fast, too much. The contact buzzes through me, galvanizing all my muscles. I grab his wrist and it's real. He's real.

Oh my God.

He grabs a fistful of my shirt and backs me toward the door. He's wading through the carpet and it's making sucking sounds like hungry mud. Half-empty cough syrup bottles clatter and bleed purple ooze as his feet knock them aside.

"I'm s'posed to..." I wheeze but can't finish.

Skippy grabs the bedroom doorknob and cranks it open. He leans in close enough for me to hear him over the buzzing in my veins. Tears roll down his cheeks, but he's smiling a goofy, reassuring smile, the kind I used to offer him.

"You don't have to save me this time, James. It's my turn. I promised. I'll keep the darkness from swallowing you up."

The book. The inscription. It *was* him. "Wait," I blurt, digging in my heels.

He shoulders me hard, sending me careening into the hallway. I hit the opposite wall with a thud that cracks the paneling. Then I slither helplessly down like a discarded puppet.

"James?" Micah calls sharply from his room.

Skippy's submerged up to his knees now and breathing hard. "Live. Okay? Stop this shit." His voice cracks. He's sinking faster and I want to crawl toward him, but all the electricity has gone out of me.

My roommate's bedroom door flies open.

"I don't even know your name." I blubber as the darkness chews my little brother up with new voracity.

"It's okay, James," he says, and he's gone before Micah gets to me. The blackness swallows him so fast this time. Then it comes for me.

I punch Micah in the face when I wake up. The blow knocks a syringe out of his hands, and he drops the cordless phone on the floor, but he scoops it up and scrambles away from me with his hand clamped over his eye.

"Hello? You still there? Yeah, he's breathing alright. He just fucking clocked me."

"Aggressiveness is common when they come to." A tinny voice emanates from the phone speaker. "Back away. Keep yourself safe. You can monitor his breathing from further away. Does he have anything he can hurt you with, or himself? Any weapons?"

Micah takes the phone off speaker and keeps backing up. "No.

I mean there's the needles."

I was right there. I was with Skippy, and I wasn't sleeping. Jesus Christ, I remembered when we were kids together.

"I wanna go back," I blubber and blink down at my legs. Two syringes are on the floor by my thigh. One full of fluid. One empty. Blood pounds between my ears, sudden and full of dangerous heat. "You inject me with something?"

"Stay down, James. Fuck sakes, I just saved your life. You stopped breathing." Micah redirects his attention to the phone again. "Yeah, well tell them to hurry up. 304. I'll buzz them in. Yeah, his lips aren't so blue now. He's trying to get up. I don't know if he'll go with them."

"An ambulance?" I choke. "Fuck no. I'm not going to a hospital." I try to stand, but my head feels like concrete. Pain lances behind my eyes and bile boils up from my stomach.

Micah doesn't answer me. He keeps mumbling into the phone to the 911 dispatcher like the two of them are in on something together. I yell at him until my throat aches. I get my feet under me, crash into the living room, and throw whatever I can get my hands on. Lamps, Dishes. Everything. I've made a hell of a mess by the time the paramedics get there. Stupid, because it's tough to reason with Micah after that.

The guys in EMS coveralls are tall and burly and they look pissed to be responding to an overdose. I'm one-hundred-percent certain I'll lose any fight I start with them, but I'm breathing fire and can't stop now. I was *with* my brother. Actually with him, and Micah took it all away.

"I'm not going to the hospital," I say through my teeth for the hundredth time. They keep flashing a penlight in my eyes and frowning.

"Well, we can't leave you here unless he agrees to be your caregiver and monitor you for the rest of the night." The medic with the flat nose thumbs at Micah. "You could stop breathing again. You don't go to the hospital, you could die. You understand, James?"

How is it that a Goddamned ambulance driver can remember my name and I can't recall my own brother's? "Tell'em you'll be my caregiver, Micah," I growl.

"No."

"What?" My hands start tingling. Did I just hear him right?

"No. You need a break, man. I'll call your parents. They'll pick you up at the hospital and take you home for a bit."

"Micah don't." I stand up. Shit. I can't go home. I have exams. I have to get my hours in. Swatting the medic away, I move toward Micah, but the guy between us is lightning fast. He blocks me and presses me back down onto the couch. "Please. I'm sorry I punched you. Okay? I'll clean up the broken glass," I blabber. "*Please*. Micah."

My roommate refuses to be my caretaker.

I go to the hospital.

They hold me for three hours until Mom arrives to sign me out. The nurse hands her a pamphlet on substance abuse resources available locally.

It's dawn when we cross the parking lot, and I can't process that the sun is rising when everything else in my life feels like it's bottoming out.

"Where's Dad?" I croak once we're in the van. These are the first words I speak to my mother.

She snorts. The sunlight turns her hair into a frizzy red halo around her head. She fires me a dead-tired gaze before answering. "He's sick. Headache. He's been home from work." We stop at two separate red lights before she adds: "He's dreaming again."

"Fuck." The word bleeds out of me. I pick at the peeling vinyl on the armrest. "I saw him, Mom."

"Who?" Her hands tighten on the steering wheel.

"The boy from the dream."

Mom is quiet for a long time before answering. She looks too tiny to be sitting in the van's hulking captain's seat. "This is my fault. I didn't want this," she mumbles. "Any of it. I never wanted kids when I met your dad."

I don't offer her a winning smile or say anything to make her feel better. We don't talk at all after that. We just drive home, silence wrapped carefully around our raw and wounded parts.

My room has new carpet. It smells like glue. I don't spend a lot of time in it. Instead, I sit on the spare room bed, with the army pamphlet and the canvas survival kit on either side of me, and I read the John Grisham novel over and over. Pages start falling out. There're no clues between the lines, I know that, but I can't stop reading it, and I can't stop twitching. I think I'm going crazy. Mom says it's just withdrawals.

Dad has barely enough energy to go through the motions of a rousing, 'What are you doing with your life?' speech before he retires to his room again. He's never had migraines before, but these ones are sucking the life right out of him. Even the twins creep around the house like the floor's made of cracked glass.

One morning, Dad dresses, shoulders his messenger bag, and announces he's feeling well enough to go to work. I'm picking at an omelet in the kitchen when Mom phones him at work to ask him to buy milk on the way home and the receptionist awkwardly tells her that Mr. Rawlingson called in sick again today. Mom freezes before thanking her politely and hanging up.

Easing to a stand, mindful of my back, I head to the living

room to peer out the picture window. It's pouring rain. The oil-stained spot on the driveway where the Ford Econoline regularly berths is empty. "He usually take the van to work?"

"God no," she answers. "It's too big to fit any of the parking spots downtown. He carpools with Gerald—who doesn't mind stopping for groceries now and then if it's just a few things."

Like I care whether Gerald is irked by after-work errands. I go back to my room and find the Grisham novel missing from my nightstand. It's not in the spare room either. Suddenly, I know where Dad is.

Mom's car is in the shop for an alternator replacement—that's why she picked me up from the hospital in the van—and the twins take the bus to work ever since their DUIs, so I call a taxi, well aware that the fare to where I'm going to rack will be one hell of a bill, but willing to cough up whatever it takes. I tell Mom where I'm headed, and she doesn't even try to stop me, just nods, and pats my arm before I go.

The rain has turned to sleet, gathering into layered clumps where the frantic windshield wipers can't reach. It takes an hour longer than usual to get there. I don't even see the Gulf station when we pass it. My taxi driver is sulking and swearing quietly while he navigates the narrow pine-lined road toward Honey Bear Hollow.

What the hell am I going to do if the van isn't here? The panicked thought hits me as we ease under the burled log arch entryway like it's a gateway to another world.

I swallow my fear, tell the driver to pull past the check-in at the Quonset, and direct him onto Sweet Bee Circle. I've never been here in the autumn before. It looks like the whole place is settling into hibernation. Maybe it's the storm. Fractal lightning reflects off the bay windows of rows of cottages as we crawl past the deserted unraked beach with the lake beyond choppy and frothing with whitecaps.

When we round the bend, the yellow summer cottage is there, same as always. Cheerful as the sun. It never changes.

The van is there too. It looks more at home here than anywhere else.

I exhale a shaky sigh, pull out my wallet, and start counting large bills, careful to include a sizable tip and a good-natured smile. The guy's eyes widen as he examines me in the rear-view mirror. It must not look convincing. He snatches the wad of bills as I pass them, and he doesn't say thank you. I guess I'm losing my charm.

Shrugging, I step out into the driving sleet. The taxi peels away as soon as I close the door. I ignore the icy water snaking down the back of my neck and run my hand along the flank of the rusty old van as I walk up the driveway. The porch light isn't on, but the kitchen light is, warm as the promise of a casserole after a cold day. Stepping onto the covered front porch, I stomp the water off my boots so Dad won't be startled by my entrance, then I open the creaking screen door, press down the worn lever on the main door behind it, and step into the cottage that cradles every memory of every summer I can remember.

I expect it to smell like home. My shoulders loosen in anticipation of wood smoke, strong coffee, and citrus cleaner, but instead, the astringent smell of industrial disinfectant and fresh paint burns my nostrils.

The cottage is gutted. All the furniture in the living room is gone and the room yawns unnaturally large. Where there used to be a wall, a bare white column supports a new laminated ceiling beam that doesn't match the rest of the open rafters. The hulking woodstove sits awkwardly in the middle of the room now, and behind it, the freshly-opened addition. I'd forgotten about the mold, how

Angus the caretaker said he was going to tear out the wall to the extension, how I was going to help.

I'm glad I didn't. I can't put my finger on why, but it looks like a bloody abomination, what they've done to the place, like an over-eager reno crew scabbed on an extra body part and made our summer cottage into Frankenstein's monster.

Dad stands in the middle of the hollowed-out room, his back to me. He's facing the empty space where the five-panel door with the crystal knob used to be, holding the John Grisham novel in one hand and a piece of grid-lined paper with square fold marks in the other. Something about the way he's swaying, how his dress shirt is wrinkled and half-untucked, makes him look like an Alzheimer's patient who's escaped their long-term care ward. He looks how I feel. Breakable. Lost, but anchored. Anchored here. To this place.

"Hey, Dad." I offer.

He doesn't turn for a long time. I wonder if he sleepwalked when he was a kid. He clears his throat and says, "He called you here too?"

"Yeah, I think he did." I wipe my feet on the welcome mat out of habit and cross the room toward him. Every footstep echoes rudely in the rafters. There's no life left in here to soften things. "What'dya got there?" I point to his hand.

"This?" He delicately holds out a crayon drawing that's been folded to wallet size so many times it's translucent at the seams.

The bright oranges and blues have faded, but I can still make out a group of fat birds with sharp beaks and stilt legs all stuffed into a nest of harsh brown lines. There's a bigger bird perched on the edge, and the smaller one's—the babies—don't have their mouths wide open for food like you'd typically see. Instead, they have slits for eyes and rows of zzzzzz's above their heads. Sleeping. Uneven five-point stars and a crescent moon plaster a black sky that some- one gave up coloring in halfway through. Below the nest, scrawled in faded, blocky pencil is an inscription. I lean forward to read it.

Sometimes quiet is best.

"Who's is this?" The bottom right-hand corner where the artist's name should be is muddled with a watermarked tan stain.

"Mine." Dad pulls the fragile artwork back, and glares at me like I'm a criminal casing out an art museum.

What the hell is wrong with all of us? My whole family, we used to be warm and loving and easy with each other. Had I imagined all that?

Dad must see the hurt on my face, because he pushes his glasses up his nose and holds out the drawing again. "It's, uh, from one of you kids. I don't know who. I spilled coffee on it." He smiles and rubs a thumb over the stained corner. "I've just kept it in my wallet for so long. Sometimes, when it's hectic at work, I pull it out and...I don't know." He heaves a sigh that comes all the way from his belly. "It reminds me of when you were all little and thought I could fix everything. Everything was easier to fix when you were small, James. And now it all feels wrong." His voice catches.

I know better than to interrupt my dad when he pauses. He clams up if you try to fill those silences with meaningless noise like Mom does. So, I just nod and shift under the weight of the cavernous room around us. He'll speak when he's ready. He always does.

Eventually, Dad takes a shaking breath and holds the Grisham novel out to me. "The handwriting matches. Especially the S's and E's. They're identical."

"What?" My face screws up.

"The inscription in your book and my drawing. The writing is the same. You can't let go of the book. And I can't let go of this. And the Goddamned dreams where the ground eats him up. I thought..." His words trail off. He presses the book against my chest, and I take it, and watch him flex his hand and blink rapidly.

My neck won't stop tingling.

"I thought coming here would help me remember," he blurts. "What's wrong with me?"

"Nothing." I grab his arm, and he winces. "Dad, we're all feeling it. It's not just you."

His hand shakes so bad that the drawing slips. The paper spins to the hardwood floor and settles over a patch where all the planks have been replaced with freshly-stained new ones. I frown down at it.

This floor was scratched. Four, long gouges. A layer of ash covering everything.

This is where I fell. This is where something came under the door and grabbed my ankle. The memories feel like being stoned, impacts thudding through me in rapid succession.

I bend over. Dad mistakes my movement and swipes the picture off the floor, but my back twinges and I can't straighten.

"Shit." I sag to my hands and knees.

"What?"

"My back."

"Okay." He snaps back to himself at the pain in my voice. "Just stay there. I'll grab some ice from the freezer."

"It's not bad, just help me—" My words dry in my mouth. From this vantage point, I can see between the claw feet of the old cook stove. The renovation crew did a sloppy job of sweeping up. There's a square of untouched sawdust under there. In the centre of the dust, is a small chunk of cast iron.

I shift toward it.

"I said don't move." Dad chides.

"There's something under the stove."

"I'll get it."

"No." I'm almost there and I sense this is important, like the book, like the drawing, and the survival kit.

I clench all my core muscles, ease down until my ear is pressed against the hardwood and reach under the woodstove. My fingers brush against metal that feels strangely warm. I tease it toward me and claw it into reach. Then I blink down at the object in my palm.

It's a skeleton key. Half of one. A broken shaft with rectangular notched teeth. And it opens every locked door in my mind in turn. Everything clicks into place. Memories flood in a torrent so strong I can't breathe against it.

Dad crumples to his knees beside me, panting. He must feel it too.

I remember.

Everything.

I remember him.

"David," I gasp. "Named after you. His name is David."

Dad nods and starts crying beside me, gulping, unapologetic sobs of relief, the kind a parent makes when they find a lost child.

The hole inside me is filling and I smile shakily.

Dad grins back. He doesn't see me gripping the broken key tightly in my fist. I only let him see the smile.

Fuck you, darkness. The key burns in my hand like it can hear my thoughts. *You hear me? He's not yours. He's ours and we're coming to take him back.*

The End

ABOUT THE AUTHOR

At a young age, SHELLY CAMPBELL wanted to be an air show pilot or a pirate, possibly a dragon and definitely a writer and artist. She's piloted a Cessna 172 through spins and stalls, and sailed up the east coast on a tall ship barque—mostly without projectile vomiting. In the end, Shelly found writing and drawing dragons to be so much easier on the stomach. Shelly writes speculative fiction ranging from grimdark fantasy, to sci-fi and horror. She'd love to hear from you.

www.shellycampbellauthorandart.com
https://twitter.com/ShellyCFineArt
https://www.instagram.com/shellycampbellfineart
https://www.facebook.com/shellycampbellauthorandart
https://www.tiktok.com/@shellycampbellauthor?

Acknowledgements

There are so many people who helped Gulf reach its final form. Special thanks to my early readers Al Hess, Essa Hansen, and Megan King for crossing the gulf to brave David's world with him. Kudos to my entire Writer Alliance crew for all your advice, help, and support while in the querying trenches. Ken McKinley, thank you for seeing David and his story and loving it—I was worried for awhile that perhaps he really was invisible! Kenneth Cain, I'm so grateful for all your work proofreading, formatting and pulling this all together into book form. Kealan Patrick Burke, your covers rock. I am over the moon to have one of my very own for Gulf. Michelle McLachlin and David-Jack Fletcher for all your help making Gulf the best possible version of itself that it could be and giving me hope that second chances really do exist.

More from Eerie River

Eerie River Publishing is a leader in independent horror, dark fantasy, and dark speculative fiction.

We are dedicated to publishing anthologies, collections, and novels from some of the best indie authors around the world. Our goal is to become a go-to resource for horror, dark fantasy and dark speculative readers, and to provide a safe space for authors to share their stories.

Interested in becoming a Patreon member?
By joining our patreon, you will be supporting our artists and authors, who work hard to produce high-quality and original content for your enjoyment. You will also get access to exclusive perks, such as early releases, behind-the-scenes updates, bonus material, and more. If you love dark fiction and want to support independent publishing, please consider becoming a patron today. Thank you for your interest and support.

www.patreon.com/EerieRiverPub

To stay up to date with all our new releases and upcoming giveaways, follow us on Facebook, Twitter, Instagram and YouTube.

linktr.ee/eerieriver

EERIE RIVER PUBLISHING

NOVELS & COLLECTIONS
Gulf: Dark Walker Series Book One (2023)
Breach: Dark Walker Series Book Two (2024)
Chasing The Dragon: Horror Vigilante Novel (2023)
The Naughty Corner: Novella Collection (2023)
Dead Man Walking: Nick Holleran Series (2022)
Devil Walks in Blood: Nick Holleran Series (2022)
The Darkness In The Pines: Nick Holleran Series (2023)
At Eternity's Gate: Empire of Ruin Series (2023)
Beyond Sundered Seas: Empire of Ruin Series (2023)
Path of War: Empire of Ruin Series (2022)
In Solitudes Shadow: Empire of Ruin Series (2022)
The Void: Sapphic Fiction (2023)
They Are Cursed Like You: Trailer Park Witches Series (2023)
Infested: Horror Novel (2022)
SENTINEL: The Bensalem Files (2021)
NOTHUS: The Bensalem Files (2022)
Miracle Growth: A Cosmic Horror Novella(2022)
Helluland: Urban Fantasy of Legends (2023)
A Sword Named Sorrow: Fantasy Novel (2022)
Storming Area 51 (2019)

ANTHOLOGIES
Year of the Tarot: Four Book Series
AFTER: A Post-Apocalyptic Survivor Series
Elemental Cycle: Four Book Series
It Calls From Series
Blood Sins
Last Stop: Whiskey Pete
Of Fire and Stars
From Beyond the Threshold

DRABBLE COLLECTIONS
Forgotten Ones: Drabbles of Myth and Legend
Dark Magic: Drabbles of Magic and Lore

COMING SOON
Hell Over Haven: Nick Holleran book by David Green
The Roots Run Deep: Collection of Horror by C.M. Forest
Rotten House: Horror Novel by by Michelle River
The Earth Bleeds at Night: Anthology of Horror

Out Now!
Breach: Dark Walker Series Book Two

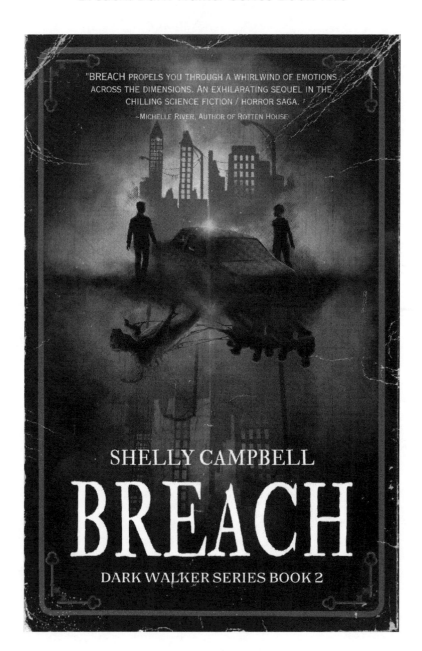

Coming Soon - Short Story Collection
The Roots Run Deep

Award Winning Novel by C.M. Forest
Infested

"The Craft" meets "My Best Friends Exorcism"
They Are Cursed Like You

Cosmic Horror Novella
Miracle Growth

Manufactured by Amazon.ca
Bolton, ON

39860305R00169